His knee throbbed
like bloody hell...

A double dose of ibuprofen had helped him walk into Kristen's office like a man. Now, an hour later, his stomach was still reeling in response to the medication on an empty stomach.

Most days he did much better. But the slow healing was driving him over the edge. He needed breakfast...or an early lunch. A good, hot shower. Much stronger painkillers. But all he could do was lie on the motel bed and try not to give in to the pain. A bull rider with enough grit and determination to follow the circuit and win surely had enough "try" to get into the shower.

But it had taken every bit of "try" Jake possessed just to get through that meeting with Kristen. God, she'd looked good.

More stubborn than ever, with that same glint of intelligence in her big gray eyes. More confident now. But he could still remember back ten years to the single night they'd shared, and even now the memory made him smile. Ten years, and he'd never found anyone else to take her place.

And for ten years, she'd avoided him like the plague.

Dear Reader,

Authors talk about writing "the book of their heart"—a story that touches them in some indefinable way, a story they would write whether or not anyone else ever had a chance to read it. I'm so happy that Superromance is bringing "the book of my heart" to you!

The world of rodeo is exciting, fascinating and dangerous. Imagine a job for which you might commute hundreds of miles, work eight seconds and then commute hundreds of miles again. Sounds like an easy work day, until you factor in the high risk of serious injury or death during those eight seconds!

Those odds have already caught up with bull rider Jake Landers, who was badly injured last year. Cowboys, bullfighters, clowns, announcers, producers, contractors and other personnel on a given rodeo circuit are often close—helping each other out, cheering each other on. Jake not only faces the loss of his career and the only life he's known since he turned eighteen, but will lose touch with the people who have become his second family.

Buying a faltering rodeo company is his ticket back into the life he loves. The one person who can help him succeed is the woman he stood up at the altar ten years before, and now they'll have to travel together for the next five months. If she'll agree…and if dark secrets from the past don't tear them apart once again.

I hope you'll enjoy reading *Rodeo!* as much as I enjoyed writing it, and I also hope you'll drop me a line to let me know what you thought. I can be reached at:

Box 2550, Cedar Rapids, Iowa 52406-2550 or online at www.pobox.com/~Roxanne.Rustand or www.superauthors.com.

Best wishes!

Roxanne Rustand

Rodeo!

Roxanne Rustand

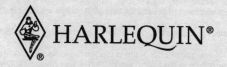

HARLEQUIN®

TORONTO • NEW YORK • LONDON
AMSTERDAM • PARIS • SYDNEY • HAMBURG
STOCKHOLM • ATHENS • TOKYO • MILAN • MADRID
PRAGUE • WARSAW • BUDAPEST • AUCKLAND

ISBN 0-373-70982-X

RODEO!

Copyright © 2001 by Roxanne Rustand.

Visit us at www.eHarlequin.com

Printed in U.S.A.

With love to my mom, who always believed I should be a writer. I should have listened to you sooner, Mom!

And to Larry, Andy, Brian and Emily, as always.

This book could never have been written without the incredible cooperation of the rodeo professionals and others who gave so freely of their time and expertise. Many, many thanks—you made the researching and writing of this story pure joy! Any mistakes are mine alone.

Endless thanks for the invaluable behind-the-scenes experience in rodeo, the introductions, research materials, and many hours of interviews, to Rory and Sheri Meeks, owners of R.M. Rodeo Productions. Sheri, who is also a PRCA (Professional Rodeo Cowboys Association) rodeo timer, and Rory, who is also a PRCA bullfighter and clown, were wonderfully patient with my endless questions.

Many thanks also to...
Dr. Kathy Ross, D.V.M.;
Fred Petzold, rodeo photographer;
Three Hills PRCA Rodeo Inc., Stock Contractors;
Donna Lucia, wife of Tommy Joe Lucia, PBR (Professional Bull Riders, Inc.) Bud Light Cup Tour manager;
Katherine Bernardi, for information on radio stations;
Chelle Cohen, for additional research assistance
And Helen Bekken, my expert on the West

CHAPTER ONE

"I'LL GIVE YOU the best dirt in the country, bar none." Kristen Davis took a slow, quiet breath to steady her nerves. "And afterwards, I'll see it's pulled up so clean you could eat dinner on that floor."

A long pause. The voice coming across the speakerphone lowered to a suspicious note. "Where's Guy McLaughlin?"

The pencil in her hand snapped. "Guy and his wife have been in Florida for the past month. He and Roy Davis, my father, retired this spring. I'm running Mid-America Rodeo now, and I can assure you I know the business inside and—"

"So who's the company's contractor?"

"Mid-America Rodeo Company is still full-service. We produce rodeos and buck our own stock. Davis Ranch is known for top rough-stock bloodlines. Last year we had three horses and a bull go to The National Finals. Now that Roy isn't on the road, Bud Bodine has been hired to manage the contracting side."

Another pause. "*Really* good dirt?"

"I figure six-hundred-fifty yards to put down a good eight inches. It has to be that deep, because of the concrete flooring in the coliseum."

"But cost-wise—"

"If it isn't done right, you'll have barrel racers and bulls sliding into home plate all day. You'll be sending contestants to the hospital." When he didn't reply, she added pointedly, "The insurance company won't be eager to underwrite your rodeo the next time around, either. I figure six hours to haul in the dirt, six to haul it out. We used Purdell Trucking out of Calderville when MRC did your rodeo last time."

"Same price as last year?" The voice turned sly. "Same arrangements?"

Kristen glanced out the open front door of the building, left ajar to welcome the fresh, early-May breezes, and silently counted to ten. He was measuring just how far he dared go—taking her for a city slicker who'd been away from the game too long. He would never have suggested that to Guy or her dad.

It was her turn to pause. She sifted through the file folder of invoices on the desk. The hauler had gone up ten dollars a load. Wages were higher, too. And compared to the records from last year, advertising was up a good six percent. But this could be the first rodeo contract for MRC since Guy and Roy had stepped down. And it was an indoor rodeo, to boot— something MRC had rarely done in the past. Success with this one could bring in more business. "Well, I—"

Staring down at the figures on the sheets spread out on the desk, she caught a flicker of movement out of the corner of her eye. Someone was standing in the doorway, leaning against the frame.

Before she could react, the man—an all-too-familiar man—walked in the door, crossed the room and met her nose to nose, his arms braced on her desk. He grinned.

Her heart bucked against her ribs.

"I think you've been at the wrong end of a bull too many times for your health, Rodale." Jake Landers's drawl was slow and smooth as honey, but the look he slid toward the phone was anything but sweet. "Maybe you'd like to drop by and discuss these figures in person."

From the sputtering coming across the phone line, that didn't appear to be the case. With a sharp *click,* the phone connection went dead.

Kristen stared at it in horror. "What have you done?" She shoved her chair back, its legs screeching against the scarred wood flooring. "I was doing *business* with that man."

Jake straightened, then sat on the edge of her desk with that damn sensual, lazy grin deepening the dimples in his cheeks and the bad-boy twinkle in his eye. "Honey, the kind of business he was doing with you, you don't want to be in."

The meaning of his words sent heat straight up her throat.

"He wasn't…taking advantage of me. I knew exactly what I was doing, and none of this is your business, anyway." She stood. "First time I see you in years, and you still manage to be insulting. Why isn't that a surprise?"

"I was being helpful."

"*Helpful?* I don't know where you're headed, but you're not welcome here."

"You mean," he said slowly, his affable grin widening, "that you can't forgive a little error in judgment after ten years?"

Little? Maybe in another fifty years. Sometimes, when she was too tired to keep her defenses high, she still thought about that awful night back in Las Vegas.

But even as she was remembering the greatest humiliation of her life, she was also remembering the feel of Jake's hard muscle beneath her fingertips...the flash of those white teeth in the silky, summer darkness as he grinned at her, winning her completely—heart and soul.

That heart and soul were now a whole lot tougher, thanks to him. Kristen would never, ever be that foolish again.

"I have no idea what you're talking about." She gave him a level look as she tapped a stack of papers into order.

What on earth was he doing out here? MRC's office was housed in a cabin on Guy's ranch, a good ten miles west of Bent Spur—a don't-blink-or-you'll-miss-it town deep in the middle of Wyoming ranch country. Visitors were scarce, and no one ever found the place without detailed instructions.

"Look, if you have business with MRC, you're in the right place. Otherwise, I'll tell you how to get back to the main road, so I can get back to work."

He shook his head slightly, his smile fading. "I'm here on business, but I guess you haven't heard."

Pale lines of strain showed at his mouth and at the corners of his eyes. She remembered him tanned and fit, with the muscular, sinewy look of an athlete ready to take on the world. And he certainly had. Twice he'd been World Champion Bull Rider.

Now he just looked…tired. Even though she'd always told herself that she would never care about this man again, she couldn't help asking. "Are…are you okay?"

His expression hardened. *"Fine."*

"Do you need a drink?" Her question must have sounded insulting because his mouth flattened. "Some water?" She amended. "Aspirin?"

"No. Thank you." He reached for something at the edge of her desk. With a loud clatter, an object fell to the floor.

She stared at him as he cursed under his breath, eased off the edge of her desk and hobbled a half-step away. He bent awkwardly to pick up the object— a cane—and sank into a chair before she could make a move.

The cane and the obvious discomfort shouldn't have been a surprise. She'd been too busy recently to look at the weekly rodeo injury reports on the Internet, but bull riders were on that list all too often.

"Bad bull?"

He hitched a shoulder in the nonchalant way of all bull riders, who relegated to minor inconvenience anything from a broken back to a ruptured spleen.

It was part of the life, facing death every time the chute opened on a ton of angry bull. The pain and risk were accepted as the price to pay for an adrenaline rush, eight seconds of glory and a shot at the Finals.

And it was all part of a life she wanted nothing

more to do with. She was going to put MRC back in the black and get it sold by the end of the season. Guy and her parents would all have a decent nest egg for retirement. Then she was heading straight back to her new condo and that job offer in Dallas.

"So what was it? Broken leg? Sprained ankle?" She gave him a thoughtful, head-to-toe perusal, trying to ignore her growing concern.

"Knee."

"How are you ranked?"

"I'm not."

Kristen's mouth fell open. "But you're always at the top! How long have you been out?"

He managed a crooked smile. "Does my heart good, knowing you've followed my career."

She gave a snort of disgust. "I haven't."

He threw back his head and laughed. "Honey, you haven't changed a bit. You're tough as rawhide."

"Why," she asked, keeping her voice dead calm, "would you think otherwise?" In a few minutes he would be gone. *I can deal with him that long.*

"Those city guys in the suits and ties won't stand a chance."

The amused glint in his eyes faded. His voice lowered. "Congratulations on that degree. I'm proud of you, Krissie. I always knew you could do anything you set your mind to." He paused, his gaze never leaving hers. "And I'm sorry about your marriage."

Her resolve wavered, as his deep voice wrapped around her, slow and easy. "I'm happy to have the degree, but the marriage was a mistake from the start. How did you hear?"

He lifted a shoulder. "Guys talk some, back of the chutes."

When they weren't busy praying they'll live through their next ride.

The rodeo world was a close one. Cowboys often traveled together, sharing mileage and expenses when the win money didn't pan out and their battered pickups bit the dust. Hitting two to three rodeos a weekend, maybe in three different states, they traveled hundreds of miles overnight to follow their dreams.

Of course, in that next town they'd often compete against cowboys they'd just seen at the last rodeo. And gossip certainly flew during those long hours of travel.

She and Jake had once given them more than enough to talk about.

"Look, if there isn't anything else, I need to get to work, here." She rose to her feet behind the desk, but he didn't take the hint.

He leaned back in his chair, settled his Resistol onto his thigh. The teasing glint in his eyes was definitely gone. "I thought they were going to call you...before I arrived," he said finally.

A chill crawled up Kristen's spine. "Who?"

"Your dad. Guy."

"Guy is out of town. I've been staying in the other part of this cabin since I came back to Wyoming, and haven't seen my dad in over a week. What were they supposed to tell me?"

"I'm going to be MRC's new owner, Kris. Providing several conditions are met."

"They *sold?*" Kristen sank back into her chair, her mind reeling. "To you?"

"We've been working out the details by phone over the past few days."

Without ever saying a word to me? Stunned, she tried to make sense of it all. "I came back a month ago when Dad and Guy decided to retire. They'd been letting the business slack off over the past year, and I figured MRC would be worth *twice* as much by the end of this season."

"Uncle Guy has been urging me to join him for years." Jake shrugged apologetically. "He called last week and said both he and Roy wanted to sell."

She fought to control her rising anger. "What the heck do you know about this end of the business, anyway?"

"Rodeo is my life," he said simply. He ran a finger along the brim of his hat as if choosing his next words with care. "I know the cowboy side. I need you to help with the rest."

"You can't possibly imagine that I'd stay with MRC now." *Most definitely not with you as the new owner.* She shoved away from her desk. "Did you buy the bucking stock?"

"I will when we finalize the deal at the end of the season. Enough bareback horses, saddle broncs and bulls to make me a fully qualified stock contractor— at least twenty-five head each, including the stock being hauled this year."

And that would be gentle old Cropduster, who loved to be scratched behind the ears yet who'd been successfully ridden only a handful of times over his

entire eight-year career. Along with Hellfire and Code
Blue and Body Trauma, the bucking mares Kristen
had raised from foals.

A sense of hurt and betrayal washed through her.
After giving up her life in Dallas to come back and
help MRC, neither Guy nor her father had bothered
to warn her about the sale.

"If this has all been decided, then I'll be out of
here on the first plane after I talk to Guy and Dad."

"They're getting a damn good price for the company." He didn't move, but the intensity of his gaze
held her as surely as if he'd come across the desk and
grabbed her shoulders. "As good—maybe better—
than they would have had later. Guy...said they both
needed the money as soon as possible."

Her breath caught on the sudden lump in her throat.
Needed? Guy had always been like a favorite uncle
to her when she was a child, and his wife Jennibelle
had been like a second mom. With their ranch just
fifteen miles away, Kristen had seen them often. And
with her mom's worsening dementia...

"Guy was eager to liquidate the company," Jake
continued. "And your dad agreed."

Liquidate. Despite her roiling emotions, she nearly
smiled at his choice of words. Hardly the down-home
vernacular of the average cowboy, many of whom hit
the circuit out of high school and never looked back.
Not many people knew Jake's background. By the
time she'd met him, he'd already left a master's degree program at Montana State to pursue rodeo full
time.

"I wish you well," she said flatly. "You'll have your work cut out for you."

Shoving a hand through his dark hair, Jake settled a little deeper into his chair. His mouth curved into a slow, sexy smile that was as much a part of him as that lean, muscular build. "And so will you."

"Not in this lifetime."

She'd heard the stories about the flocks of buckle bunnies who followed him on the circuit, offering companionship and a whole lot more. Jake Landers's reputation for booze, brawling and women had started before he hit twenty-five, and had built into legend since then.

That killer grin was one reason Kristen believed the rumors were true. Once it had led her straight into disaster.

"Look," he said softly. "I know we have… history. This won't be any easier for me than it is for you. Thing is, Guy and Roy have this chance to sell out now for an excellent price. But the deal only goes through if you agree to stay with MRC and help me get through this first season."

"*What?*" Kristen stared at him in horror. "My *father* agreed to this?"

Jake's mouth tipped into a lopsided grin. "It's not like they sold you into slavery. I said I needed help for a season. Neither one of them wanted to come out of retirement. It's up to you whether or not you'll stay on." The laugh lines at the corners of his eyes deepened. "You would have been running the company this season, anyway, right?"

She looked pointedly at the door. "True, but my answer is still no."

"Think, Kris. You want the company back on its feet so it can be sold. What if there *isn't* a buyer in the fall? Will you stay year after year, trying to keep the company afloat until that finally happens? It'll all be on your shoulders. Your dad has your mother to worry about, Guy can't travel..."

Kristen turned and moved over to the window, where she leaned her forehead against the cool glass. Outside, arid grassland rolled ten miles east to the empty Main Street of Bent Spur, a town so quiet that a pickup rattling through made people turn around and stare.

A thousand miles south lay Dallas, and all Kristen's dreams. Her pretty condo—currently occupied by an old college friend—overlooking a small park. A plum job as assistant brand manager for a top-notch company.

She'd devoted eight challenging years to that future. The hard-won four-point GPA in business school, the two years with an investment firm in Chicago. Her marketing MBA from Northwestern. She'd had four good job offers and had accepted the best— but delaying her start too long might lead Lambert & Anderson Associates to withdraw their offer.

And away from the campus recruiting system, it would be much, much harder to start over.

"Why not hire some cowboy friend of yours? Or lure someone away from another company?"

"You grew up with MRC," he said simply.

"I tagged along as a kid, sure, but I've been away for a long time and never *managed* any aspect of the company."

"I need a mentor—someone who has strong busi-

ness sense, who understands the clients. Someone
who cares whether or not the company survives." He
lifted a shoulder. "That's you."

At her frown, he added, "Look, I know this isn't
easy. I understand you're raring to get on with your
life. But this will be better for all of us—Roy, Guy,
me, and even you."

"Me?"

"Think of your resume. The MBA is great. Add
that you put a failing company back on its feet during
your first six months out of school, and your career
ought to take off like a bull out of the chute." The
warmth in his eyes belied the businesslike tone of his
voice. "I've always been sorry about what happened
between us, Kris. Don't let our past stop you from
helping Roy and Guy."

Images from childhood came to her: Guy picking
her up and twirling her in the air; Jennibelle buying
her ice cream and lemonade. Her father, now at home
taking care of Mom. All of them needed the money
from MRC. Perhaps more desperately than she knew.

"I don't want to do this," Kristen said finally on
a drawn-out sigh. "But I'll stay through this season—
til October first. After that, you can ask Guy or Roy
any questions that come up while you're planning the
next season. You'll be able to take over easily."

When Jake rose stiffly to his feet, his face paled
and pain flashed across his face. But that easygoing
smile was still in place, his handshake warm and sure.

"You've got a deal."

A DOUBLE DOSE OF IBUPROFEN had helped him walk
into Kristen's office like a man. Now, an hour later,

his stomach was still reeling in response to the meds on an empty stomach, and his knee throbbed like bloody hell.

Most days he did much better. But the slow healing process was driving him over the edge, and yesterday he'd pushed himself too hard—forced himself to try alternately walking and jogging a half-mile. His knee had given out within five minutes, and now he was paying the price.

He needed breakfast...or an early lunch. A good hot shower. Much stronger medication. But all he could do was lie on the motel room bed and try not to give in to the pain.

Maybe—in a half-hour or so—he'd be able to make that long journey into the shower and turn it on high. A bull rider with enough grit and determination to follow the circuit and win was said to have "try."

It had taken every last bit of *try* he possessed just to get through that meeting with Kristen, and every silent prayer he could think of to make it a success.

God, she looked good.

More stubborn than ever, with that same glint of intelligence in her big gray eyes. More confident now. But he could still remember back ten years to the single night they'd shared, and even now the memory made him smile. Ten years, and he'd never found anyone else to take her place.

Ten years, during which she'd avoided him like the plague.

The night he heard about her marriage, he'd been so torn up inside that he'd gone on his one-and-only, all-night, hell-raising drunk—and got so sick he hadn't touched a drop of liquor in all the years since.

Jake opened his eyes and surveyed the dreary little room. Skimpy, faded curtains barely covered the windows. Below the air-conditioning unit, the fake pine paneling had buckled far enough away from the wall for a possum to crawl through.

And the carpet— Hell, he'd slept in motels far worse over the years. Sometimes even slept in his truck, when he couldn't drive another mile. But the thought of stepping on the carpet in his bare feet made him think of—

A sharp rap sounded at the door. "Hey, Landers, you in there?" Bud Bodine's voice bellowed through the thin wood, nearly loud enough to take the door right off its rusted hinges. Bud didn't hear very well, but anyone he talked to sure did.

"Yeah. Just a minute."

Twenty seconds of silence. "You gotta woman in there or something?"

If the rest of the patrons of the Tumbleweed Motel hadn't heard that, they were either deaf or dead.

"Just hold on a second." Jake's stomach gave an extra pitch as he eased to the edge of the bed and carefully positioned his bad leg.

Cold sweat covered his back by the time he found his cane and hobbled to the door. This wasn't how he wanted to meet Bud again. Leaning the cane against the wall, he straightened to his full height, managed a lazy grin and flung the door open.

Pushing fifty, Bud was an ox of man—a good six foot three, barrel-chested, beer-bellied, with the ruddied look of a guy who had an affair going with his favorite whiskey and wasn't planning to break it off anytime soon. He was Kristen's cousin, but there wasn't one bit of family similarity between them.

He peered into the room, then punched Jake in the shoulder. "And here I thought I might be interrupting something *good.*"

The physical greeting nearly sent Jake to his knees. "Come on in, stranger." He waved Bud toward the farthest of two orange vinyl chairs and then sank into the one by the door.

Bud grinned. "I sure never imagined seeing you in a place like this—figured a big rodeo star would have champagne and silk sheets."

"In Bent Spur?"

"Good point. Why aren't you staying at Guy's? Or out at Roy's?"

"Guess I just thought this place was too darn pretty to pass up," Jake drawled.

Both Roy and Guy had offered their places, and had sounded offended when he'd declined their Wyoming hospitality. But right now he felt more comfortable with solitude. If he was having a bad day, he wanted to be alone with his pain.

Bud frowned. "You okay, Landers? You look a mite poorly."

"Just one too many bulls down in Silver Spring, but I'll be back in the arena in a few months," Jake said easily. "Guess you and I are going to be working together now, or did Guy forget to tell you, too? Kristen was sure surprised."

Bud guffawed, tipping back in his chair until it creaked ominously under his massive weight. "I just heard from Guy *and* Kris. Doesn't sound like he handled this deal too well."

"You have any problem with it?"

"Hell, no. Since Roy quit the road I've managed the contracting side of the business. I handle the stock, haul it to the rodeos, take care of my own payroll. I'll keep on doing that, if you want me. Things will be better with you in charge." He tugged a pack of Camels from his breast pocket. "You mind?"

Jake managed a nonchalant shrug, as Bud lit up and sent a cloud of smoke toward the ceiling. The thought of smelling Bud's stale smoke all night, long after the man left, made Jake grit his teeth. But the effort it would take to stand and follow Bud outside was more than he could manage right now.

With waves of pain rolling up his thigh, he could only imagine how good it would feel to lie back down, even though that bed was lumpier than a plowed field.

Bud drew deeply on his cigarette and gave an appreciative sigh. "I was just coming through town, so I figured I'd let you know that this deal is gonna work out. We're booked through this season, and...Kris is booking for next year. We'll do good, even with the old guys gone."

Jake didn't have to guess at his hesitation over Kristen's name. Many of the contractors he knew were hardworking, hard-drinking charter members of the good-old-boys' network, where the macho camaraderie of rodeo created a strong brotherhood of friendship and support.

Women were accepted as event timers, rodeo secretaries, barrel racers or helpful wives, but some of those guys could make life tough for a woman trying to break into their ranks as a contractor or producer.

Until now Jake hadn't thought about just how tough it was going to be for Kristen to get through this season. From the edge he heard in Bud's voice, he realized that difficulty was going to exist even on her home turf.

"What's the schedule like?"

"Mendota, Nebraska, this weekend. That's a three-day rodeo starting May thirteenth. The following week we head for Colorado." He thought for a minute. "In June MRC has a few venues in the Midwest, but we ain't contracting bucking stock for those. After that, hell. I think we have three dates a month through July and August, and two in September."

"So Kristen's management hasn't hurt business."

Bud snorted. "Guy set up the schedule last year. Some ain't happy, but they signed a contract and it's too late to back out. Next year, we'll be lucky to book half what we got now. No one's gonna trust some fancy Ms. MBA to know rodeo." He spat out the last words.

"Isn't she your *cousin?*" Jake fought to keep his voice level. "I thought you two would work well together."

Learning the business would be hard enough without immediately replacing the man who managed MRC's stock contracting, but right now Jake wanted to haul the guy outside and rearrange his face.

Though at the moment, just standing on his damn right leg would probably take more *try* than Jake could muster.

"I ain't saying she don't know anything. Hell, she tagged along with her daddy all the years she was growin' up." Bud shook his head slowly. "But a woman producer has a tough haul, and she's been out East a lotta years. Right there, she lost ground.''

''I've seen women who do darn well as contractors and producers.''

''Some—but they all have more experience than Kris.'' Bud glanced at his watch and whistled. ''Gotta go. Tina and the kids are at a team penning practice out at the Foster place, and I gotta get there before noon or there'll be hell to pay. Tina gets reeeaal testy.'' At the door he looked back, that easy grin back in place. ''Come out, and I can catch you a run with some good cowhands. You can use my gelding.''

''Thanks…maybe another time.'' *Like in another year—if I'm lucky.*

After Bud's truck roared out of the parking lot, Jake got up as slowly as an old man, cautiously testing his ligaments and joints. Grabbing his cane, he hobbled at a snail's pace toward the blessed heat of a good hot shower. He took four steps before turning back to lie down on the bed in defeat.

Closing his eyes, he wondered bitterly just how much help a crippled cowboy would be in pulling MRC out of its looming failure.

CHAPTER TWO

KRISTEN HADN'T THOUGHT to ask where Jake was staying overnight. After discovering he hadn't gone to Guy's ranch or Roy's, she assumed he must be at the dreary Tumbleweed Motel—the last place on earth anyone would imagine finding a rodeo star of Jake Landers's stature.

Over the years he'd become a cult hero among the rodeo fans. Two Web sites had been started in his honor, where cyber-fans posted notes about his latest rides and big wins, and gushed about seeing him in person.

Kristen didn't glorify the rodeo life the way the fans did. She knew that the quest for a world championship was grueling—cowboys lived on coffee and hope and far too little sleep. It was a wonder that more of them didn't end up as highway statistics in the process.

Now, as she stood outside the Tumbleweed's room number 4, with a warm late-morning breeze at her neck and dust swirling around her battered Tony Llamas, she tried to imagine what could have brought Jake from that life of excitement to a faltering rodeo company and this weather-beaten motel on the edge of a Wyoming town smack dab in the middle of nowhere. His injury—or something else?

Whatever his reasons, the outcome of this meeting would be the same: she'd had second thoughts and could no more stay with MRC than she could have worked side-by-side with her stubborn father. Some relationships were hopeless from the word *go*.

She knocked lightly—then scowled and knocked harder. It was already nine, and even a cowboy used to all-nighters on the road ought to be up by now.

No answer.

Maybe he was hungover. She knocked harder, hoping each sound was blasting through his brain like cannon shot. "Landers? Are you in there?"

His truck—a gleaming ebony Dodge with Colorado plates—was parked right at her heels. He had to be in there. There was absolutely no place worth walking to, just a deserted highway out front and a dusty town a half-mile up the road. The only place to eat in Bent Spur was The Lone Steer, a roadhouse at the far end where the entire menu consisted of decent hamburgers, and the bagged potato chips that hung on a rack by the cash register.

"Hey, are you okay?"

The door was warped, much of its red stain beaten to bare slivered wood by time and wind and blowing grit. Kristen tested the handle; it wobbled in her hand. It looked like the push-button type, and she'd bet he hadn't bothered with any safety chain or dead bolt. Especially if he hadn't been thinking too clearly the night before.

She gave the doorknob a sharp rap with her palm.

It held. But when she rammed her full weight against the door, it sprang open and she lurched inside, barely catching herself before falling unceremoniously into a heap on the threadbare carpet.

"Jake?" The room was dark. Dead quiet. In the silence she heard something skitter inside the walls.

Anger built inside her as she surveyed the gloom for whiskey bottles, expecting to find at least one empty. She'd tried to ignore the stories about Jake Landers, but a man known for bulls, booze, brawling and buckle bunnies tended to generate a lot of talk.

All successful rodeo cowboys commanded respect as athletes, but there was a special mystique and sense of danger surrounding the bull riders. The fans loved the sport, and savvy producers kept interest high by scheduling the bulls at the end of every rodeo.

More than any other contestants, the bull riders stared down death with every ride. Many of them lived high and hard, were the biggest spenders, the most reckless gamblers. She had no doubt that Jake had lived as wild as the rest of them.

She stepped farther into the room and snapped on a bedside lamp. The bedspread was rumpled but had not been turned down. Maybe he'd winked at some woman out at the roadhouse, and she'd whisked him off to her ranch, and even now…

Kristen shook off the thoughts, irritated at the flash of unwanted emotion that coursed through her.

It didn't matter if he slept with the entire female population of Texas and Wyoming combined. She only needed to talk herself out of this deal and then get back to Dallas—and hope that Lambert & Anderson would let her start work right away.

Steam curled under the bathroom door, eerily backlit by the dim light from within. "Get the hell out of here." The usual deep rumble of his voice was gone, replaced by the hollow sound of exhaustion.

The lack of power behind his words gave her license to ignore them. She strode to the bathroom door and rapped on it. "We need to talk. Are you coming out anytime soon, or do you want to work this out through the door?"

She heard the rustle of a shower curtain being shoved back, and caught her breath. What on earth was she doing here? Planning to confront a naked man?

An image of Jake, all powerfully sculpted muscles and lean hard planes, his sun-bronzed skin gleaming, slammed into her brain. Closing her eyes she could almost feel the corded mass of his arms, that indentation down his spine.

She could imagine all too much.

On a quick, indrawn breath, she spun toward the door. "I'll be back...later," she tossed over her shoulder. "An hour—probably two."

She was closing the door behind her when she heard the crash of something metal against a ceramic floor. A heavy *thud*. And then a long, low, almost feral groan.

He can sleep it off right there on the bathroom floor. She took another couple of steps toward her truck. *On the other hand, maybe he'd hit a sharp counter edge on the way down and was in there bleeding to death from a head wound. He could be unconscious....*

She was tempted to keep going, for her own good. But the inner sense of responsibility that made her pull over and help duckling parades and turtles cross busy highways forced her to stop now.

Exasperated at her own weakness, she turned back and walked through the motel room to the bathroom door. "Are you decent?"

"Go away."

At least he was conscious. "Are you bleeding?"

"No."

"Hurt?"

No answer.

She tried the handle. This one wasn't locked, either—no surprise. She hadn't left a bathroom door unlocked since she'd seen an old rerun of *Psycho* in high school, but Jake didn't seem to be overly concerned with security. "I can't leave until I know you're okay."

When he still didn't answer, she pulled the door open.

Through a haze of warm steam she could see Jake sitting on the edge of the tub, his head lowered and hands braced on his thighs. All he'd put on was a pair of unsnapped, faded jeans, and from the looks of him that process had been exhausting. He wasn't hungover, he was in a lot of pain.

Worry lanced her. "Let me help you." Moving across the slick tiles, she automatically reached out to lay a comforting hand on his shoulder.

At the look of frustration and anger in his eyes, she hesitated, then drew her hand back.

"I don't need help." He bit out each word with savage intensity. "Just leave."

"No." She hadn't grown up with a dad like Roy Davis for nothing. "Now what do you want—can I get you your pain meds? Help you into the other room?"

His hands clenched his thighs. "I just want to be left alone. I'll be okay in a minute."

"Have it your way." She closed the lid of the toilet and sat on it, then crossed her legs and studied her fingernails. "I've got time." She held her hand out inches from his nose. "What do you think—Carefree Coral, or would Crimson Passion be better?"

With any other man—with a stranger—she wouldn't have been so nonchalant. But whatever his reputation, however badly he'd humiliated her years ago, she knew Jake would never touch a woman in anger.

Drawing in a ragged breath, he straightened a little, then silently lifted his head. Those white lines of tension at the edges of his eyes and mouth were stark against his tan. His eyes betrayed just how much he was hurting. But oh, Lordy—her memory and imagination hadn't served her as well as she'd thought.

He'd changed from that rakish, handsome daredevil in his twenties into a man—bigger, more massive through the chest. With the seasoned, cynical look of someone who'd been down a lot of miles and had seen far too much.

She instantly knew that this was the real Jake Landers—not that easygoing charmer who'd stopped in her office yesterday.

One corner of his hard mouth curved up just a fraction. "I...just lost my balance pulling on my jeans. It's nothing."

"And I'm Annie Oakley." She glanced down at his right leg. "So how bad are you, really?"

"It'll heal. Yesterday I worked out a little too hard, and that set me back."

Kristen snorted. "A little? What did you try—the Boston Marathon?"

He didn't answer.

There were new scars on him: neat, pale lines over his left shoulder and right elbow. They told stories that he probably wouldn't—of rank bulls and heart-stopping rides, of long surgeries and slow recoveries.

Beneath his jeans she knew of another scar that snaked up the back of his calf a good eight inches, courtesy of a bull known for charging anything that crossed his line of vision.

"You had surgery on that knee yet?"

He shrugged. "Twice."

"Physical therapy?"

"Look, I don't need your help. I'm sure you have lots of things to do. So if you don't mind..."

"Fine." She stood. "All this steam is playing havoc with my hair, anyway. Meet me at The Lone Steer in a half-hour. If you don't show up, I'll be back with Lenny and the rescue squad."

Stubborn fool, she thought to herself as she closed the motel room door behind her and headed for her truck. Just like the men she'd been around while growing up at the ranch. Just as hung up on macho pride, just as determined to avoid help or advice.

If he didn't agree to let her go, it was going to be a very, very long season.

"WELL, LOOKEE HERE. It's Krissie Anne Davis, come back from the city!"

The ever-present wiping cloth in her hand now stilled on the gleaming surface of the bar, Maude Hallahan beamed at Kristen. A tall, angular woman who hadn't been seen in anything but jeans and colorful western shirts in fifty years, Maude was well-known throughout the entire county for her good heart and love of gossip.

"I suspect you already know why," Kristen said dryly as she crossed the floor to the bar and slid onto one of the stools. "Nothing in this town has gotten past you for decades."

"True." The smile faded from Maude's broad, wrinkled face. "I sure am sorry about your mom's Alzheimer's, honey."

"She's still pretty good—mostly just forgetful, but she has wandered a time or two. I know my dad has his hands full."

"It's gotta be hard on both you and your dad, seeing her like that." Without asking, she scooped up a glass of ice, then filled it with diet cola and slid it in front of Kristen.

"Thanks." Kristen reached for some money in the back pocket of her jeans, but Maude waved away her effort.

"On the house. The boys tell me you're taking over

MRC for the season. I sure wish you luck. It isn't gonna be easy, stepping into Guy's shoes.''

Kristen took a long swallow, then set her cola down on its coaster and traced lines in the condensation forming on the glass. ''I'll be okay. I don't want a career in rodeo, but I grew up in the business and...''

''Wayne tells me MRC was sorta slowing down before Guy retired. And you being a woman, well...''

Maude's son Wayne, known as Hoot by everyone except his mother, worked as a bullfighter for most of MRC's rodeos. He favored wild clown makeup and polka-dot pants, but he had the most serious job in all of rodeo—saving the lives of bull riders once they hit the ground. ''It's a testosterone-laden business. I know that as well as anyone, but I—''

From behind Kristen came the squeal of the front door hinges, followed by heavy footsteps.

Maude drew in a sharp breath. ''Lord have mercy, is that Jake Landers? *Here?*''

Kristen sighed. ''Guess you haven't heard about this part of the deal yet. Personally, I wish I hadn't, either. Thanks for the soda, Maude.''

Jake was fully dressed now—the regulation jeans, long enough to wrinkle deeply at the top of his western lacers, a subdued navy plaid shirt, his Resistol in one hand. Nodding toward Maude he slid into a chair close to the door. *I'll bet he doesn't want to walk another step farther,* Kristen thought. ''Had lunch?'' she asked as she strolled over to his table. He shook his head. ''One double cheeseburger, one single,'' she called out to Maude over her shoulder. ''And...'' She paused as if trying to remember, though it didn't take a second's thought. "A Coors?"

"Just water these days."

She must not have hidden her surprise very well, for he shook his head slowly. "You sure haven't wasted time thinking good thoughts about me," he said flatly. "You believe all you hear?"

Sliding into the wooden chair opposite him, she rested both arms on the table. "Jake, I don't want to mix past with present here. We should both take a hard look at this situation, weigh what's important, then make sound decisions on the facts. I am," she added carefully, "sure that you've had time to think this over and come to the same conclusion that I have."

He lifted his gaze slowly from her clasped hands, up her shirt, and then finally to her eyes. "Which is?"

"I'm superfluous, now that you're buying MRC."

He snorted. "*Superfluous?* Is that a business term?"

She gave an impatient wave of her hand. "You can't pull the dumb cowpoke routine with me. I know where you went to school, and I know how well you did."

"Yeah, right. Papered my family room with degrees."

"You could have, if you hadn't decided to go pro and chase gold buckles instead of more four-point GPAs." She took a deep breath. "Look, that isn't the point. Roy did the contracting, while Guy handled the rodeo production side of the business by himself. You've got Bud for the contracting, so you'd be better off if I told you what to do, and then left. If two people take on Guy's job, they—''

''Will make it easier?''

''No, there'll be conflict. Confusion. Spur-of-the-moment decisions that clash.''

''Last I heard, good communication can take care of that.''

''As if you'd know!'' The words were out of her mouth before she could call them back.

Kristen sat back in her chair as warmth crept up her cheeks. She hadn't spent the past ten years thinking about him. Not at all. It was embarrassing to think that now he might assume just that. ''I—I'm not sure why I said that. Everything was for the best. No one knows that better than me.''

His expression grew pensive, his eyes filled with a regret she wouldn't have expected. ''I never meant to hurt you. I'm truly sorry about Las Vegas. Looking back, I feel worse now than I did back then.'' He flashed a quarter-smile. ''We never had a chance to talk afterwards, and I'm sorry about that, too.''

''We were young and stupid. It never would have lasted.''

''I really did care about you, Krissie. Maybe it could have, if we'd both—''

''Shown up at that chapel?''

He laughed then, the same low, lazy laughter that had once charmed her completely, had made her fall in love with him six ways to Sunday the summer she'd followed the circuit as a barrel racer.

She'd loved everything about him—the sexy sparkle in his eye, his intelligence, the easy sensuality that made her heart tumble whenever he glanced her way. She'd been young and stupid, all right.

"I'm not asking you to forgive me."

"It doesn't matter. Look, I can stay a week or two to help you, but I simply don't want to stay longer." She tried for a vaguely apologetic smile. "Do you have any idea what the job is like?"

"I'm just asking for this season, Kris. Not a lifetime."

He winced a little, and she wondered if it was at his choice of words. Then he continued in a lower tone. "I know rodeo from the back of a bull or a bronc. I know what the cowboys need and want out of a rodeo. Hell, I've lived out of a duffel bag and pickup truck for so many years that I wouldn't know what it's like to have the same roof over my head five days in a row. But you're right, I *don't* know the business end."

"So I can't convince you that this is a big mistake."

"Nope. I want you to stay."

He held all the cards, and he knew it.

She gave up the debate. After all, she had been prepared to stay longer to make sure the business sold for a good price. "You probably already know this, but MRC mostly does summer circuit rodeos. Our first rodeo of the year is in Nebraska next weekend, so I leave tonight. When I get back, I'll clear it with Guy or Dad, and then you can come to the office so we can start going through old business records. I can explain how—"

"I'm coming with you."

"But—"

He reached out and laid a hand on hers.

Kristen snatched hers back. "Don't even *think* this will be anything more."

"Sorry…reflex, I guess."

His earnest smile might have fooled someone else, but not her.

"I'm not going to interfere," he said, "but I need to start learning it all. The records will keep until sometime when we aren't on the road."

Maude rounded the bar with a tray in her hands. "Here you go, a single and a double cheeseburger, a water and another diet cola. Anything else?" A light pink flush brightened her cheeks and her hands trembled even as they maintained a death grip on the tray.

Kristen quickly reached to capture the beverage glasses, just in case.

To his credit, Jake didn't seem to notice the older woman's obvious adulation. "This looks great. Thanks."

He looked up at her and flashed his trademark smile—deep dimples, with the half-shy look in his eyes that had always appealed to women of all ages.

An image of Maude keeling over like a felled redwood flashed through Kristen's mind. "Thanks, Maude," she said a little too loudly. "We'll yell if we need anything else."

Maude seemed to shake herself out of her reverie. "Right." She headed back to the bar. "I'll just be over there. Be sure to ask. For anything at all."

"Guess the stories are all still true," Kristen whispered. "Even Maude isn't immune."

Jake looked up from his cheeseburger. "Stories?"

Kristen rolled her eyes. "About you and all those women in every town."

"Every town?"

"Everywhere."

"*Lots* of women?" He shook his head in disbelief as he finished a bite of his sandwich.

Kristen couldn't help but laugh. "Then tell me how you *avoided* all those women!"

"Who had time? When my traveling buddies and I stepped off our bulls after one rodeo, we'd maybe drive all night to the next one. Or drive like hell to catch a charter plane. Half the time, contractors were holding our bulls 'til last so we wouldn't turn out."

Maude strode across the room with a water pitcher, and pounced on those last two words with relish, even though Kristen was sure Maude knew what they meant. "Turn out?"

Jake lifted his gaze and winked at her—and from her answering smile, it was clear his simple gesture had turned her into two hundred pounds of pudding. "Once you enter a rodeo, you owe that entry fee no matter what, and they load a bull into the chutes for you. If you miss your turn, they turn that bull out of the chute without you. You lose your entry fee *and* your chance at the prize money." He snapped his fingers. "Often a hundred bucks or more gone on the entry fee, just like that. Not including travel."

"A big gamble, ain't it," Maude marveled, topping off two inches on Jake's water glass. She hovered nearby. "Anything else you two need?"

Clearly, the older woman wanted to sit down and

chat, and any other day Kristen would have welcomed her into the conversation. But this was business. "Thanks," she said gently, "but I don't think so. We need to discuss a few things."

Looking crestfallen, Maude returned to the bar and began cleaning its gleaming surface once again.

"I'd forgotten just how hectic the rodeo cowboy's life is." Kristen shook down the ice cubes in her glass, then took a sip.

"As soon as the last eight-second horn blew, we'd be racing to the next town." He paused, considering. "Though chasing women does sound better than driving night and day with two guys who snore and one who chews tobacco."

"Right there, you've destroyed the last romantic image I held about cowboys." She pushed away from the table. "I'll stay until October first if we come up with an equitable salary arrangement. Oh, and if you want to go to Nebraska, that's up to you—you're the boss. I leave tonight so I can be there Wednesday morning, but the boys are taking the chutes and arena fencing on Thursday, and Bud will haul the rough stock on Friday. You could probably ride with him."

"I get the feeling you two aren't very close."

"Bud?" She firmly reined in the frustrations that were better left unsaid. Bud defined the term *male chauvinist,* but he was good with the stock and his wife was one of the best rodeo secretaries in the business. "We'll do...fine."

The slight lift of Jake's brow told her that he'd noticed her hesitation. "You leave tonight?" he asked.

"Er...that's right. But Bud—"

"I need to be there early to see what's done from the start."

There were lots of reasons she'd rather he didn't go with her. But if she wanted the sale to succeed for Roy and Guy's sakes, she would need to cooperate.

"I'll pick you up at the motel by five-thirty." With a brief nod in his direction, Kristen stood and headed for the door. "I've got a little business that can't wait."

It was time to straighten out a few things with her father.

THE DRIVE FROM Bent Spur to the Davis Ranch took her through thirty miles of open country that became more hilly with each passing mile.

The ranch—actually two ranches, consolidated after her grandparents died—nestled in the foothills of the Rockies and commanded a beautiful view of the mountains to the west. From a promontory in one of the pastures, one could look out and see the foothills fade into nearly level rangeland to the east.

As soon as she'd crossed the cattle guard at the main gate and topped the first hill, Kristen could see the lifeblood of the operation—a small herd of the more than five-thousand purebred Canadian Hereford cows and their calves grazing up on the hills. Soon they would be trailed into the upper summer ranges.

Kristen sobered at the thought. She'd wanted to pursue a career outside the insular boundaries of this isolated area, but those seasonal cattle drives were the highlight of her year. Even now she could smell the pines and the scents of cattle and horses, could hear the creak of saddle leather and taste the trail dust.

Since leaving home she'd always come back to help. This year she might be in any one of ten states working on a rodeo, when the cattle were moved.

By the time she reached the house, she'd worked herself into a fair state of melancholy. It was compounded the moment she walked in the door.

Maria Vasquez, the family's part-time cook and housekeeper for the past fifteen years, looked up from the stove and smiled. The widow of the ranch's long-time foreman, Maria hadn't wanted to leave the home she'd had for years, and Kristen's family had been more than happy to keep her on.

"So, you come to see your momma before you leave town?" Maria waved a spoon toward the living room. "She's in there, already waiting for supper, though she just had her dinner. She forgets."

"Is she having a good day?"

"Not so bad. She remembered my name today, and dressed on her own. Got everything right except the shoes."

"Where's Dad?"

Maria's beautiful, aristocratic face broke into a smile. She had to be over fifty, but her smooth brown skin and sparkling eyes made her seem much younger. "Where else? Out with the bulls, deciding which one is his new champion. Now that you've left, they are like his children."

Kristen smiled her thanks as she crossed the

kitchen and headed for the living room just beyond. She paused in the arched doorway to study her mother.

Ada Davis sat in a chair at the window, fingering the pages of a magazine in her lap. Slender, tall, she'd been a true beauty in her day, but at sixty-seven, the passing years had softened her aristocratic features, leaving deep lines in her parchment skin. Her soft, silver hair still swept in natural, deep waves away from her face.

She looked like the quintessential grandmother—until one looked into her eyes and discovered that Ada Davis didn't truly live in this body anymore.

"Hi, Mom." Kristen stepped forward and pulled a footstool close to her mother's chair, then sat down in front of her and quieted the woman's restless, ever restless hands within her own. Ada's fingers twitched, as if still turning those magazine pages, and she continued to silently stare out the window.

"Are you feeling okay today?"

Silence.

Kristen sat with her for an hour, reading to her from the paper, offering to fetch her things. After painting Ada's fingernails shell pink, she lifted those fragile hands for inspection. "What do you think, is this glamorous, or what?"

Ada's gaze dropped to her hands. A soft smile wreathed her face. "Lovely."

The lucid response touched Kristen's heart. Her mother had been a city girl who loved pretty things yet had chosen the hard life of a rancher's wife. Through all the years of Guy's rodeo days as a contestant and later as a contractor, she'd been out on this isolated ranch raising her child alone. She'd never once complained.

Kristen stood and enveloped her mother in a long, gentle embrace, feeling a stab of sorrow at how bony and fragile Ada was beneath the thick pink sweater she insisted on wearing every day. "I love you, Momma."

Ada's arms fluttered upward and caught Kristen in a weak embrace, then fell back to her lap. "I missed you. You've been playing outside too long today."

"I missed you, too, Mom."

A soft smile lit Ada's face, and with it shone a hint of just how beautiful she had been, long ago. A good ten minutes passed before she spoke again, her voice now soft as the beat of a butterfly's wings. Kristen had to lean close to hear the words.

"I always knew."

"Knew what, Momma?" Kristen turned to follow her mother's gaze.

Through the window she could see her father standing beside a pasture fence on the hill rising behind the cattle barns. In that pasture were fifteen of his beloved Brahma cows and a dozen calves.

A tear glistened on Ada's eyelashes. "I always knew."

KRISTEN CAUGHT UP with her father near the large pens holding this year's lineup of bucking bulls. Nodding a casual greeting to her, he continued to fill the feed bunks with prime alfalfa out of the back of a pickup.

It felt good to be back, she thought, breathing in the scents of alfalfa and cattle and crisp mountain air. She glanced with approval at the massive weight and overall condition of the bulls. Good contractors took better care of their livestock than of themselves. It was a business yet much more than that—for these animals were the stars of the rodeo, each with different talents and personalities. Good ones could sell for over twenty-thousand, and the biggest stars could go for far more.

"I see you've still got 88 and Tornado Alley penned alone," she called out.

Roy threw the last of the hay over the fence—a perfect launch into the long bunk running parallel to the lane. "Have to, after what happened in Fort Wayne."

Kristen shuddered, remembering. She'd gone along on that trip to secretary the rodeo. Usually a group of bucking bulls could be penned together, but the night before, 88 and Tornado Alley had taken a younger bull down and relentlessly mauled him, ignoring all efforts of the cowboys to get them apart. In the end, the downed bull had had a rib driven into its lung and had had to be humanely destroyed.

But a few, like Cropduster, were gentle attention-seekers away from the bucking chutes, and when ridden pulled Jeckyl-and-Hyde personality changes that left most cowboys face-first in the dirt.

Duster left his hay and sidled over to the fence. Kristen obediently scratched the powerful animal behind the ears. "How're you doing, buddy?"

"He's doing good," Roy said as he jumped down

from the back of the pickup and ambled up the lane to join her. "Dumps most of his riders in under four seconds. With another year of experience, he oughta qualify for the finals."

Roy had topped out at five foot ten—tall for a bull rider—during his last year of competition, but had kept the wiry, athletic build and still looked like he could go out and compete with some of the best.

"Is Duster going to Nebraska this weekend?" she asked.

Nodding, Roy ticked off the numbers and names of the others that would be hauled.

"Pretty easy life. Best care and feed in the world for eight seconds of work every now and again." She reached a little farther through the fence to scratch behind the bull's other ear, then withdrew her hand and straightened. "How's Mom doing these days?"

The light in Roy's eyes faded. "Not any better, but okay."

"Does she talk much?"

He gave an impatient shrug of one shoulder, as if trying to dislodge a load too heavy to carry. "Some."

"Do you…try to talk to her, Dad?" Kristen asked, choosing her words carefully. "The days are long for her, just sitting at that window. Maybe if—"

"You aren't here day and night. You don't know." He sliced the air sharply with his hand. "Maria and I do our best. When that's not good enough, we'll have to…put her in some home. God willing, that won't be for a long time. The money…"

Kristen almost reached out and laid a hand on his

arm, but it had been a long, long time since she'd touched her father. "I'm sorry. I know it's hard."

Shrugging irritably, he turned toward his truck.

She took a deep breath. *On to the next topic.* "Why didn't you tell me about the sale of MRC?"

He stopped but didn't look back.

"I think I had a right to know."

With a sigh, Roy turned to face her. "Guy called, said Jake made a good offer. We took it."

"But I had no clue until Jake walked into the office this morning. Didn't I deserve to be told?"

"You found out today, didn't you?"

Frustration swept her. "I should have been warned. I'd have got everything ready for him to take over on his own."

"You won't work with him?" Roy scowled. "You just need to teach him how to run the business."

"Surely you of all people know that I wouldn't ever want to work with—"

"I know two kids nearly made a stupid mistake. That has nothing to do with this deal."

Perceptive and sensitive as ever. Kristen thought back to her father's anger at the rodeo in Las Vegas, when she'd announced her sudden wedding plans.

He'd disappeared for the next few days, then shown up at the chapel voicing suspicions about her being pregnant, embarrassing her in front of the handful of friends who'd come to attend the ceremony. When Jake failed to show up, Roy clearly had been pleased. There had been no comforting words from her father, even while she stood in that chapel and cried.

It had taken years before she could talk to him with as much civility as she did now.

"You aren't...selling now because something is wrong with you or Guy, are you?"

Shaking his head, he fixed his attention on the bulls ambling up to the feeders.

She felt immense relief, even as she faced the inevitable. "Jake says the deal won't go through unless I stay on."

"Is that so hard? You would have been here running the company that long, anyway."

"Why the rush to sell now?"

Roy chewed his lower lip—a habit he'd developed after finally managing to quit chewing tobacco—and she could tell that he found the next words hard to say. "Feed prices went up again...taxes...Ada could be in a nursing home by winter. We need this sale to go through."

Kristen sighed, knowing that there would be no request, no simple "please and thank you" out of her father. "I told Jake I would stay until October first."

Roy held her gaze for a split second, then looked away. "Good."

They fell into an uneasy conversation about safer topics—the weather, cattle prices, Kristen's upcoming trip to Nebraska—until she glanced at her watch.

"I need to get back to the office, Dad. I'll call from Nebraska to check on Mom, okay?"

Roy hesitated for a moment, then grunted a farewell and turned toward his pickup.

Kristen sighed again as she headed back to her own truck. She knew that he would never change.

But as she drove away, her thoughts weren't on her stubborn father's heart. All she could think about was her mother, who sat at her window day after day and cried silent tears over the past.

CHAPTER THREE

AFTER A LATE START out of Bent Spur, they crossed the Nebraska state line and pulled into Mendota by midnight. All things considered, Kristen found herself surprisingly at ease with Jake's quiet presence in the truck.

Thinking of him as a distant relative helped.

He certainly wasn't a high-maintenance passenger who bored her to death with constant chatter. Instead, he occasionally tossed out questions about the business and acted truly interested in her responses.

If things had been different, they might even have had a chance to become good friends.

"Here we are," she said, peering up at the hot-pink neon sign flashing "Stardust" above their heads.

Despite the surprisingly comfortable camaraderie they'd developed during the long drive, she felt a sudden flicker of awkwardness now—like that moment at the end of a first high school date, when one didn't quite know how to handle farewells on the front doorstep.

"I reserved two rooms, so we should be fine. Are you hungry? After I check us in we can go hunt down some all-night truck stop."

Jake had been lounging at the opposite side of the

cab as if it were an easy chair—maybe it was, for a guy who lived on the road. He straightened, wincing as he moved his knee, and gave her an amused glance, then nodded toward Main Street.

A black hole in space couldn't have been darker than downtown Mendota at midnight.

"I think you lost your last chance to get food when we crossed the border."

Actually I was just launching into nervous babble. She was pretty sure Jake recognized it for what it was—emotional remnants of the past that would collide with the present for as long as they continued this brief business relationship.

"That last chili dog did me in," she said. "Road food doesn't hold a lot of appeal."

"That's where you're wrong. You just need to know where to go."

"Then you'll have to show me, or I'm not going to last long at this." She turned off the crew-cab truck's motor. "Be back in a second."

He eased out of the truck, swearing softly as he put weight on his injured knee. Earlier on the trip he'd managed without his cane, but now he retrieved it from the back seat of the truck.

The grim set of his mouth told her that he loathed every step he took with that cane, but still he followed her determinedly to the motel office door.

"I'll take care of my own bill," he muttered.

"MRC has a budget for travel. It's all part of the standard expenses." She reached into her leather purse and withdrew the VISA she'd used for gasoline along the way. "You just bought the company, for heaven's sake."

"Provided you stay for the entire season."

"We're both here, aren't we?" Exasperated, she held out both hands, palm up.

"So far. I'll keep my expense records for taxes."

"Suit yourself." If some sort of cowboy code of ethics was going to make him pay his own way, so be it. The season would be over soon enough, the deal would be finalized, and he could do whatever he liked.

When an elderly face peered through the curtained window of the door, she gave her brightest smile. "We've got reservations!"

After a moment's hesitation, an old man unlocked the door. "Cain't be too careful," he muttered as he rounded the desk and pawed through some papers. He glanced up at her. "Must be a mistake. You want one room, right?

"Two."

"Adjoining?"

"No. Two *totally* separate people, believe me."

Jake snorted.

Mumbling under his breath, the old man snagged keys from opposite ends of his pegboard and tossed them on the table along with a pair of registration cards.

Minutes later, after refusing Jake's help in retrieving her luggage from the back seat of the pickup, Kristen found him standing to one side, watching her.

"What?"

Moving had apparently eased some of the discomfort in his knee, because now he managed a grin. "I was just thinking about how much you've changed in the past ten years."

"Thanks." She shouldered a suit bag and grabbed a suitcase in each hand. "That's exactly what a woman wants to hear. 'Hi, sugar, you sure look old today!'"

"You look better than ever. But you were just a kid back then. What—eighteen? Sorta shy, didn't have much to say. I think you would've fainted if you had to stand up to anyone."

She set the suitcases back down with a thump. "I wasn't that bad."

"Darlin', you blushed five shades of pink if someone complimented your boots."

The parking lot was dark, save for the rosy flash of light from the motel sign and the moth-wreathed security lights at either end of the parking lot.

There was a certain inherent intimacy, standing in the darkness bantering with the most handsome man she'd ever laid eyes on—the man she'd once thought would be her husband until the day she died.

And if she stood here much longer, listening to the seductive warmth of that familiar baritone voice, she'd be thinking about things that did not fit in with her career plans, her new life in Dallas. She might even forget why he was the last man on earth she would ever trust again.

They were two adults, far from home, but there was no way she was going to risk involvement with Jake Landers.

The last time had broken her heart.

SHE'D SET HER ALARM for six on Wednesday morning. He was pounding on her door at five.

"I drove out to the truck stop for coffee and doughnuts. I'm setting a bag by your door. You awake?"

"Arrgghhh," she mumbled as she peered at the alarm clock on the bedside table. Bleary-eyed, she sat up and squinted at the darkness outside, visible through a slit in the curtains. "Is there a reason for this, or do you just like being up early?"

"I run—well, a little. I picked up a new knee brace before we left."

Run? She thought of him wincing as he'd climbed out of the truck last night. The frustration in his eyes when he'd had to use his cane. "I thought running got you into trouble last time. Should you be doing that sort of thing?"

"Moving is good therapy. Want to come along?"

A trip from the bed to the bathroom sounded just about right. More than that, no dice. "Uh...maybe later. You go have fun."

After he left, she flopped back onto the sheets and rubbed her eyes. How long had it been since she'd found time to run, or to do any of those little extra things for herself?

She'd gone after her MBA with single-minded determination, and between the first and second year she'd had the ideal summer internship—working on a brand management team for a high-profile pharmaceutical company. Countless hours, endless copy to write, monumental stress.

But she'd embraced each challenge with excitement because every step along the way meant another step away from the kind of isolated and dreary life her mother had led. For a girl from a flyspeck town on a Wyoming map, the internship and her new career were a dream come true.

She should have been launching into that career right now. Then again, maybe this was a chance to recharge her soul before starting up the corporate ladder.

"Wait!"

He didn't answer, but she got up anyway. She found the coffee Jake had left and took a swallow as she pulled on jeans, a T-shirt and a scuffed pair of Nikes. Within minutes she was outside her motel door, breathing in damp, cool air as she did some stretches and then started off at an easy pace toward the darkened streets of downtown Mendota.

She hadn't gone fifty yards before she heard footsteps behind her.

"It's just me," Jake said. He'd already been walking far longer than he should have, if the lines of strain on his face were any clue.

"I heard you say to wait, so I just went around the block." His teeth flashed white as he spoke, and in a torn, sleeveless T-shirt and sweatpants, he looked muscular, trim and—if one ignored his knee—very, very fit.

"Maybe we should just sit down and have those doughnuts, and the coffee while it's still hot."

"I'm going to walk for ten minutes more, then try jogging for five." He shortened his stride and fell in step with her. "With ibuprofen, the new brace and a good adhesive tape wrap, I figure I should be able to get up to an hour by next week. Maybe,'' he added with a rueful smile.

"Not that I expect you to believe me, but sometimes rest and healing are even better than blind determination."

He shot her a patient look. "I'm already doing better than the doctor's predicted."

"How did it happen?"

They passed a darkened gas station, a beauty salon and two bars before he finally answered. "Silver Springs, last year." He fell silent for a few strides. "The bull turned back hard, took a wild, high jump. Coming down, he slipped in the mud and flipped over. That broke my leg—but before the bullfighters could get there, he got up, spun and hooked me. He sorta doubled the damage."

A chill coursed through her. She'd seen those train wrecks happen...had heard the horrible silence sweep through the crowd, as if every person were breathing a prayer. It wasn't just riding the bull that was dangerous—reaching safety afterwards could be much, much worse.

"So what broke?" She tried to sound nonchalant, but couldn't quite still the waver in her voice. As they walked through the dim illumination of a street lamp, she saw his sardonic smile.

"A compound, comminuted fracture, just above my knee, and a shattered patella. Two surgeries—the second because all the pieces weren't healing right." He gave a short laugh. "Between this and my other ankle, I'll set off metal detectors at airports for the rest of my life."

"One heck of a way to retire."

"Retire?"

"Surely you aren't going back."

"I'm not going out this way."

"But at thirty-four—a lot of guys quit before they're thirty!"

"I'm going to heal, and then I'm going back to ride one last bull to the buzzer."

She walked along in silence for a while, measuring her words. "My cousin shattered his knee and never dared go back on the circuit. The docs said a new joint could last fifteen years or more given normal use, but there were only so many times they could drill bone for a replacement. By the time you're fifty, sixty—what then?"

"I'm not planning on a full season—just one good bull. I'm going to retire with success, not failure."

"That one time could be disaster."

A muscle in his jaw jerked. "It won't be."

As they passed the next block, Jake's stride started to falter. "Should we turn back?"

"No." He glanced at his watch. "In another three minutes I'll try jogging."

"You're already limping!"

He touched her arm and pulled to a halt, then turned to face her. "I appreciate the concern. But I'm doing this my way."

"You're crazy. Be thankful that you're still able to walk, and that you had a great career…and move on." She slammed a hand on one hip and glared up at him. "What happens if you do get on a bull one last time—and when you get off, you can't run fast enough for the fence? What happens if you break those bones again?''

"Kris—''

"You go on." She turned back toward the motel. "I'm going back to bed for an hour or so. Be ready to start working at nine o'clock.''

He started to speak, but she held up a hand. "You're right. It's your life and absolutely no concern of mine.''

Without looking back she knew he was following her, making sure she got back safely before going back out on his fool's mission.

She'd never forgotten his warm smile, his charm. His genuine interest in others that made women from nine to ninety sparkle in his presence. But she *had* forgotten his stubborn streak—the one that made him push himself too hard, too fast, no matter what the price.

This time, it could cost him his life.

"HERE'S THE AGENDA for this morning," Kristen announced a few hours later as they pulled into the parking lot of the *Mendota Gazette*. "We schmooze with as many people as possible in this town—the rodeo sponsors, local organizations and businesses, anyone who can provide us with good publicity. Advance posters were sent out, but now we need to make sure the town is covered. I'm going in to talk to the newspaper staff to try to set up some coverage. Do you want to go out and work on the posters, or come in with me?''

Jake looked faintly amused. "Schmooze?''

"It's all good public relations, and important for ticket sales," she said briskly. "Some rodeos are organized by various clubs or a town committee, but this one is MRC's own venture. We've kept the same local sponsors over the years, but it's our baby. We take the risks, we get all the profit."

Leaving his cane in the truck, Jake trailed along behind her as she strode up to the front desk inside the newspaper office. "We're here to see Ned Dawson. Is he in?"

The matronly woman at the desk looked up and smiled. "Yes, he's..." Her gaze shifted up toward Jake and her voice trailed away. "He's..."

"He's in?" Kristen offered. "Can we talk to him?"

The older women shook her head, as if to clear her thoughts. "Uh...sure. Who are you?"

"We're with the MRC Rodeo. He should be expecting us."

Fumbling with the papers in front of her, the woman grabbed at one sheet that nearly slithered off the side of her desk, then tapped them all into a haphazard pile. She led Jake and Kristen back to a cluttered corner office.

"Thanks, ma'am," Jake drawled.

Giving them both a nervous smile, the woman retreated to her desk in front.

"How do you *do* that?" Kristen whispered. "She could be your grandma!"

"Do what?"

"You said two words and made that woman melt."

A corner of his mouth lifted. "Manners."

"Trust me. That's not it."

Ned, a gaunt man in his sixties with thick glasses and thinning hair, reached across the stacks of papers on his desk to shake hands, then settled back in his chair and waved them to the chairs in front of his desk.

He pursed his lips. "The rodeo has been here in town for—what, maybe six years? I haven't had a chance to meet you two, though." He regarded Jake with a thoughtful look. "Son, you look mighty familiar."

Jake shifted uncomfortably in his seat.

"This is Jake Landers. He won the world championship in bull riding twice, and now he's in the process of buying MRC. I'm Roy Davis's daughter, currently managing the company during the transition. We'd like to arrange some interview opportunities. Our bullfighters and the announcer will be in town tomorrow, and—"

"World champion, eh?" A gleam of interest sparkled in Ned's eyes. "Now I remember. There was a lot of news about you a year ago—just before the end of the season, I think."

It struck Kristen that bringing Jake in hadn't been such a bad idea, after all. Publicity, whether on the bullfighters or on Jake Landers, still called attention to the rodeo, and in turn, sold tickets.

Jake had leaned back in his chair and was studying the brim of his hat, so Kristen took over. "He drew a killer bull in Silver Springs," she said, with just the right note of awe. "He was in the running for a third championship—everyone figured he was unbeatable.

His bull took a spectacular fall, then hooked him in the air—'' she drew an arc skyward with a hand ''—and he sustained severe injuries.''

"Kristen." Jake still sat back in his chair as if he were on the verge of a nap, but she could feel a sudden crackling of tension in the air.

"He doesn't like to talk about it much,'' she added blithely. "You'll have to ask him the rest—or you'll find articles on some of the rodeo Web sites. Now about the bullfighters and announcers...''

The bullfighters in full clown paint and the rodeo announcer with his extensive knowledge, were ideal interviews to schedule and would provide good copy. Apparently the editor agreed, because within a few minutes the appointments were set and Kristen had provided her printed information on the rodeo.

"Well, thanks again, Ned,'' she concluded, rising from her seat and extending a hand across his desk. "This rodeo is a wonderful event for your community. We hope to bring out big crowds and give everyone more than their money's worth.''

But Ned wasn't quite done. "In all the years of MRC coming to town, I don't think I've ever had the pleasure of doing business with a young lady. That's pretty unusual in rodeo, isn't it?''

"Actually, there are some women who are successful contractors and producers, but yes—it's less common.''

Ned tapped a finger thoughtfully against his thin lips. "Would you say there's—an element of conflict, working as a producer in a male-dominated sport?''

Jake snorted. "Yes, it's—''

"No," Kristen countered. "I think in this day and age the rodeo world is enlightened about the value and capability of women in any career capacity. I appreciate your time, Mr. Dawson." She handed him a couple of complimentary tickets, then smiled sweetly at Jake. "It's time to run—we have *lots* of stops to make."

Grabbing at Jake's arm, she started toward the door.

Ned rose from his chair and nodded, as Kristen waved goodbye. "My reporter will be talking to some of the folks beforehand, but I think I might be stopping out at the performances myself. Sounds like it will be a very newsworthy event."

AS SOON AS THEY WERE in the truck, Kristen turned on the ignition and then rested one wrist on the steering wheel. "We need to talk about interviews."

Jake lifted his arm and laid it across the back of the seat, but his narrowed eyes didn't appear friendly. "And also about where you learned to lie so well. *Enlightened?* Even ol' Ned knows that rodeo is still a male-dominated sport."

The counterattack was no surprise. Jake probably wasn't accustomed to being told much of anything, and some men—like her dad—could never be told anything at all if they didn't want to hear it. But Jake had to understand, or there would be hell to pay.

"There are some topics that are off-limits. Some things that…can be misinterpreted, pounced on by a reporter and blown out of proportion. You must have done thousands of interviews. You know what I mean.''

He gave a short nod.

"We can't control what they write, but we can give them the solid, accurate information they need to do their job fairly.''

Jake lifted a brow. "And your concern is…''

"Give a reporter any hint that some male chauvinist jerk has made things hard for me, and the story hitting the stands could have awful ramifications. These stories don't die. A lot of them end up available on the Internet and can be accessed by anyone.''

"You're saying you've had no problems at all? I've been around for just a few days, and I've seen it happen more than once.''

"I don't want newspapers implying that I'm a little girl who's all upset because the big, bad men won't give her a chance. That kind of publicity would damage my credibility in the industry *and* my value to MRC.''

"Fair enough. And while we're at it, my past and my injuries aren't material to toss to some reporter in hope of extra publicity.''

They stared at each other a moment. "Fair enough,'' she said finally. "I'm sorry. People aren't going to forget who you are and what you've won, but no one will hear anything about you from me.'' Shifting the truck into reverse, she checked the rearview mirror and then swung out onto the highway. "Now we have to call on our sponsors. Do you have any questions about how the sponsorships work?''

"I've been involved from the cowboy side. I wore

the shirt and patches for several companies over the past few years. The companies paid me, provided clothing and logo patches, set up public appearances."

"It's similar on this side of the business. Staging a rodeo can cost twenty to thirty thousand, so it really helps to get some sponsorship money up front. We give the sponsors VIP treatment at the performances, announce them during the event, hang their banners around the ring. The company name goes on the tickets and printed programs. They also receive lots of publicity and appreciation from the community."

In the next hour they visited the car dealer, the grocery and a western store—all sponsors of the rodeo—chatting with the owners and distributing VIP tickets for the performances.

Once they were back in the truck, Kristen flipped through her notebook. "Much of your time before each rodeo will be spent on public relations and promotion," she said with a grudging smile, "and you're a natural. Next we hit the radio station here in town to make final arrangements for some interviews."

"You don't just call ahead?"

She nodded. "I did, but we need to stop and discuss the details, drop off comp tickets. Interviews are often done by phone, and the station plays the tapes later just as if they were live. Here, we've got a live call-in program—that's even better."

They found the station in a small cement-block building on the edge of town. The disc jockey had twenty minutes before going on air and was more than willing to chat. His eyes lit up when Kristen handed him a dozen complimentary tickets.

"Take your wife to the rodeo. You can use the other tickets for some sort of give-away contest if you like." She fished through her canvas tote, then withdrew a stapled set of papers. "Here are some trivia questions you might want to use for the interview."

"Interview?"

"On the rodeo. We're scheduled for a call-in show tomorrow afternoon."

"Not anymore." The DJ frowned. "That's filled, but—"

"Filled?"

"Yeah. We were lucky to find something at such late notice, too."

"But our announcer and the bullfighters are coming in early for that interview. They're great on the air."

He glanced up at the calendar on the wall. "Our schedule is full. I'd be run out of town if I preempted the game coverage scheduled Thursday evening. Our most popular talk show is Wednesday evening—tonight—and we can't move that..." He thought for a minute, then shrugged. "If you come in early tomorrow, maybe we can fit you into Mortie—uh, Quinn Phillips's morning show. It's the best I can do."

Kristen stared at him. "I called last week and set this up, and sent a follow-up letter."

"Oh, I saw the letter, and Bob mentioned your call last week. But when you changed your mind, we didn't book a slot in any of the programs."

"Changed my mind?"

"Sure. When your manager called Monday to say you wanted to cancel, we rescheduled the slot."

"*Manager?* I'm the manager, and I sure didn't call."

The disc jockey's smile slipped, and he gave an impatient wave of his hand. "Look, honey. I've got to cut this short so I can get ready for my show. I'll do the best I can for you. But I can't help it if your company screwed up."

She stared back at him, stunned into momentary silence. Who would have canceled that interview, and why?

CHAPTER FOUR

THEY WERE FINALLY DONE for the day. He hoped. His knee hurt like hell, and the painkillers hadn't helped for the past hour.

After leaving the radio station, they'd stopped at every gas station and store in town, the feed elevator, three bars and two insurance agencies, giving a complimentary ticket to anyone willing to post the flyer in a front window.

In the process, Kristen found out where to rent a forklift and a tractor for the best price, and who would be on duty for emergency medical coverage on the grounds. Their last stop had been at the local vet clinic, where she'd made final arrangements for veterinary coverage of the performances.

She'd smiled, she'd worked efficiently and she'd presented a professional front to everyone she met. But that incident back at the radio station had upset her more than she would admit. That, and the fact that the same radio station had been announcing the possibility of rain for Thursday night through Saturday.

"Look, it's already five o'clock. Let's head out to that steak house south of town," he suggested, as they drove down Main Street for the twentieth time. "You have to be hungry by now."

She barely glanced in his direction. "I need to get back to my room and check the Weather Channel. You can take the truck—"

"I don't want to eat alone, and you need a decent meal." He reached over and gave her shoulder a playful shake. "Lighten up a little. You aren't going to change the weather by listening to a report."

"But I can better prepare for it," she snapped, her knuckles white on the steering wheel. "It's serious business on this side of the fence. The cowboys arrive, ride and leave, but every last detail of our planning matters a great deal."

"Yeah, we cowboys have an easy life," he drawled. "We just sort of drop in, a few of us get hurt, and then the rest aimlessly wander away and enjoy the sights."

She flushed. "I didn't mean it that way."

"You were Ms. Cool until we heard about the canceled radio interview. If it means that much to you, I'll go do the blasted thing tomorrow. Hell, I've done so many of them, I can give a good interview in my sleep."

He'd thought she would be relieved at the offer. Instead, she worried her lower lip with her teeth as she gave a distracted nod. "Yeah—that would be good."

He waited patiently for her to elaborate, but she just kept her gaze pinned to the road ahead and maintained a death grip on the wheel. "So what's wrong?"

"Nothing."

"There you go again. When did you start parting company with the truth?"

She lifted one hand from the wheel and gave a dismissive wave. "The canceled interview couldn't—*shouldn't*—have happened. There's no one at MRC who would have done that. The only person working on the production side is me."

"Call Roy and Guy. Maybe someone from the station called Wyoming just to verify the time, and one of them misunderstood. Thought it was some radio calling about a contest or something."

"But someone called this radio station, not the other way around."

"It doesn't matter, does it? Maybe the DJ forgot, double-booked the slot and was covering for himself. I'll do the interview, or you can. You'll still get the free airtime to promote the rodeo."

Her shoulders relaxed slightly. "I suppose you're right. You'd be the best person for the job, if you don't mind." She flipped on the left turn signal and slowed to a stop in front of the motel. "I can't guarantee the disc jockey will stick to the questions I sent in, but I'll print an extra copy of them for you to look over."

She looked so earnest, so concerned, that he had to hold back a chuckle. "I think I'll manage."

"It won't be just about cowboys. Do you know how many broncs and bulls will be coming in? Who the big-name entries are this weekend? How many people we expect? How many pounds of hot dogs we'll go through? Or who had the record rides here over the past five years?''

She had him there. ''Run in and get your list, and then you can go over the material while we eat supper.''

''No, I really—''

''I could come by your room a little later, instead.'' He lowered his voice just a notch. ''We could relax, and you could give me all the information I need.''

She drew in a sharp breath. ''Dinner,'' she shot back, ''would be just dandy.''

Interesting. Maybe beneath that cool, businesslike exterior, she still had some remnant of feeling for him. It would only be fair, after all. Even after all these years, he knew he'd done the right thing when he'd walked away.

But he'd never quit wishing things had been different.

THEY ARRIVED at the radio station fifteen minutes early on Thursday morning. A short, balding Humpty Dumpty clone stood at the front desk, talking to the receptionist who'd blushed so deeply when Jake had smiled at her the day before.

Today, she didn't so much as look in Jake's direction, but she must have been talking about him, because the man turned and smiled.

''You're Landers? I'm Quinn Phillips, Mendota's King of Country.'' He gave a self-deprecating laugh as he extended a hand. ''Otherwise known as Mortie Kowalsky. I get to be King because there's only one station in town.''

As they shook hands, his gaze dropped to Jake's gold trophy buckle. He gave a low whistle. "You bet I'd like to have you on a show. Our listeners ought to *love* this. Have a good trip here?" Without waiting for a reply, he turned and signaled to a secretary. "Hey, take these two into the lounge and get them some coffee."

Mortie scurried into a small office behind the secretary's desk and flipped on a computer, then plopped into a chair and disappeared from view behind the monitor. "I'll be on the air in about eight minutes," he called out. "I'll get to you at about ten after, okay?"

"He certainly doesn't look intimidating," Kristen murmured to Jake, as they followed the secretary down a short hallway. "The only problem might be getting a word in edgewise. Everything should go fine. Just remember the crib sheets I gave you, and be careful not to wander off the subject."

The secretary ushered them into a dank, harvest-gold room with a magazine-strewn table and four chairs upholstered in torn red vinyl. The room smelled like a musty basement. With quick efficiency, she poured them coffee from the coffeemaker on a card table in the corner, and dropped a basket of creamer and sugar packets between them.

"Thanks, ma'am," Jake drawled.

"Well, yes—of course." A flustered pink rising in her cheeks, she gave a distracted nod to Kristen and backed through the door.

"You are going to give that woman heart failure,"

Kristen warned. She took a sip of coffee, then eyed the contents of the cup and slid it away from herself.

"How the Sam Hill would I do that?"

"With—with those shy-cowboy grins—" she lowered her voice to a gritty baritone and gave him an exaggerated, heavy-lidded look "—and that 'thank you, ma'am' stuff."

"I can't be polite?"

She gave a sound of frustration as she folded her hands neatly on the table. "If the DJ asks you about the states MRC covers, you say…"

He could picture her as a schoolteacher with her hair skinned back into some sort of knot on her head, tapping a ruler against her palm, with a room full of kids staring obediently back at her. "Just about anywhere we can find on the map?"

"No." Her stern schoolmarm expression darkened. "You say we cover states east of the Rockies, north of Texas, generally this side of the Mississippi. How many contestants are expected this weekend?"

"I think you're just a little tense about all of this. It'll be fine."

"How can it be fine? I'll bet you didn't even *read* those pages again after supper last night!"

"It'll be fine, because you're going in."

That stopped her cold. "What?"

"You know all these details."

"You promised!"

"You can come along," he continued patiently, "and if there's anything that throws me, you can whisper it or write me a fast note. Or point it out on those blasted sheets of yours. Heck, you might just want to jump right in and take over. I sure won't mind.''

Her gaze flickered. ''I don't think—''

''Darlin', you think on your feet just fine. The time will go by so fast, you won't even realize it's over.'' He bit back a smile. For all that businessperson bravado she'd acquired over the years, she was afraid!

Once again, the years slid away to the time when he'd first seen her—a shy, slender girl who'd materialized like a blond angel out of the roiling dust and heat of that rodeo in Scottsbluff. At just the sight of her, his heart had pounded in his chest—and time had stood still.

The memory touched him, warming areas of his heart he'd shut away years ago—areas he had no business going into after all this time. It might have been a poor match before, but now it was absolutely impossible.

She had a bright future ahead of her in Dallas and had worked darn hard to make it happen. He could no more live within fifty miles of a city than a paint horse could change spots. Even weekends spent at indoor rodeos—which were always held near large towns—made him edgy.

And the last thing she needed holding her back was some broken-down cowboy.

''Hell, I might get nervous, say the wrong thing and destroy MRC's future in one fell swoop.''

He was teasing her, and she knew it. But when the secretary appeared at the door and motioned them to follow, Kristen stood and followed Jake into a cramped studio.

There was barely enough space for Mendota's roly-poly King of Country and all the radio paraphernalia. He sat behind a control board the width of an old Cadillac's dashboard. Racks of CDs hung slightly askew on the walls to his left, competing for space with shelves holding CD players, an old reel-to-reel tape machine, and stacks of what looked like eight-track cassettes atop something resembling a VCR.

If the lounge had been depressing, *this* room would make Martha Stewart weep.

Yellowed linoleum curled up from the floor; avocado shag carpeting covered the wall, molting in damp shreds. Kristen had a sudden vision of just what might be living in that carpet. Centipedes… millipedes…

She edged closer to Jake to avoid touching the walls.

"Okay, folks, that's your mike. And as you can see, you'll have to get real friendly if you're both gonna talk into it. We got a little over a minute left until this song is done, and then you're on. Any questions?"

Jake eased into one of the chairs at the mike and grabbed Kristen's hand, pulling her down into the chair next to him.

He drew in a sharp breath as her knee collided with his.

Behind them, the secretary quietly shut the door.

"I don't want to be in here," she said through her teeth.

He winked at her. "Too late."

She could feel the warmth of his thigh against hers,

and in the oppressively tiny room she imagined she could hear his heartbeat. Hers seemed to thunder clear down to her fingers and toes, though whether from tension at the tight space or her proximity to Jake Landers, she didn't want to guess.

Business. This is only business. Forcing herself to take a deep breath, she focused on the wall above the console, where a clock silently ticked away the seconds. Beside it, a tattered two-foot square of white tagboard showed another clock face—drawn with a careless marker—indicating the segments of an hour. News feed at the top. Commercial. Music from ten after the hour to twenty after.

A bright pink scrap of paper taped onto the board at five after the hour read: ''Jake Landers, World Champion Bull Rider.'' Not the MRC Rodeo company, or the Mendota Annual Rodeo.

Just Jake.

Frowning, she turned to Jake and started to speak, but the DJ held a pudgy finger to his lips as he flipped a switch and launched into a rollicking, down-home presentation of the local news and weather.

She nudged Jake with her shoulder, then pointed to the schedule on the wall. *The rodeo,* she mouthed, hoping he got the message.

He grinned down at her before looking up at the tagboard. His smile faded as his gaze veered over to the papers in front of the DJ. She could feel the tension grip him as his mouth flattened into a hard line.

Curious, she peered past him, but couldn't make out the words on the papers. Probably the questions she'd provided, she reassured herself. At least the DJ was efficient. Not all men were capable of following simple instructions, but when one did, things went so much more smooth—

Jake stood up abruptly.

Alarmed, the DJ drew back, his eyes wide. "And that's it for the local weather, folks," he said hastily, flipping a switch to start a commercial. He rolled his chair back from the microphone. "What's going on?"

Jake jerked his chin toward the schedule on the wall. "This interview—you were planning to focus on me?"

Confusion washed over the man's doughy features. "Well, sure. Why else are you here?"

"To promote the rodeo, not my career."

"But—"

"The *rodeo*. Or nothing."

The commercial ended. Quinn hit another button, and a soft country ballad started. He glanced uneasily up at his schedule on the wall. "Fine…we'll talk about the rodeo. But you're quite a draw, Landers. I guarantee, people will keep listening if we spend a little time on you, start taking call-ins right away, and then segue into the rodeo promo. It's gonna stir up more interest that way."

Jake looked down at Kristen. "Whatever you think."

The DJ was probably right—and any airtime was better than none, especially if it was free. She nodded, and Jake sat back down.

The call-ins started almost immediately. House-wives, ranchers, teenagers who should have been in school. The air of reverence was palpable, as they asked questions. *What was your most dangerous ride? Who's gonna win the World this year? How many days a year did you travel?*

Kristen leaned back in her chair and watched as Jake drawled easily into the microphone, his almost courtly manners and deep voice clearly charming the socks off every female listener within range of the airwaves.

It should come as no surprise. Even in his twenties he'd had that same effect on women...on her.

She had been so sure they were in love, making plans for the future, wrapped in that passionate glow of youth and anticipation. But her doubts had been there all the same. With constant temptation facing him, how could she hope to compete? When he turned on the charm for fans who wanted an autograph or a photo of rodeo's hottest new talent, she'd seen her father, and had remembered just how faithful *he'd* been when on the road. That alone had made it easier to move on after Jake left her at the altar—

Quinn's voice broke through her reverie. "Well, Jake," he was saying, "Tell us about the wreck in Silver Springs that destroyed your career. I heard that was one heck of a bad bull."

He glanced down at the papers in his hand, and Kristen could now see that they were printouts from some rodeo site on the Internet.

"The doctors figured you wouldn't make it to the operating table due to a severed artery, and afterward said you wouldn't walk again." Quinn chuckled. "But folks, I'm here to tell you that he came into the studio on his own power and still looks darn good. He's proved them all wrong."

Kristen drew a sharp breath. He'd talked about broken bones...but the doctors hadn't even expected him to *survive?* Even with him sitting so close, his presence clear evidence that the docs had been wrong, an unspeakable sense of fear flooded her.

She turned away to compose herself. *He could have died.*

Silence filled the air.

The DJ tried again. "So, what are you planning to do? It's gotta be hard, leaving rodeo behind. But with the risks so high for you now..."

Jake's easy grace and relaxed sprawl turned to granite.

Kristen placed a warning hand on his arm.

After a moment of silence, Quinn gave a nervous chuckle. "Well, it's been great having you on the show today—"

"I'm in the process of buying a rodeo company," Jake broke in, his voice dead calm. Mid-America Rodeo has been producing rodeos for over thirty years...."

He found that easy drawl once more, though Kristen could still feel his tension beneath her fingertips. As if he'd been a producer for years, he covered the material she'd provided and much more—anecdotes about bullfighters, some of the great names in rodeo and the records that still stood after years, poignant recollections about the people who'd become like family to him during his career.

If he hadn't just single-handedly sold out every performance over the coming weekend, she would eat her new Resistol.

When the show ended, the DJ's relief was palpable. Popping a cartridge into the machine, he turned to face them as another commercial played quietly in the background. ''Thanks, folks. That was dynamite.''

Jake didn't answer. He stood, gave the man a curt nod and stalked out the door.

THE SEMI AND A LOWBOY TRAILER loaded with chutes and arena fencing arrived at the fairgrounds on the edge of town by late Thursday afternoon, followed by a Ford crew-cab pickup filled shoulder-to-shoulder with five burly men. Jake had seen most of them around the rodeo circuit for years.

Kristen looked up from the boxes she was counting in the food stand, then motioned to Jake and sauntered across the parking area to greet them.

The cowboys piled out of the pickup and headed for the semi.

''Wait a minute, guys,'' she called out.

They halted and turned back toward her. The two younger men broke into appreciative grins at her approach. The others bore the expressions of indulgent uncles.

She stood in front of them. ''This is Jake Landers, who will be MRC's new owner this fall. Jake, Hoot Hallahan and Kenny Asplund, the bullfighters.''

Hoot, maybe five-nine and pushing forty, had put on a lot of muscle since his bull-riding days, but he was fast on his feet and had a real flair for comedy routines. Jake had seen him delight crowds at rodeos all over the Midwest.

Kenny was much younger, not as sure, but his broad farm-boy grin and eagerness showed promise.

Both men had saved Jake from more than one set of deadly horns. He grinned at them, and they nodded back.

"Rowdy and Tom are MRC's pickup men," Kristen continued.

Jake nodded. "They've both helped me off saddle broncs a time or two."

"I'm sure those broncs were mighty glad to see you gone." Lou grinned. "Don't reckon I ever saw you takin' flight lessons before the buzzer sounded."

"It happened."

Laughing, Tom punched him in the shoulder. "Not that I ever saw."

Big men with massive shoulders, they couldn't have been more opposite—Rowdy was a gentle bear of a man with a shy smile who rarely spoke, while Tom's broad grin and love of practical jokes were familiar features behind the chutes.

She nodded toward the lanky youth hovering awkwardly nearby. A good six feet tall but matchstick wide, he blushed bright red when she looked over at him. "This is Kip. He works out at my dad's ranch with the stock and travels quite a bit with us."

Kip touched the brim of his hat and shuffled his feet, apparently struck mute. From the puppy-dog look he shot Kristen, the kid was long gone, Jake thought, but she didn't seem to notice. Instead, she turned toward Hoot and started asking him questions in a low voice.

Jake felt a flash of sympathy for the boy. Ten years ago Jake had probably looked just as lovesick as Kip did now. He'd found any excuse to hang around Kristen whenever she showed up at the same rodeo. He'd even started choosing rodeos she might attend, which was a damn fool way to choose the rides that could make or break his career.

The briefest courtship on record and their near-wedding had seemed inevitable, given the overpowering desire that had rocketed through him from the first time they'd met. For just a while, blinded by the all-consuming emotions of youth and an overload of testosterone, he'd allowed himself to believe that it might work.

In the ten years since, he'd tried not to think about how things might have been.

Out on the highway, a pickup and trailer bearing a rented forklift turned onto the dirt road leading down into the fairgrounds. Dust billowed across the grounds as the driver pulled to a creaking stop next to the semi.

Kristen lifted her hand to suppress a sneeze. "Let's go on over and help out. Ever put up an arena and chutes?"

Jake grinned. "As you remember, I'm one of the guys who just drift in when the real work is all done, ride my bull, and then drift on."

She had the good grace to drop her gaze. "I'm sorry for that. And I can't imagine why you'd ever have been around for a setup, either. C'mon, and you can work with me.''

She went ahead, her stride long and confident, that heavy fall of blond hair swaying with every step. She'd been beautiful before, in a shy-fawn sort of way. But now she was so much more—and worlds beyond the reach of a crippled ex-bull rider whose last chance in the rodeo world might well end in defeat.

Gritting his teeth, he started after her, ignoring the searing pain that shot up his thigh with every step. Maybe he'd been pushing himself too much, trying too hard to heal. But he didn't have forever to make it happen.

Younger bull riders had an advantage, until age added height and muscle, altering the low center of gravity that helped them withstand the force of a spinning, twisting bull. Most successful older riders were small and wiry, though not many rode successfully past their early thirties.

Jake had always compensated for his six foot height and muscle mass with sheer skill and strength. But even he couldn't keep at it much longer.

Kristen glanced over her shoulder at him when she reached the semi. ''The arena fence panels are all stacked in just the right order on the trailer, and fit together like a puzzle. The sections are assembled with steel pins—just like any fence panels you've seen before—but we wire the panels together for extra security. Otherwise, a bull could hook a horn between the bars and jerk the panels apart.''

''Got it.''

Her brow furrowed with concern as she watched his approach, then her gaze skidded down to his injured knee. "We've got a good crew here, so it won't take long. Maybe you should just step back and watch this time."

She hadn't meant to insult him, but if she'd thrown a gauntlet at his feet, the challenge couldn't have been more clear to the cowboys standing nearby. They shuffled their feet and showed sudden interest in either the horizon or the toes of their boots.

"I can probably figure out what to do," he said through gritted teeth, forcing himself to ignore the pain throbbing with every heartbeat. He'd work until every last panel and chute was in place, or die trying.

"But—"

"I'll work here, so you can do something else," he bit out. "I'd hate to see you ruin that manicure."

Her eyes flared wide, and he knew he'd hit his mark all too well. He wasn't the only one of them with stubborn pride.

Tom climbed behind the wheel of the forklift. He backed it down the ramp, then spun it around and headed for the lowboy trailer. As soon as the guys released the nylon strapping around the panels, Jake began unloading sections of fence and the chutes.

Kristen edged closer and lowered her voice. "Tell me one thing. Are you forcing yourself to get stronger, or are you really just hoping for a nice wheelchair once you damage that leg beyond repair?"

But before he could reply, she'd walked away.

CHAPTER FIVE

AS SHE STRODE toward the clapboard announcer's stand at the rodeo grounds on Friday afternoon, Kristen gave her fingernails a rueful look.

Jake hadn't been far off when he'd taunted her last night. As a teenager she'd helped her dad and his crew set up more rodeos than she could count. But back then, she hadn't sported acrylic nails. What had looked nicely professional and competent yesterday looked hopelessly out of place today.

With luck, the town of Mendota would have a nail salon that could simply remove them. With better luck, Jake might catch on really fast, decide she was simply in the way, and release her from her promise to stay with MRC until October first.

The announcer's stand was the size of a single-stall garage, with a second floor offering a good vantage point from which to view the performance. Inside the lower level, she found Bud's wife Tina scowling at the screen of a laptop computer placed on a card table next to a phone-fax machine.

"Hey, Tina, how's everything going?"

"Hold on a minute—I need to get this e-mail sent." She started typing on the keyboard, then clicked the mouse and looked up with a smile.

A small, muscular woman in her early fifties with man-cut hair the color of fresh asphalt and sun-cured skin, she served as the on-site secretary for MRC's rodeos. She was a good ten years older than Bud, and rumor had it that she ran their marriage with the same steely determination she used to secretary rodeos and manage Tina's Wave and Curl back in Bent Spur.

There was a certain element of justice in the fact that Bent Spur's most notorious fourth-grade bully had married a woman who could make men turn tail in terror at the sound of her voice. For that alone, Kristen had liked Tina from the start.

"You don't look happy," Kristen murmured, rounding Tina's chair to peer over her shoulder at the screen.

Tina took a deep drag on her cigarette, her eyes half closed as if she were kissing a lover goodbye, then aimed the cloud of smoke toward the ceiling. "We've had three bareback event turnouts for tonight. That leaves just four riders."

And less spectacle for the fans paying good money for the show. "How come?"

Tina tapped the screen. "This doesn't tell me, but one of the boys said that a couple of the guys were injured last weekend, and one had his pickup break down outside of Denver. I don't know about the fourth. He probably drew a better bronc at another rodeo. If he doesn't report in, he'll be fined."

"And the rest of the events?"

"Just got the day sheets, and the entries look good. Jim Holiday, who made the finals last year…Deke

Clover...Spence Marshall... Hey, does Jake have a brother who rodeos?''

''He has a younger brother, but I don't know how old he'd be now.'' Kristen gave Tina a quick shoulder massage and then moved to the big open window facing the arena.

Bud was out there circling with a tractor and harrow, working up the soil into loamy softness to receive any cowboys who ended up being airmailed during the performance. Hoot and Kenny were walking the perimeter fence, checking to make sure it was secure. Everything—even the weather—was going as planned.

Tina took another deep drag on her cigarette. ''We got a guy on the list named Tucker Landers. Haven't seen him before, but maybe he's been riding a different circuit. Oh, and the photographer confirmed. She'll be here by six to get set up.''

''Have you met Dixie?''

Tina snorted. ''You'd have to be blind and deaf to miss her.''

''It's all an act. She's really this quiet, demure little spinster, and—''

''And my grandma won the World in saddle bronc last year.''

Kristen laughed. ''You're right. Did she say anything else?''

''Hmm...something about turning this town upside down tonight, and you'd better be ready.''

''Want to come with us? We'd be more fun than sitting in a motel room. Maybe pizza, or a roadhouse close by?''

Tina's fingers started flying across the keys of the laptop. "I'll think about it. Bud usually has a date with the boys and Jack Daniel's every night we're on the road. I'm not sure if I should stay and baby-sit him, or just let him suffer in the morning."

"Suffering might be good."

"It never teaches him anything—the man has more hangovers than a dog has fleas. He's incapable of associating the next morning's misery with the bottle he had in his hand the night before. Or maybe he does, and just doesn't care."

Or can't help himself, Kristen thought, remembering stories of the hard life of constant travel and inconsistent paychecks. Bud had been one of the rodeo cowboys with moderate determination and not much talent, and he'd been a member of the party scene long before he met his wife.

From the second floor of the wood-frame booth came the whine and static of an audio system, then a resonant, booming voice that vibrated the entire structure. "Helloooooo, ladies and gentlemen—" A pause, more static, and then, "Hellooo, ladies—"

"Stan's in good form today," Kristen ventured, listening to him adjust the system.

"He's been doing better," Tina said dryly. "But he's still the most boring announcer I ever heard— even the bulls fall asleep."

"Why was he contracted?"

"Guy booked this whole season a year ago, but the announcers he wanted were already taken for some of our dates."

Out in the middle of the arena one of the bullfighters, still dressed in jeans and a western shirt, gave the announcer's stand a thumbs-up and then jogged a dozen yards away and cupped a hand to his ear. Again, Stan bellowed out his greeting.

The bullfighter staggered as if hit by lethal sound waves, spun in a drunken circle and collapsed, his hands neatly folded over his chest.

"Guess that worked," Kristen observed, watching him jump up and jog farther down the arena.

The bullfighter adjusted his microphone set, checked the wire going to the pack at his belt, and called out in a reedy falsetto, a perfect imitation of Stan's much deeper voice, "Hellooo, everybody!"

"The last rodeo we did last fall didn't go well," Tina muttered. "Had a couple of broncs go down in the chute, then a doggin' horse went berserk and it took ten minutes just to get him headed in the right direction for the steer wrestling. The announcer's sound system went out early on, and we had a lot of dead airtime."

Kristen could well imagine impatient kids squirming in the seats, parents glancing at their watches every few minutes. But a good specialty act, talented bullfighters who could do a little clowning if need be, and a top announcer could turn every delay into an entertainment opportunity and keep the show moving. The crowd wouldn't even be aware of any problems in the chutes.

"I'll keep my fingers crossed for tonight," she said fervently. "This is my first show on the road, and I want it to be perfect."

"It'll be fine. Do you want a copy of the day

sheets? Guy always made copies for the spectators so they could see who was in each event. Gives 'em a chance to follow the action a little better.''

Kristen nodded. ''I'll run into town to find a copy place.''

''That youth group is over at the food stand getting set up, by the way. They've got some problems and need to see you.''

On her way over to the food stand, Kristen flipped through the notebook in her hand, checking food order receipts and notes.

When MRC produced a rodeo for a community or organization, local people generally took over the food and ticket sales, car parking and the myriad other details.

For rodeos like this one, financed and staged entirely by MRC from the rental of the grounds on up, every aspect had to be planned and managed.

In the food stand she found a dozen teenagers arguing over assigned chores, and one harried adult.

The woman—the local high school band instructor—shoved a hand through her gray curls and gave Kristen a desperate look. ''We're having a bit of trouble here. We don't have as many tasks since we don't have the menu we'd expected.''

''Menu?''

''Yes, well, I remember that you and I had discussed this earlier—barbecue pork sandwiches and hot dogs. There's plenty of buns and barbecue, but without hot dogs, the menu is awfully limited.''

Kristen frowned as she stepped behind the counter and headed for the row of antiquated refrigerators across the back of the food stand. "Forty pounds of hot dogs were delivered yesterday. I put them away myself so they could thaw safely in the refrigerators."

The teenagers stopped squabbling and watched with open interest as she pulled open one door, then another. She gave them a narrowed look after checking the last refrigerator. "Is this a joke? The hot dogs are gone."

"No, ma'am. And no one else has been in since we got here," a taller boy volunteered. "The door was locked, too."

Kristen had given the teacher the key a few minutes earlier, so now she turned toward the older woman. "Locked? *Both* doors?"

"Tight as a drum. I saw your list on the counter and checked. The beverages, the cases of candy and chips were untouched."

A short girl with a riot of freckles across her nose moved forward. "Does this mean we won't have enough food to sell?" Her voice rose, edged with panic. "We needed this money for our band trip. Not all of us have the money to go, and—"

Kristen gave the girl a comforting smile. "I'll scout around in town to see what I can come up with, after I call the sheriff. We'll figure out something, okay?"

At a collective sigh from the other girls in the group, Kristen lifted her gaze and found Jake standing in the doorway. Apparently oblivious to the girls' awed expressions, he stepped past them and lifted a brow at the band teacher. "Bud's wife said there were some problems over here. Need any help?"

In the cramped confines of the food stand, he appeared much broader, much larger, and that damnably effective charisma of his had apparently rendered the woman speechless.

"We're missing a good part of the supplies that were delivered yesterday," Kristen said. "The door was locked the entire time and nothing else was taken." She nodded at the cell phone in Jake's shirt pocket. "We need to call the sheriff and also start tracking down some replacements."

Their eyes met, and she wondered if he was remembering the canceled radio interview. One problem could be attributed to bad luck. Two, in such a short span of time, hinted at something more.

For the next two days, she would be keeping a close watch on the spectators, cowboys and crew. Radio interviews and hot dogs were minor inconveniences, but there were a lot of things that could go wrong at a rodeo, and lead to injuries or worse.

She wasn't about to let that happen.

BY FOUR O'CLOCK that afternoon, Kristen had made a thousand copies of the day sheets and had raided the local grocery store to replace the missing supplies.

The youth group was now in business—looking forward to twenty-five percent of the net profit on the food stand for their efforts; the ticket sellers were in place; and the pots—double-decker livestock semis—had just pulled in.

"I can't believe the sheriff didn't even dust for fingerprints," Kristen muttered, as she and Jake walked toward the arena. "They always do that on television."

"I don't think he gets too excited over hot dogs," Jake said dryly. "He said if he hears anything, he'll check it out. It'll probably happen—there aren't many secrets in a small town."

"But someone broke in, and stole from us!"

"And given the size of the crime, it likely wasn't anyone on the Ten Most Wanted list. Probably some teenagers picking up supplies for a beer party, and their fingerprints probably wouldn't be on file, anyway."

"Tell me that in five years. Today, hot dogs. Tomorrow—a Nebraska Savings and Loan."

Jake laughed and looped an arm around her shoulders. And though yesterday she would have pulled away, now it seemed...comfortable.

Kristen glanced down at the notebook in her hands. "You probably know this already, but the pots are always the last to arrive and the first to leave," she murmured to Jake. "Contractors want to stress their animals as little as possible."

Both she and Jake hooked a boot heel on the arena fence and watched as the men unloaded the bulls and bucking horses into the arena, where another group of cowboys sorted them into the appropriate holding pens.

Bud stood off to one side, barking orders as he checked off livestock against the list in his hand. After a few minutes, he strolled over and leaned against the fence.

"We've got good stock here this weekend. Some of our highest scoring bulls and last year's top bronc," he said, glancing at Jake. "Oughta be a good show. We had a slow start out of town, though. Didn't have our health papers in time because the vet hadn't been scheduled.''

Kristen looked up in surprise. ''I called him last Monday and again on Wednesday. It was all set.''

''I'll just call him myself next time,'' Bud muttered, not looking at her. ''We couldn't even unload here without those papers.''

Kristen took a deep breath and counted to ten. ''I'm aware of that. The vet was contacted and had agreed to come.''

''That's not what he said.''

Out in the arena, a Brahma made a dash to the far end of the arena instead of heading through the gate into the holding pens. Two cowboys on horseback went after him.

''Guess I'd better get back to work.'' Bud slapped Jake on the shoulder and strolled to the center of the arena.

''There are a million things to take care of. I have lists. I check things off as I do them.'' Kristen glared at Bud's back. ''I definitely called that vet.''

Jake shrugged. ''I get the feeling he isn't exactly pleased with the arrangement this season.''

''Bud? He undoubtedly expected to take over MRC. In this business, it's probably a little hard being sidestepped in favor of a woman—especially one twenty years younger.''

''Why didn't he take over? He's a relative—that would have kept the business in the family.''

''He would have run the business into the ground. He's good with the stock, but occasionally has a little trouble with the bottle. And he has the people skills of a door. Ninety percent of this job is communication—endless phone calls, meetings, e-mails…there's a stack of faxes every week. And to get good sponsorships takes some personality and salesmanship.''

They stood watching the cowboys move more bulls into the holding pens. ''I recognize a few old pals out there,'' Jake said, waving a hand toward a massive cream Brahma. ''Isn't that Cropduster?''

''Sure is. Some bulls are dangerous night and day, but he's one of my favorites. He loves to have his ears scratched.'' She squinted at the animals through the rising dust and began calling out the names. ''That black bull is Sixty-Four, and behind him are Hellfire and Code Blue and Body Trauma. Some of the others are newer and haven't proved themselves like those old boys. Actually, some of the younger stock was sired by those bulls, and out of top-flight bucking stock on the dam's side as well.''

Jake watched the stock, his face expressionless. When he took off his sunglasses to clear away a film of dust, she could see the bleak expression in his eyes.

''Have you had to sit out a season before?''

He gave a curt nod. ''A few rodeos here and there.''

Though he made it seem like nothing, she'd seen cowboys go out on bucking stock with splints, even a cast on their free arm, rather than sit out the event. ''Anything serious—before this last injury?''

He pinned her with an intense look. ''Never.''

And not now, either. The unspoken words hung in the air between them as if said aloud.

And so he punished himself every morning with exercise his knee probably couldn't tolerate, she thought, took ibuprofen like he had stock in the company, and by evening moved like an old, old man.

It was all part of that damnable rodeo cowboy's code—wrecks happened, and short of paralysis or death, a man who had *try* just kept going. A tough man—a *worthy* man—never complained.

With a sigh, she turned back to the cattle. It didn't matter. It *couldn't* matter.

Before long she would be back in Dallas starting her new job, pursuing her dreams of a challenging and exciting career, a steady income and decent benefits. The vagaries of rodeo crowds, bucking stock and the weather, and the grueling days of rodeo travel, would be in the past. Exactly as she wanted.

Except that a small corner of her heart had never forgotten her first, wild love.

Now the object of that love had grown into a man, and all the promise of his youth had been fully realized in sculpted muscle and a wicked grin that spoke of long, dark nights and fantasies fulfilled...

Distance. She needed to keep her distance.

Clearing her throat, she turned toward the long trailer parked near the announcer's stand. "I'd better go over to check on Bud's crew."

She'd only gone a few yards when a petite figure emerged from the announcer's stand and headed straight for her.

Big, *big* platinum-blond hair...movie star sunglasses...a hot-pink "Cowboys Do It Better" T-shirt and tight jeans molded to every curve of her voluptuous body—there was no one else on earth like Dixie Galbraith.

"Hey, sweetie!" Dixie called out, sauntering across the broad grassy area toward Kristen. "You're lookin' *good!*"

There wasn't anyone else with a set of lungs like that, either. Heads turned, cowboys grinned. For all Dixie's flash, she had the morals of a nun and the heart of a dedicated social worker, and she'd befriended many a down-and-out cowboy over the years.

Kristen embraced her old friend and then held her at arm's length. "You're looking pretty good yourself. It's been way too long—two years? Three?"

"You took off and went back to school and left us all behind. I'm really proud of you for all you've done." Dixie looked over Kristen's shoulder and flashed a smile at Jake. "Hi, sugar. It's good to see you back."

"Dixie." He touched the brim of his hat in greeting, then turned back toward Hoot Hallahan, who was now lounging against the arena fence with one arm slung over the neck of his paint trick mule.

"What's this?" Dixie added in a lower voice. "You two back together?"

Kristen briefly explained the sale of MRC and the bargain she'd made with Jake. "Strictly business."

"Tell that to those cowboys on the fence, not me." Dixie looped an arm through Kristen's and started for the bleachers. "Come talk to me before this place gets crazy."

"Maybe later—"

"Now." Dixie flashed one of her trademark mega-watt grins. "You need to talk to Momma, whether you know it or not."

There was a lot left to do, but stopping Dixie on a mission was like trying to corral a tornado. "Five minutes, tops."

They settled on the top row of the bleachers, side by side. Below, the cowboys ran the last bucking horse out of the arena and into an alleyway, and Bud made a final mark on the notebook in his hands. Farther out into the arena, one of the specialty acts—a blond Adonis with a trio of Border collies—started putting them through their routine. Scents of cattle, horses and dust filled the air.

"How long have we known each other?" Dixie asked, watching Adonis with keen interest.

"Since the summer I spent running barrels—when we were both eighteen." Kristen smiled. "A summer to remember in so many ways."

"We were so young. First time away from home, first real loves…we thought we had the world by the tail, didn't we? You were going to travel the rodeo circuit with Jake Landers until you were both old and gray."

"And you were going to do the same with Clint Williams."

"And look at us now. Two old ladies—"

"We're twenty-eight!"

"Yep, two old ladies without a prospect in sight."

Kristen laughed. "Believe me, if you crooked your little finger, you'd have half the population of Wyoming lined up at your doorstep. Every cowboy here nearly went into cardiac arrest when you showed up.''

"One of 'em sure didn't.''

Kristen scanned the rodeo grounds. "*Clint's* here?"

"No. When he quit rodeo he quit for good and never looked back...never once tried to call or write. I'm talking about Jake. That man is watching *you*, sweetie.''

"He has to. He's learning the business, and I agreed to stay just through the season.''

"Still as perceptive as dirt.'' Dixie threw up her hands in mock exasperation. "Did you *really* get a master's degree?''

"Look, I remember the old days, too. But those times are gone.''

"Tell me that you've never thought about him since then.''

"He was part of that first, exciting summer out of high school, the first season I traveled on the rodeo circuit as a competitor. How could I forget all of that?''

"Have you ever forgiven him for what he did?''

Kristen snorted in disbelief. "It was humiliating, standing at the church alone. And after I found out where he was...with some other woman...''

After a long silence, Dixie laid a hand on Kristen's arm. "Maybe it wasn't what you think. Maybe he had a good reason—''

"*Reason?* Another woman?''

"Did you ever find out who he was with?''

"No one told me, and I never wanted to know.

Putting a name and a face to the person who mattered more than me would have made it that much harder.''

''I still wish I could have been at that chapel with you. I didn't hear about it all until later.''

''I didn't have many people there at all, thank goodness. We decided to get married, then MRC went to Las Vegas to put on a rodeo and Jake had to be in another state. He was going to meet me in Las Vegas in time for the ceremony. Ours was probably one of the briefest engagements on record.''

''Well, you deserved much better.''

''At least I found out about him *before* the ceremony. I considered myself lucky.''

''*Lucky?*''

Kristen fixed her gaze on the Border collies, who were obeying their handler's hand signals from across the arena. Perhaps she'd lied to herself for the past ten years, but lying to an old friend was harder. ''Not entirely lucky... I felt as though my heart had been cut out and placed, still beating, on the ground. Marrying Steve a year later was a mistake, and the divorce was an awful experience. I'm just not cut out for marriage.''

''That's 'cause you married the wrong guy. Maybe this business deal is offering you a second chance.''

''I don't want it. I could never believe that Jake would stick around when he saw a pretty face. Heck, with just a smile he practically charms the pants off women old enough to be his mother, and he isn't even *trying.*''

''That doesn't mean he would stray.''

''Right. Like any man is going to ignore every opportunity that comes along. Even if he did, I've seen the kind of life my parents had. My dad traveling with the rodeo, my mom at home. The worries back at the ranch about cattle prices and weather. I want dinner meetings instead of road food. A condo in suburbia.'' Kristen thought for a minute. ''And a fluffy little dog.''

Dixie stared at her with an expression of horrified fascination. *''Truly?''*

''Look, I appreciate your concern. But my father thought his marriage license was a permit for hunting other women. I was dumped by the one man I loved. And my one-and-only marriage lasted less than a year. Believe me, I'm a whole lot better off making a life of my own.''

Dixie just looked at her and smiled.

CHAPTER SIX

JAKE'S ADRENALINE started kicking in as he surveyed the empty parking lot of the rodeo grounds late Friday afternoon.

He'd always had an uncanny sense of awareness—like an internal radar system—as he neared a rodeo site. Even if he'd never been there before, that edge of impatience would start coiling in his gut miles before the arena came into view, warning him that he was close.

Even now, he could taste that old, familiar sense of building anticipation. *Feel* the sticky rosin of his bull rope as he jerked a suicide wrap around his palm and waited for that perfect, still moment in time—when the bull was head-up and primed for eight seconds of hell.

But now, for the first time, he was on the rodeo grounds long before the livestock came, before all the cowboys had pulled in. Before the crowds started streaming in through the gates and up into the stands. He wasn't urging the pilot of some charter plane to fly faster, or driving his pickup ninety miles an hour across the prairie trying to make it in time for his bull....

The stark reality of it hit him like a charging

Brahma. Unless he pushed himself harder, ran faster, punished his weakened muscles into condition, he was going to be on the ground for the rest of his life.

With a start, he realized that Hoot and his paint mule had sauntered off, and Jake was alone at the arena fence. Cursing under his breath, he glared at the leather rodeo planning folio in his hand and fought the temptation to pitch it into the nearest trash can. *As if that would change anything.* His anger was better directed toward forcing himself back into shape.

He lifted his gaze to find Kristen, but found Dixie instead, kneeling next to the arena a few yards behind him, burrowing through an oversize camera bag at her feet.

She glanced up at him. "Hey, there, cowboy, how's the new career?"

"Sorta like taking your daddy's '63 Buick after piloting a Lear." He shrugged. "It's all transportation, but the similarity ends right there."

Her hearty laughter rang out. "It has to be better than riding fence for some rancher, though." She deftly loaded film into a battered Nikon F4S, then lifted it for a careful inspection. "I carry four camera systems, but this one is my all-time favorite. Every one of them has quirks, and it sometimes takes time and effort to get it right, but this one was worth every moment."

The gleam in her eye told him she wasn't talking about the Nikon. He started to edge away, looking for an escape.

Lacquered fingertips landed on his arm faster than a tripped coyote trap.

Over the years they'd bumped into each other at rodeos across the country, continuing a friendship that had never led to more, and by now she was like a sister. Her breezy banter and forthright common sense were a welcome contrast to the sometimes desperate flirtations of the buckle bunnies who lurked around the chutes.

She was, however, completely without reservations about offering personal guidance.

"Kristen and I aren't getting back together," he said quietly.

"But you never married, and that brief marriage of hers was a mistake from the word *go*. Ever wondered why you both are still single after ten years?"

"Uh…luck?"

"No. *Fate.*"

Holding up his hands in self-defense, Jake started backing away, but she stayed right with him. There wasn't a more passionate speaker on the planet than Dixie when she got on a roll. "Kristen will meet the executive of her dreams when she goes back to Dallas."

"That's not fair. As you well remember, *you*—"

"Sorry—I need to check on the lineup." Gently extricating his arm from her grasp, he gave her a quick nod of farewell and spun toward the holding pens behind the chutes.

He couldn't think of anything much worse than talking about his personal life—or, God forbid, *feelings*. Especially with a flock of grinning cowboys perched on top of the chutes at the south end of the arena observing them with interest.

''Poor ol' Jake has more women than he can handle,'' one of them called out with mock concern.

''I'm gonna be a world champion someday so I can fight off the women, too,'' yelled another.

The others guffawed. And then another voice, lower, slid through the laughter. '''Course, *ex*-rodeo stars prob'ly don't have much trouble with an oversupply of 'em.''

Standing next to the others was an older man—burly, well past the age of rough stock. Jake had seen him a few times over the years in bulldoggin' or team roping events. Louis…no, Lew.

There was no laughter in the man's voice, just a thread of pure disdain as he continued. ''I hear Jake's buying MRC. Oughta be interesting, seeing if he makes it to the eight-second buzzer on *that* deal.''

The other cowboys glanced back and forth between Jake and Lew, their grins fading at the clear challenge.

Most competitors were friendly and would do anything to help one another. A few, however, succumbed to resentment and bitter rivalry. And from the sour look on this old guy's face, the past years hadn't done him much good in or out of the arena.

From the corner of his eye Jake saw Hoot step forward, but Jake waved him back. ''Guess I'd better use extra rosin and hold on tight,'' he said mildly. ''Anyone seen the chute boss back here?''

One of the younger cowboys on the rail jerked his chin toward the semis and stock trailer parked behind the pens. ''I think he's checkin' on the kids.''

With a nod of thanks, Jake circled the pens and

headed for the dozen palomino saddle horses tied to a fence beyond the trailers.

A bevy of teenage girls—daughters of Bud, Vance and Hoot—were busy washing the animals and laying out equipment for the Grand Entry.

Vance, a stocky man who'd been with MRC for several years, looked up from the bridle and the tin of saddle soap in his hands. "Everything under control?"

"Guess so. Did the stock make the trip okay?"

"One of the lead mares for the Grand Entry came up lame, but we'll be all right. Buckshot has done it a time or two."

"The hippodrome ride?" Jake thought about the girls who stood in the saddle and rode at a dead gallop around the arena gripping a flagpole, with the American flag streaming out behind them. They rode in opposite directions, criss-crossed the arena a few times, then pulled to a stop in the center for the anthem. One false step, or a horse suddenly veering away from something in the stands...

"Susie is a tougher hand than most of the cowboys here."

"Maybe just one flag should go out tonight."

"Nah, she'll be okay." Vance gestured toward the girls, who were splashing each other and seemed to be wearing every bit of dirt they'd washed off the horses. The horses, veterans of too many rodeos to count, ignored the ruckus and munched from the hay bags strung along the fence. "These teenagers keep me on my toes. I finally had to send the *boys* off to clean out the trailers."

"Let me know if there's anything I can…" Jake's voice trailed off.

Over by the arena, looking straight at him, stood a lanky young cowboy with a rebellious tilt to his chin and a sneer curling his upper lip.

Vance peered around Jake. "Someone you know? I don't think I've ever seen him on this circuit."

The cowboy met Jake's gaze, then shook his head and turned for the announcer's stand.

"Whoever he is, he sure has a chip on his shoulder. We'll have to keep an eye on him. Crowd gets nervous if there's trouble behind the chutes."

"There won't be." Jake gave a long sigh, wishing he could turn back the clock and change the past. "I'm the only one here he'd like to tangle with, and I won't let that happen."

Vance whistled through his teeth. "You'd better have some backup."

"I won't need it." Jake gave him a weary smile. "He'd probably just as soon see me dead, but there isn't gonna be any fight."

They both watched the cowboy stalk away. He looked ready to take on the world in a barroom brawl.

"An old competitor of yours?"

"Might be easier if he was. That guy is certain every bad break in his life can be attributed to me. He's my kid brother, Tucker."

"HELLOOO, LADIES AND GENTLEMEN! And welcome, to MRC's first rodeo of the season!" The announcer's deep, resonant voice boomed through the loudspeakers.

The overflow crowd cheered and rose to its feet as two teenage girls—Bud's daughters—raced into the arena on matching palominos, with American flags held high. They ran their horses flawlessly once, twice around the perimeter, standing above their saddles, their long hair flying in the breeze in blond counterpoint to the flags they held.

"Lord almighty," Hoot muttered, when they stood at last in the center. "Like to give me a heart attack when I saw Susie come in on Buckshot. That mare isn't near as steady as the one they always use."

He'd always been like a mother hen, worrying over all the kids who followed their rodeo parents from one venue to the next, and he'd always taken younger contestants under his wing. He helped novice rodeo clowns and bullfighters as well, often working with one for an entire season.

Kristen leaned over and bumped him on the arm with her shoulder, as everyone stood for the anthem. "They did just fine. Are you and Kenny ready?"

"Sure enough."

His voice sounded a little too cheerful. As soon as the anthem ended, she continued. "It's always hard, getting used to a new partner. Does he still have just his first-year membership status?"

"Yeah." Hoot lifted a shoulder. "But he's had this dream since he was a kid. He'll do."

"That doesn't sound like a ringing endorsement."

"He's getting better with every time out."

They both watched the girls circle the arena at a gallop, this time side-by-side, then come down the center of the arena and pull to a sliding stop at the gate. Behind the arena, a group of cowboys milled around—some shooting the breeze, some getting ready for their rough-stock events.

The girls disappeared into the crowd, and Kristen heaved a sigh of relief. "How many rodeos has Kenny—"

From the far end of the arena, a horse squealed above the sound of the cheering crowd. A girl screamed. Men shouted and rushed forward.

Even through Hoot's garish clown greasepaint, Kristen could see his face fill with worry. He pivoted and headed toward the melee at a dead run, Kristen close at his heels.

By the time they fought their way through the crowd, the EMTs manning the ambulance—required at every rodeo performance—had reached the gate and were hovering over the prone figure of a girl. The doctor on call was there, too.

Susie.

"Oh, God, is she all right?" Hoot dropped to his knees and reached for her hand.

An EMT looked up. "Are you her dad?"

"No, I am." Bud shouldered his way through the cowboys. "What happened, honey?"

Susie opened her eyes. A tear streaked down her cheek. "Buckshot was steady as a rock 'til I got out of the gate, and then she blew for no reason. She reared *way* up, and there was a little girl in the way— we were going to come down on her!"

"Susie pulled her mare over backwards to avoid that girl, Bud." Jake leaned down and gently ruffled Susie's hair. "You're quite a rider, kid."

Bud grabbed the doctor by the shoulder. "How is she?"

"Let go, sir. I'm trying to get another blood pressure, here." The doc bent to his task, then straightened. "We're going to take her in, but so far things look good. She can move her extremities, her pupils are equally reactive. With luck, she's just shaken up a little. She took quite a fall."

Kristen slipped back out of the crowd and circled until she found Jake. A few feet away, Buckshot stood tied to the fence post. "Let's take a look."

Together they walked around the quiet mare. Kristen inspected her hooves for glass or nails, while Jake ran a hand over her sleek golden hide.

After putting down the last hoof, Kristen came around to where Jake stood. "Nothing wrong with her feet."

"That wasn't the problem, and she sure didn't blow out of spite." Jake gave Kristen a grim look, then stepped aside.

Blood dripped steadily from a small, neat wound in the mare's lower chest.

JAKE, KRISTEN, the sheriff and the MRC crew crowded around the vet, as she finished with the mare.

"I can only probe a track of about three inches," the vet said, giving Buckshot a final pat on the neck. "I couldn't find any foreign objects."

"Your best guess?" Jake asked.

"A puncture wound—something long and straight. A protruding metal rod of some kind, or maybe a long nail."

"There isn't a sharp projection *anywhere* on the arena or gate," Kristen said. "These chutes and the arena are put up and taken down all the time. The crew would have noticed."

"I saddled that mare myself, and she was fine before she went in," Vance said, his voice grim. "So I just walked the entire arena and checked the gate she came through. *Nothing.*"

"The horse blew right *after* Susie came out of the gate," one of the other cowboys muttered. "Not before. It wasn't the gate or the fence panels."

"Anyone see anything? Know of anyone wanting to cause trouble?" The sheriff looked at each person surrounding the mare. "Know of anyone with a grudge?"

The gathered cowboys and crew shrugged, shook their heads.

"Kristen, Jake—what do you think?"

"We...had some problems with a theft earlier, as you know, but nothing indicating any physical threat," Kristen said.

The sheriff scanned the area. "I'll call in some deputies, and we'll patrol the area. You might want to have your people keep an eye out, as well, but I wouldn't argue if you want to finish the rodeo."

After a quick conference with Security and the county sheriff, Bud went to the hospital with Susie, and Jake stood sentry behind the chutes. Kristen kept watch at the far end of the arena.

Murmurs spread through the crowd when several deputies arrived and stood at strategic locations. Some of the spectators left.

By the time the bulls were being moved into the chutes for the last event, Jake was bone-tired and his leg throbbed. Somewhere back in the pickup was his bottle of ibuprofen, but it might as well have been a thousand miles away.

When Tucker walked past, Jake did a double take. He'd wanted to find Tucker right away, but Susie's accident had taken priority. "Hey, stranger, what are you doing here?"

Tucker jerked a shoulder and kept walking.

Maybe it was the late hour. The stress. He'd never risen for a fight and had never gone after someone to argue, but suddenly his baby brother's attitude pushed him to the edge.

"At least show some manners, Tuck."

Tucker stopped and wheeled around, his eyes glittering. "If I'd known you were here, I wouldn't have entered."

Jake stared back at him. The events had rolled on through the evening like clockwork, but he hadn't watched a single one. He hadn't been listening to the constant banter of the announcer, either. "What event were you in?"

Tucker snorted. "Nothing ever changes. I'm just *real* glad that you've taken such an interest in my career."

"It's a little hard, when you up and take off without a word. You don't return phone calls, you don't write. Hell, half the time the family doesn't even know where you are." Jake wanted to take Tucker by the shoulders and shake him, then tell him just how hard that had been on his mom and dad. But from the surly expression on his brother's face, Jake guessed the words wouldn't even register.

"Guess maybe I wanted my chance, too."

Tucker turned away and kept walking, and then Jake noticed the duffel in his hand. A feeling of dread crawled up Jake's throat. "Tucker!"

His brother just hitched a shoulder, then climbed up onto the catwalk behind the chutes. He settled behind chute 4 and a big mottled gray Brahma the size of Rhode Island.

Oh, God. Jake motioned for Vance to keep an eye on things and then headed straight for the chutes.

The announcer's voice rose, inciting the crowd to greater excitement over the last event—the headliner—the most dangerous one of all. A theme song from a major action film burst through the loudspeakers.

"And now, in chute 1, we have Billy Joe Duncan on number 222—a bull that qualified for the finals *twice*. Billy Joe is third in the standings..." The announcer's voice receded, as Jake reached his brother's side.

Images of his brother as a toddler—Jake had been fifteen when Tucker was born—dressed in cowboy pajamas flew through Jake's mind, interspersed with images of bull riders who'd staggered into the center of the rodeo arena, concussed and confused, only to be mowed down by a bull the bullfighters hadn't been able to turn back.

Images of the cowboys who'd been hooked, and then airlifted to the hospital.

Images of the ones who hadn't lived long enough for transfer.

"Talk to me, Tucker. How long have you been doing this?"

Tucker lifted his bull rope out of his bag and shook some rosin into the palm of his glove, then began working the sticky substance into his rope. "Got nothin' to say."

He'd left home a year-and-a-half ago. At eighteen, he'd been old enough to enter bull riding. "We've all missed you, Tucker. We haven't heard from you in months. Where've you been?"

Out in the arena, the first rider lasted two hard jumps and a sharp spin to the left; then his bull switched direction in midair and landed like a pile driver. Before the guy even hit the dirt, Hoot, now in full clown gear, was in position to draw the bull away.

Kenny hung back by the clown's barrel, not nearly as aggressive as his partner.

Tucker watched dispassionately as the cowboy limped out of the arena, then rubbed more rosin into his rope. "I've been riding fence for an outfit up north, hitting some local rodeos. Now I'm starting on the circuit full time. But why should you care?"

"You're my brother, for God's sake."

Tucker looked up then, his expression fierce. "If you cared so much, then why did you leave me behind—with *him*?"

In that moment, Jake suddenly was back at the ranch, with Tucker and Mom and all the hands...and Dad. "He was a hard man, but—"

"But, nothing. Now get out of my face, *brother*. You have no say over what I do."

From behind the chutes came Vance's voice, calling for Jake.

"After the rodeo, let's go to that truck stop on the edge of town."

"I'll be on my way to another rodeo."

Jake glanced back at Vance, who was gesturing impatiently. "If you ever need anything—"

"I won't."

"You can contact me through MRC, out of Bent Spur, Wyoming. Call me collect."

Tucker flushed, and suddenly he looked like the nineteen-year-old kid he was. "I'm not broke."

"I know how it is in rodeo. Flying high one minute, down the next. I've been there. If I don't see you after your ride, I want you to call me sometime, okay?" Jake fished through his pockets and withdrew an MRC business card, then reached out to stuff it into his brother's hand. "Keep safe, Tucker."

Vance met Jake the minute he was back on the ground. "We got a witness. A lady standing in line for the rest room, who said she saw some guy move real close to the horse a split second before it reared. Then he disappeared into the crowd as if he was trying to get away. Why on earth would anyone try to hurt Susie and her horse?"

"No clue, but I'd sure like to get my hands on him...and Bud would probably tear him apart." Jake shook his head. "Any description of the guy?"

"Nope. She was too far away. Said he was 'average' height, with a dark shirt and a black hat. He kept his head tipped down.''

The two men looked at the crowd, then at each other. ''That would describe a few hundred guys here,'' Jake said.

Vance nodded. ''I'll still keep watching for anything suspicious.'' He paused and listened. ''Hey, didn't the announcer just call a Landers for gate 3?''

Without a word Jake spun away and headed for the arena fence, his pulse jerking in his throat.

Respect for the bull and a certain edge of fear had always been there when he rode, but that's when *he'd* been the one on the bull. In control of his own strength, his own sense of balance.

When he slid into the *zone*—where the noise of the crowd faded, time stood still and he became a part of the bull—the exhilaration of that adrenaline high had been incomparable.

Standing on the ground, waiting for his baby brother to come launching out of chute 3, was sheer hell.

He could see the crown of Tucker's hat. A second ticked past. Two. Three. Then the hat dipped down and the chute gate flew open.

Two thousand pounds of violence exploded into the arena. The bull spun hard to the left, drove its front legs deep into the earth and then launched upward in a wild twisting jump that rocked Tucker back on his pockets.

The rest would be history, Jake knew. As the bull landed with the force of a head-on collision, Tucker tipped forward over his rope hand. From the side of the arena, Dixie crouched over her camera, taking rapid-fire photographs.

Jake scanned the arena for the bullfighters. Hoot was again in good position—each bull was different, and he'd clearly paid attention to Bud's instructions on where he needed to be. Kenny lurked behind him.

A split second later, Tucker was airborne. But like a rag doll, he hung from his bull rope, his hand held tight in the wrap.

The crowd gasped. Hoot charged forward and ran alongside the bull, frantically pulling at the rope. The bull jammed to a stop and spun into Hoot, trying to hook him, but Hoot danced backward, barely beyond reach of the horn.

A heartbeat later the rope fell away, and Tucker dropped to his knees, his head bowed, his left hand clutching his other arm.

Get up—get up—get up!

Jake reached for the top of the arena fence, ready to pull himself over, but the pickup men charged forward on their horses, shouting and slapping their chaps.

The bull pivoted toward them and lowered its head. After a moment of indecision, it gave a last shake of its horns, wheeled and nonchalantly jogged out the open gate leading back into the stock pens.

As Tucker stumbled to his feet, Hoot reached out to help him, but he angrily shook off the attempt. Amid deafening applause and cheers, Tucker made it back to the chutes.

And then he collapsed in the dirt.

CHAPTER SEVEN

INJURIES WERE COMMON at rodeos.

The physician in attendance and the EMTs always saw action—strains, sprains, fractures, concussions, and sometimes much worse. The chiropractors who set up tents behind the chutes were busy, too.

Jake had experienced his fair share of treatment by both, but none of those experiences had ever given him the rush of fear he felt today as he raced to the ambulance behind the chutes.

Memories of bull riders—his friends—who'd died beneath the bright halogen lights of a rodeo arena merged with images of his four-year-old brother roping bales. Riding calves. Trying to emulate rodeo cowboys in every way.

Had Jake ever given him enough attention? The fifteen-year span between them meant Jake had been gone before Tucker started school. But he could have come home more. Spent more time…

Kristen was standing by the gurney holding Tucker's hand, when Jake got there. Tucker lay there, pale, his eyes closed. A swathe of bandages stabilized his left arm next to his body. An EMT was putting away supplies, while another wrote up a report.

Kristen reached out to take Jake's arm. "The physician rode to the hospital with Susie. The EMTs here say Tucker's a little shook up and probably has a broken wrist, but otherwise they haven't found anything.''

One of the EMTs looked up. "Are you family?"

Jake nodded.

"The judge just sent over a signed rodeo insurance form, so we're ready to send this cowboy in. Does he have other insurance?"

Jake looked blankly back at the paramedic, but Tucker stirred and opened his eyes. "Nope—just the rodeo coverage."

The hospital wouldn't deny his care when given that documentation, but considering the high deductible, he'd better have some money stowed away somewhere.

"I'll follow the ambulance."

"No."

All eyes immediately turned to see Tucker's mutinous expression. Dixie appeared out of the darkness, a camera still slung around her neck, to stand by Kristen.

"You want family along, don't you, son?" the doctor asked.

"I don't need a baby-sitter."

The older EMT gave him a knowing look. "I understand all that. But you'll need a ride somewhere after you've been seen. You probably have your truck here on the grounds, right?"

"I'll find a way." He shifted as if to sit up, then winced and clasped his free hand over the bandages.

Jake turned away and lowered his voice. "I'll follow.'' He lifted his gaze to meet Kristen's. ''Unless there's something I need to stay here for?''

''Of course not. You brother is far more important than anything here. While you're there, can you check on Susie?''

''We got word back on her, ma'am,'' the younger EMT said. She's fine—one tough little gal. They haven't found anything wrong, so she should be back here later tonight.''

''Thank God for that,'' Dixie replied. As they prepared to put Tucker into the ambulance, she leaned down close to his ear and whispered something.

Tucker shook his head—winced—then lay still.

''Honey, you pay attention to the people who love you,'' Dixie drawled as she straightened, laying a hand on his shoulder. ''Don't get so prideful that you go makin' things harder on yourself, you hear? You have more talent than I've seen in years, and I want to make it to some magazine covers with the pictures I take of you on those bulls.''

A blush stole across Tucker's cheekbones as they moved him into the ambulance.

''Thanks, Dix,'' Jake said, as the ambulance pulled slowly out of the grounds. ''He's got quite a chip on his shoulder. What did you say to him to get him to cooperate?''

Dixie chuckled. ''I just told him about the pretty gal in the front row who was watching him like he was the coolest thing she'd ever seen. Offered to find out her name so he could let her know about his next rodeos.''

''He won't be doing any bull riding for a long time

to come, if he broke that arm." Kristen looked up at Jake, her gray eyes filled with concern. "Will he go back to your family's ranch while he mends?"

"He took off without a word. I think he'd rather die in the desert than go back."

"I've seen him at rodeos up in Montana," Dixie said. "He shows a lot of talent. Almost always covered his bull and earned day money, but didn't win often enough to have much set by. I'd offer to take him in, but I'm on the road all the time."

After what Tucker had said tonight, it obviously wasn't going to be easy to convince him. But there was only one good option unless he'd made some awfully good friends in the past year.

"I'll try to get him back to my motel, then see if he'll let me take him back to Wyoming." Jake raised an eyebrow at Kristen. "Okay with you?"

"Of course it is. He could stay out at my dad's ranch. If it's going to take a long time to mend, he could do some odd jobs and feel like he was needed."

Jake reached for the set of truck keys in his pocket. "Thanks, but Guy offered me the use of one of the cabins at his ranch until this season is over. Tuck could stay with me."

"I'll call both Guy and my dad tonight to let them know."

"Tucker may refuse. He's turned into one hard-headed kid."

Dixie laughed. "Absolutely nothin' like his big brother, right? I think we can convince him. If not, we can just hogtie and blindfold him, and throw him in your truck."

THE LOCAL HOSPITAL was the size of a small grade school, with a tiny emergency room and one doctor. When Tucker walked out of the ER with a cast from elbow to palm, his anger was gone. He looked defeated, exhausted and lost.

"Hey, stranger," Jake called out from his chair at a far corner of the waiting room. "How's that arm?"

"It hurts like h—" He caught himself and started over. "It's fine."

"Need a ride somewhere?"

"No." Tucker looked around the otherwise empty room, and his shoulders slumped. "Yeah, I guess so. I don't even know where the hell we are."

Knowing how much that admission had cost Tucker, Jake waited until they were nearly back to the rodeo grounds before discussing the future. "Are you traveling with some buddies?"

"Yeah."

"They heading out tonight?"

"Yeah."

"How long are you going to be in that cast?"

Tucker slumped a little more. "Six weeks or so."

"Think you'll go on with your friends?"

"They can't afford to pack someone who can't pay his own way."

"What are you going to do?"

Tucker glanced at the darkened houses as they drove through the empty streets of Mendota. "Maybe get a job, hole up for a while, then get back on the road as soon as I can."

Jake let a silence lengthen between them, time for his brother to think about the likelihood of any job opportunities in this small town. "I broke my wrist once. Luckily, it wasn't my right hand, like yours, but that wrist was weak for a long time after the cast came off. Have you thought about going back home?"

Tucker stared out the window, a muscle flicking in his jaw. "Only if I was in a pine box."

"Then come with me. At least until you're completely healed. I'd like that, Tuck."

"I'll bet," he retorted bitterly. "I saw that woman you're with. I bet she'd be just reeeal happy to have me show up."

"She's a business partner. We have separate rooms at the motel, and I have a cabin back at the MRC's base ranch. What do you say? You'd have a roof, and meals. Remember Uncle Guy? You could work for him if you wanted, or help me."

By the time they pulled to a stop at the rodeo grounds, Tucker still hadn't answered. Jake tried again. "Guy's ranch is four hundred miles from Dad's place. It wouldn't be like you were going home. Guy is Mom's brother, not Dad's. I don't remember Dad ever going there for a visit."

"I'm not afraid of him," Tucker retorted.

The unspoken words hung in the air. *Not anymore.*

"But you don't want to go back like this."

"I'm never going back."

Jake turned off the engine and pocketed the keys. The rodeo events were over now, the stands were emptied and stragglers were heading out to their cars. A trio of young cowboys stood by a battered truck at the gate with duffel bags and bronc saddles at their feet.

"Pride is a good thing, but take it too far and you only hurt yourself. Looks like your friends waited for you."

Tucker opened the door, awkwardly supporting his cast as he climbed out of the truck. Without a backward glance, he joined his friends.

Kristen appeared by the passenger door of Jake's truck. Her pale blond hair gleamed like silver under the bright lights, but the shadows under her eyes resembled bruises. She looked completely exhausted. Suddenly Jake wished he could bring her back to his own room. Just sleeping with her, nestled close and warm, would feel so damn good.

"Any luck with Tucker?"

"Guess not, but I sure as hell tried. Everything under control here?"

She lifted a backpack. "The food stand is closed and locked, I've got the cash box here, and Tina has everything from the announcer's stand. Bud's crew takes care of the livestock and grounds for the night." Opening the door, she climbed in and dropped the bag at her feet. "We're free to go."

Jake turned on the motor and put the truck in gear, but held it steady as he watched Tucker and his friends saunter away. "I hope he's going to be all right."

"He's a big boy, Jake, and you're just his brother. You can't make him do anything he doesn't want to do, even if he's being completely stupid."

Even after a long day and longer night, she smelled like some sort of flower, light and fresh. Just a hint of it that made him want her closer. "You look tired,'' he murmured. "Slide over and you can lean on me."

"You sound like the big bad wolf."

He grinned back at her. "Maybe I am. Come over and find out."

"I really don't—"

A sharp rap on the door startled them both.

"Guess I could use a place to crash tonight," Tucker mumbled, not looking either one of them in the eye. "If it's still okay."

"Of course!" Looking a little too relieved, Kristen slid over to make room for him.

"Good decision, Tuck." And probably a lucky one for Jake, as well. He'd been ignoring his instinctive reaction to Kristen, and had been doing pretty well. Until now. Having a surly chaperone might just be the best thing that could have happened.

BY SUNDAY NIGHT, Kristen was ready to hit the road and drive all night—anywhere—just to be in the quiet confines of the pickup.

Saturday's rodeo had gone better than Friday's— no injuries, no major problems. Unless one counted the hours of rain that fell throughout the morning, which turned the arena into nearly impassable mud.

The sun came out by late afternoon and the crowd was fair, but some of the bulls and broncs bucked poorly on the heavy footing, and cowboys slipping and sliding in the mud made poor times or missed altogether in the calf roping and steer wrestling events, muting the crowd's enthusiasm.

Sunday had gone much better—except for the sullen figure of Tucker Landers moping around the chutes, and Jake, who had slipped into a state of almost total silence.

"So," Dixie was saying, as they surveyed the departing crowd from the top rail of the chutes. "This was your baptism by fire?"

"We had everything *but* fire. I don't remember anything going wrong when Dad and Guy put on rodeos."

"Honey, you were just too young—or too preoccupied—to notice what they were dealing with behind the scenes. You put all of that rough stock, a bunch of cowboys and a passel of spectators in one place, and things just happen."

"I won't have much time to dwell on anything— we're off to Colorado next week and have a pretty full schedule from that point on. How about you?"

"Covering rodeos like always. This year I'm trying to finish pulling together a strong portfolio. I'd like to take off for six months next year and work on a book—a photo-essay on rodeo."

"Hey, that's wonderful! And I can say, 'I knew her when.'"

"I'd just like to have something permanent, for when…" Her voice trailed off and her smile faded, then she gave a forced chuckle. "It depends on the shots I get this year, and how the money holds out."

"I'll sure be looking forward to the dates you scheduled for MRC."

Dixie thought for a minute. "Four weekends?"

"Five. And one of those rodeos is just outside Bent

Spur.'' Kristen gave her a wicked grin. ''Maybe you can stay with us a few days.''

Stiffening, Dixie looked away. ''I don't even know why I asked to cover that one. It was a moment of sheer stupidity. I'll probably just head to something farther west.''

''Chicken.''

''You know Clint will be there. I just couldn't—''

''He isn't married.''

Dixie stilled.

''He's not engaged, either. He was for a while, but that fell through. I still keep in contact with his sister—we were friends on the horse show circuit when I was a kid. We e-mail each other now and then, and I keep tabs on him for you.''

''Kristen!''

''What are friends for?''

Dixie's smile faded. ''It never would have worked, anyway, you know. He had all the makings of a world champion and was solid as Gibraltar—but he rodeoed just long enough to finance college and then he went back to school.''

''So?''

''There was nothing he wanted more than to get off the road. There's nothing I love more than to be on it. If I stay in one place more than three days, I'm ready for a straitjacket. He wanted six kids and a picket fence, and the only thing I know about kids is that they are shorter than me.''

''You couldn't work things out?''

Dixie looked ruefully at her scarlet satin blouse and

skintight jeans. "Do you really think rural Wyoming is ready for this?"

"So buy your clothes from a farm supply store instead of Frederick's of Hollywood. If you really love someone—"

"Can you see me in flannel shirts and work boots?" Dixie gave a forced laugh as she absently stroked the Nikon in her lap, her gaze following the livestock semis as they pulled away from the grounds. After a long silence, her voice lowered to a whisper. "But that wasn't the real issue. He'll have my heart until I die, but it doesn't matter. He said he didn't love me."

"I *saw* how he used to look at you. What was Scarlett O'Hara's last line—something about 'another day'?"

Dixie stood abruptly and shouldered her camera bag. "I just don't think I have enough of those left."

TUCKER GLANCED at the alarm clock on the bedside table—it was already mid-morning—and then glared at the narrow confines of his bedroom.

Okay—so it wasn't so bad, having a decent bed and clean sheets. After three months on the road with the guys, he'd slept on more motel-room floors than he cared to count.

He didn't need to look to know that Jake was already up and gone. Running, no doubt, though anyone could see that it wasn't going to do him any good.

A sharp rap sounded at the door of the cabin, followed by the squeal of hinges and a hearty

"Howdy!" that shook dust from the open beams above Tucker's head. *Uncle Guy.*

With a growl, Tucker jerked on a pair of jeans and ran a hand through his hair, then shuffled out into the main room of the cabin. "'Lo."

Sometimes people and places didn't look as big or imposing as you remembered, and Tucker hadn't seen Guy since early grade school at best. But Guy was just as tall and formidable as ever, despite being old as the hills.

"Thought I'd stop by and welcome you to the Triple L." He'd brought a coffee mug in with him, and now he lifted it in salute. "It's been a long time since you boys were here last."

"I was in fourth grade—you let me ride your cuttin' horse, and I got dumped in the dirt on the first turn."

Guy chuckled. "That would have been Sandy. She could turn inside out before you could blink an eye." He took a long swallow of coffee, then glanced at Tucker's arm. "I hear you had a run of bad luck."

"Not a *run.* Just one night." That had sounded just like a sullen kid out on a playground, and Tucker knew it. He tensed, waiting for Guy to launch into some big tirade about stupid kids and useless dreams, but, unlike Dad, Guy just lifted an eyebrow as he took another swallow of coffee.

"You're doing good?"

"Making my way."

"So after you're healed, you're going back on the road?"

"'Course."

The lectures he'd heard from his dad spilled into Tucker's thoughts. *You ain't gonna make it, kid. You ain't like Jake. You don't have what it takes. Stay on the ranch and make something of yourself.* And like always, anger built in his chest, sending his adrenaline soaring.

"I'm not quitting 'til I'm at the top, either."

Guy just looked at him, long and hard. "I hope you get there, son. In the meantime, you're welcome here until you heal. I could use a little help. Or if you want to go on the road with the company, they could use you, too."

For years, a stubborn edge of rebellion had eaten at Tucker day and night, making him want to go toe-to-toe with someone—*anyone*—who stood in the way of his dreams. But with Guy talking to him like just another man, like an equal, he found himself easing up inside. "Uh…thanks."

Guy nodded toward the little kitchen along one wall. "You boys can cook out here, but you're surely welcome to join us up at the house. Your aunt Jennibelle makes a damn good breakfast." He glanced at the clock on the wall. "'Course, you gotta show up a little earlier—we're all done and out of there by seven. But I bet, this once, she'd be glad to rustle up something for you right now."

Even as he shook his head, Tucker's stomach growled at the thought. When had he last eaten? There'd been those three-for-a-dollar hot dogs back at some truck stop outside Mendota—they'd tasted like the bottom of someone's shoe, and he'd pitched them after the first bite. Before that…

A smile played at the corners of Guy's mouth. "Don't be bashful, kid. She's just your aunt Jen, and I know she's looking forward to seeing you. Grab a shirt, and I'll go back up to the house with you."

OVER IN MRC'S CABIN, Jake glanced up from the papers spread across Kristen's desk to look out the window, then whistled under his breath. "Well, look at that. People say Guy can charm the birds out of the trees. Now, I believe it."

Outside, Guy and Tucker sauntered toward Guy's house, and from Guy's animated gestures, it looked like he was probably telling some tale from the old days of rodeo.

"Tucker *would* be the ultimate test," Kristen retorted dryly. "That kid didn't say one word to either of us the entire trip back here."

"He was probably tired, and maybe a little woozy from the painkillers the doc gave him. Driving all night probably put him to sleep." Jake leaned back in his chair and stretched, then set aside the calculator and looked at her. Some crazy impulse made him want to scoop her up and haul her into his lap, but he suspected it might be a dangerous move.

"No. He was awake. Now and then I'd glance back to say something to him, try to make him feel welcome. A porcupine couldn't have looked more prickly."

Tucker's words kept coming back to Jake. *You left me there…with him.* "Your dad and my uncle were partners for what—maybe sixteen years?"

"That sounds right. I think I was twelve when I first started tagging along with Dad."

"By that time I'd left home to follow the rodeo circuit out in California for a while. Did you see Tucker much when he was a kid?"

"Nope. I rarely saw him or the rest of your family here at Guy's. Why?"

Was Tucker happy? Did he look scared? But asking wouldn't change the past, and would betray the basic tenets of family loyalty.

"Nothing." With a shrug, Jake reached for another sheaf of papers on the desk. "So what about these?"

She leaned forward and peered at them, her arm brushing against his. "These show you how MRC handled advance publicity for several rodeos last year. The kind of things we did in Mendota. How we usually start is…"

The warmth of her arm against his radiated through him, landing in his chest where it changed into that same, unaccountable hunger that he'd felt before. The scent of her was like flowers and sunshine, teasing at his senses, making it hard to concentrate on what she was saying.

"…and that's usually very effective."

He stared at her. "Huh?"

"You had a question?"

Yeah. What would you do if I kissed you, right now? Ran my hands through your hair? Pulled you close? "Tell me about public relationships again."

Her expression darkened. "Public *relations*."

"Right."

He turned toward her, hoping she'd feel he was

paying more attention this time, and casually draped an arm across the back of her chair. "Is there…uh…a certain percentage of the budget set aside for that?"

"You're thinking about *advertising*," she ground out. "Are you sure you want to go over this stuff today?"

"Absolutely." He eased his arm a little closer, until he could stroke her shoulder with his thumb. Gently, as if it were just a reflex, or a gesture between friends.

She stilled. "Jake…"

Looking down into her flashing gray eyes, he saw the unmistakable warning, but then his gaze slid down to her mouth, and it was as if he'd been slammed back through time.

Once again she was that shy, pretty eighteen-year-old, impossibly sexy and totally naive, and he was twenty-four—old enough to know better, but so in love with her that he couldn't eat, couldn't sleep, couldn't even concentrate on his next bull without thinking about her.

He hadn't planned it.

Knew she didn't want it.

But suddenly, here and now, he was kissing her once again. And the sheer pleasure of it made him feel as if he'd finally come home.

She stiffened and pressed her hands against his chest. But then, Lord have mercy, her mouth softened, and she opened to him, warm and sweet. Her hands slid up his chest and slipped around his neck, drawing him closer. Everything else faded as the desire held in check for ten years exploded into a searching, demanding kiss that nearly sent him straight over the edge.

And then she was gone.

Wild-eyed, panting, she stared at him, one hand at her throat. "My God," she breathed. "I didn't want... I mean, I didn't mean..."

He had to wait until his heart slowed before he could speak. In those moments he saw deep regret replace desire in her eyes...followed by a spark of anger. And then he knew just how badly he'd once hurt her.

"I'm sorry," he said quietly. "It won't happen again."

"No, it won't." As she stood, she kept her gaze fixed on the papers strewn across the desk. "I know exactly how much this sort of thing means to you."

At the door, she stopped and looked over her shoulder, her expression devoid of emotion. "Look through those things, and we'll discuss your questions a little later. I think I'll go for a run."

And then, just as he'd been on their wedding day ten years ago, he was alone.

CHAPTER EIGHT

ROY GLANCED at the calendar, then wolfed down another forkful of scrambled eggs. Mid-May. He'd always been on the road starting another rodeo season. And now...

Across the table, Ada hummed a never-ending series of Christmas carols as she pushed her food into little piles on her plate, then rearranged them into patterns only she could understand.

Once a gracious woman with a quiet sense of humor and a pretty smile, now she had some days when she seemed happy and would talk as if she were normal. Other days she didn't even seem to realize that he was in the room.

There'd been a time when he'd been jealous of every guy who gave her a second look and had wondered about how faithful she was when he was away. He'd seen Guy look at her often enough, though both she and Guy had vehemently denied doing anything wrong.

"Ada?"

She pushed another lump of scrambled eggs across her plate.

"Ada!"

When she finally lifted her gaze, a glimmer of a smile deepened fine wrinkles at her eyes.

"Kristen oughta be back at Guy's by now. Maybe she'll stop here before heading to the Colorado rodeo tomorrow."

Ada showed no sign of recognition. She was dressed in a faded blue dress today, her buttons askew, her baby-fine hair wisping out of the knot on her head. Just sixty-seven years old, she already looked as if she should be in a nursing home.

He choked back a bitter laugh, remembering how he'd thought retiring from MRC would lead into one long, wonderful vacation. Old age and fate and Ada's failing health had betrayed him, leaching away every measure of enjoyment he'd earned after decades of hard work. He'd sacrificed so much. Damn it, he deserved much better.

Maria turned away from the kitchen sink and moved behind Ada's chair. "Ada will like it if Kristen comes. Won't you?" Maria bent low and gave Ada's bony shoulders a quick hug. "But we'll get along fine either way. We got some new seed catalogs yesterday. She likes looking at pictures."

Picture books. Hours spent staring out the windows. An empty life, for what was now the empty shell of a woman he'd once loved. Ada's vacant expression and wrinkled flesh contrasted painfully with Maria's smooth, gleaming skin and the lively twinkle in her eyes. Roy had to look away.

With a growl of frustration he shoved his plate back and stood, needing an escape. "I'll be moving cattle up onto the north ridge today. I'll carry the phone, just in case Kristen shows up or—'' he nodded toward Ada ''—you need anything.''

Maria followed him to the door and lifted his hat from the hook on the coatrack, while he jerked on his boots. ''This is hard for you, I know. It is sad to see a loved one fade away.''

When she handed him his hat, she held on to it for a split second longer and met his eyes. She moved no closer, but he could feel her reaching out to him, offering what she dared not offer with Ada in the room. ''You're such a good man, Roy. I wish I could help you more.''

A man had needs. Deserved a little attention. He'd taken comfort in the arms of a few women during all those lonely years on the road with MRC, when he'd worked to support his wife and daughter and keep the ranch going through lean times—but he'd made sure that none of that ever touched his life back at the ranch. No one had been hurt.

Still, he knew an invitation when he heard it. Maria's silent message came through loud and clear. And Ada would never know the difference.

So why, after all these years, did he feel a stab of guilt?

THREE DAYS LATER, Kristen and Jake were in Pine Bend, Colorado, starting the promotion process all over again.

This time, the rodeo was an annual event put on by the local hospital auxiliary. The committee organized the food vendors, concessions, ticket sales, medical coverage and traffic control. MRC took care of the rest. Because it was a popular town event, there were numerous businesses that had agreed to provide sponsorship.

"So," Kristen said, as Jake drove MRC's truck through town on Wednesday morning. "Want to solo, or come with me?"

He could easily have met with sponsors, distributed half the promotional materials and done whatever needed to be done, but doing it alone didn't sound like nearly as much fun. "Uh...I think it would be better to work with you."

After ticking off a few items on the clipboard in her lap, she lowered her sunglasses with a forefinger and looked at him over the rim. "We could each take one side of the street and distribute posters, then meet at the far end and go from there."

"Or we could go together and scout out who's behind the counter—you hit up the guys, and I'll go in if there's a gal in charge."

After a moment's thought, she tipped her head in acknowledgment. "Whatever."

He pulled into a parking space at the far end of the business area, and they each gathered up a sheaf of rodeo posters and a packet of complimentary tickets.

At each place of business, they peered through the door at the person behind the cash register. Then one of them sauntered in with a big grin and offered a comp ticket in exchange for the right to tape a rodeo poster on the front window.

By the time they reached the end of the street, Jake was no longer sauntering—he was favoring his leg— but every place in town sported an eleven-by-seventeen poster plus an employee enthused about a free ticket to the rodeo. A person who would likely encourage friends and neighbors to come, as well.

During the evening, they called on most of the sponsors in town, who'd donated money for rodeo expenses in exchange for VIP seating, advertising, special recognition during the performances and comp tickets.

And by the time they were finished for the day, they had eased back into the same casual camaraderie they'd shared before he'd kissed her. Almost. Kristen still kept a careful distance, and there was still an edge—an uncertainty, an undeniable awareness—that made him hesitate over his words.

She felt it, too—he could see it in the way she focused so intently on every detail of their promotional efforts. Now, seated in a restaurant on the edge of town, at a small corner table with a dark tablecloth and candlelight, Kristen studied her clipboard for the hundredth time, holding it up to catch enough light from the candles.

"Sponsors. *Done.* Posters. *Done.* The committee has arranged for the forklift, tractor and harrow. We need to check on their coverage for ticket sales, parking, and—" she flipped the page and made another mark "—the concessions. There shouldn't be any problem with the medical coverage with this group."

Jake speared the last chunk of his rare steak. "Do they realize they need a physician on-site during every performance, though? And a vet?"

"We talked about it on the phone, but I'll verify that." She circled a few lines. "The committee wisely arranged sponsorships by the local paper and a radio station, so we've already had considerable coverage there.''

"Are there any interview times set up?"

"I confirmed everything twice." She thumbed through the papers on her clipboard, then tugged several sheets loose and handed them to Jake. "Here are copies of some of the radio spots and press releases I sent them earlier."

He couldn't read them in the poor light, so he handed them back. "It's a big job."

"And fun, really—for the most part. I can see lots of ways to do better next season, now that I'm on the road with this. I'll...I'll leave you notes on some ideas."

For once she'd left her hair loose to cascade down her back. Part of it now hung over her right shoulder, and he found himself mesmerized by the molten gleam dancing across those deep waves as she spoke. It looked like a waterfall of spun gold.

She'd worn some sort of skimpy, snug T-shirt with a low neckline, and the shadows also did very interesting things to the hint of a valley between her breasts. If that top were just an inch or two lower...

"Actually, the Association has wonderful resources, including extensive checklists to follow on everything—personnel, the arena, stock, a thousand details. Jake?"

Startled, he lifted his gaze and found her frowning at him.

She kept right on going. "I hope you like talking on the telephone, because there are countless decisions along the way. While you're working at one rodeo, you'll be busy via phone, fax and e-mail on the details for each venue during the coming year. Things *really* get hectic as each date draws closer.''

''You were right.''

She paused to spear a forkful of lettuce. ''What?''

''You once said that just showing up for the bull riding and then taking off for the next rodeo was a whole lot easier.''

''There's a first—a man who agrees that I'm right.'' For the first time that day, she gave him a genuine smile, and her laughter sounded low and sultry as she slowly shook her head. ''You're definitely smarter than most.''

He didn't care about being smarter than most. He wanted to reach across the table and capture a handful of that silky hair, just to feel it slide through his fingertips. He wanted to trace the soft curve of her cheek with his fingertips, and settle his mouth on hers.

She would taste much, much better than that triple-chocolate cake on the menu.

The last kiss had been one major, unforgettable mistake.

It had brought back memories of a night spent in heaven, followed by far too many years spent alone with regrets, and wishes that couldn't be fulfilled. They were from two different worlds, and he had no business even thinking about her. But...

''...the schedule. What do you think?''

She looked at him expectantly, but he hadn't heard a word she'd said.

''Uh...yes?''

"I was asking how you wanted to frame up your schedule for next year, geographically speaking," she said dryly.

Jake tossed his napkin on his plate. "Let's discuss it while we walk."

"Aren't you tired?" She frowned and glanced at the cane leaning against their table. "I mean, maybe you should just rest."

"Nope." He tossed a couple of twenties on the table and stood, then offered his hand. "It's better if I keep moving, and I get a little edgy if I stay too long in one place."

She hesitated, then stood and accepted his hand. "I remember." There was a hint of sadness in her eyes. "You were always looking ahead to the next rodeo, taking off with your buddies right after the last eight-second buzzer. I used to watch you, you know...well before we met. When I was a teenager, I thought you were the cutest guy in rodeo."

He gave her a sidelong look as they stepped out into the night. "You must not have been looking very hard."

"Oh, but I was." She drew a deep breath, then sighed. "Those were the days, weren't they? No responsibility beyond getting to the next rodeo...every weekend a new challenge."

"I remember," he said dryly. "Like it was just last year."

Squeezing his hand, she laughed. "Sorry. For you, it was. For me, it's been a long time."

When she started to pull her hand from his, he held on gently. "Friends?"

They were at the end of the parking lot before she finally answered. "It'll be a long season if we aren't."

It felt right, walking with Kristen in the darkness. He'd forgotten just how much he enjoyed the lilt of her laughter. The intelligence and loyalty that were as much a part of her as that golden waterfall of hair.

How long had it been since he'd spent any time at all with a woman? One day he'd been on that hectic schedule of racing from one rodeo to the next. The next, he was pursuing recovery with single-minded intent that left no time for anything else.

Somehow, with Kristen, he no longer felt the driving need to push himself past the limits of his endurance. They walked slowly, past darkened houses, with fireflies dancing in the air before them and only the distant cry of an owl or yip of a coyote to break the silence. The heady fragrance of wild roses drifted from an unseen flower bed. Then the earthy dampness of a pond.

Somewhere along the line, he put his arm around her, and she didn't resist. Instead, she slipped her arm around his waist, then hooked her thumb in one of his belt loops.

A casual response, without a hint of flirtation.

He wanted more.

"You were going to explain next year's schedule," he prompted, seeking safer ground.

The moonlight and shadows had turned her pale hair to a molten river of silver, now. Shimmering. Inviting. When she tipped her head up to look at him, there was laughter in her eyes. "I know you are absolutely *fascinated* with that subject. Where should we begin?''

''Wherever.''

Soon they were back at the motel, standing beneath the No Vacancy sign. June bugs bumbled against the lights above.

A car with Just Married emblazoned across its rear window crunched across the gravel parking lot and stopped in front of a room several doors down from Kristen's, and a tipsy couple climbed out. As they made their way into a room, the man swung the woman up into his arms and staggered over the threshold. From their shrieks of laughter, they must have collapsed just inside.

Kristen's cheeks darkened, and she looked away. ''I think it's too late…maybe we can talk tomorrow.''

''Or maybe not.'' He moved closer, tipped up her chin with a forefinger. ''Maybe it isn't too late at all.''

''No, Jake. I…''

Her voice trailed off as he looked down into her eyes, willing her to agree, hoping she felt the same rush of attraction he'd been feeling all night. He dropped his cane onto the grass at his feet, and with both hands sifted through the spun silk of her hair, then cupped her face gently and lowered his mouth to hers for a brief kiss.

Her skin was impossibly soft, gleaming like flawless ivory beneath his work-callused fingers. He drifted one hand lower to catch the erratic pulse at her throat.

What he'd felt with her ten years before had been no fluke, no figment of his imagination. It pulsed through him once again—heat and need and a nearly overwhelming desire to possess her rocketed through him in the space of a heartbeat.

No other woman had ever made him feel this way.

And when she looked up, her eyes filled with stunned recognition, he knew she felt that same avalanche of emotion.

Glancing at the parking lot and empty street, she gave a weak smile. Her voice was breathy, uneven when she spoke. "I'm not one of your little buckle bunnies. But maybe the street isn't the place to continue this, ah...discussion..."

Maybe it wasn't. But after ten long years, his motel room was just too far away. The possibility that she would follow him there was even more remote. "I want you, Kris. You can't even begin to imagine just how much."

He caught her mouth once more and held her in a crushing embrace, dropping a hand to the pockets of her jeans to hold her closer still. And when she finally opened to him, welcomed him, he felt totally, irrevocably lost.

She pulled away, shaking her head. "I—I'm sorry. This might be a casual thing for you, but it isn't for me."

Casual. He choked back a bitter laugh. Given what she believed about the past, he didn't blame her. But a vow he'd made ten years ago meant she could never learn the truth, and she was probably better off not knowing. He could offer her so little—and staying with him would destroy her chance to reach her dreams. She deserved much more.

He stepped back, and uneven gravel shifted beneath his boot. His knee twisted, buckled. A searing sensation rocketed up his thigh.

With a soft curse he bent over, his hands cradling his knee, and focused on slow, steady breathing to move past the pain.

"Oh, *no*." Kristen rested a hand on his shoulder. "What can I do? Should I get the truck?"

"No." Clenching his teeth, he grabbed his cane and slowly straightened. "If I were a horse, someone would shoot me. I'm beginning to think that's a damn good system."

"Just take your time," she said. "When you're ready, you can lean on me."

"I—don't—need—help."

"Yes, you do. What are friends for?"

Friends?

Looping an arm through his, she continued. "We'll get you back to your room, and I'll get your pain meds for you. Do you need a hot-pack of some kind? Ice?"

"Kris—"

"If you need something else, I can run to the Wal-Mart on the other side of town. I think the sign said that they're open twenty-four hours—"

"Kris!"

She stopped chattering and glanced up at him with a haunted look in her eyes, and he realized that she'd been affected as deeply as he had a few moments earlier.

"It's okay."

"I—I don't know what to say." Her gaze slid away.

He did, but it wasn't going to be easy. "This is just a business deal. We'll keep it that way?" He gave an offhand shrug, as if none of it had mattered. As if her presence didn't affect him, heart and soul. "I guess the moonlight and the motel sign just went to my head. Habit."

Her eyes narrowed. "Sort of like that salivary response of Pavlov's dogs anticipating food—show you any motel and any woman, and you get *hot?*"

She was so wrong. He never pursued a woman in the face of hesitation, never slept with anyone he didn't care for deeply. And as long as he was with Kristen, he couldn't imagine wanting anyone else.

This rodeo season was going to be a long one.

TUCKER ARRIVED with Bud and the two livestock semis on Friday afternoon, and went out into the arena to help sort the bucking stock. Jake watched him with an approving smile.

"I'm glad to see him pitching in. He ought to be a little easier to live with if he has something to do."

Hoot rubbed Petunia behind her ears. "Gotta be hard, coming off the road like that. A kid that age has a lot of big dreams." In response to an invisible signal, the mule nodded her head vigorously. "Even Petunia agrees."

"He's got a real attitude. Doesn't want to listen, figures he's heading right back out on the circuit as soon as his cast is off."

"That doesn't sound like anyone *I* know," Hoot

said with a wry smile. Petunia lifted her head and curled her upper lip into a horse laugh, and he slipped her an alfalfa cube as a reward.

"We all look out for each other at the rodeos, but I've never been responsible for anyone until now. Knowing how the bulls are, knowing how green he is—I wish he'd go back to the ranch."

Hoot stroked his mule's splashy bay-and-white hide. After a few moments he looked up and measured his words carefully. "He's of age, can make up his own mind. He isn't gonna appreciate you being his mother." Hoot's gaze lifted to something over Jake's shoulder, then he frowned. "Maybe you'll want to check that out over there—Bud's been a little riled today."

Jake turned. Over in one corner of the arena, Bud was standing nose to nose with the chute boss, his fists clenched. Vance's reddened face and belligerent stance indicated the situation was escalating.

"Thanks." Jake hadn't slept well at all—had tossed and turned, then paced the floor until nearly three. He was in no mood to deal with trouble. Luckily, his knee was okay today—a different brace and a double dose of ibuprofen were doing the job, despite that moment in the parking lot last night.

By the time Jake was twenty feet away, Vance and Bud turned to face him.

"Need something?" Bud's fists were still clenched, but he bared his teeth in a welcoming smile.

"Any problem?"

"No." Vance shot a venomous look at Bud, then pivoted on his heel and walked away.

"Anything that needs to be figured out before the performance starts?"

Bud watched Vance head for the chutes, grab a jacket off a rail, then head out to the parking lot. "It's done."

"He's *leaving?*"

"Fired."

"Got a reason?"

"I won't tolerate anyone who don't treat this stock better than his own family," Bud spat, rolling the tension out of his shoulders.

"What happened?"

"I handled it."

"And I want to know."

Bud gave an irritable shrug. "Carelessness. The fool didn't set up the ramp right, and Grizzly caught a hoof while being loaded. Take a look—he's by himself in the pen behind me."

Jake stepped up on the bottom rail of the fence and looked over into the pen at the mottled gray Brahma. The animal stood with a hind foot cocked, lifting it intermittently. "Talked to the vet?"

"He's already on his way here for the evening performance."

Jake shook his head. "Grizz has to be out of the lineup for tonight."

"He'll be out for weeks, maybe longer. I won't buck any stock that ain't in top-notch condition."

Bud might be genetically lacking in people skills, but his concern for the animals was evident in their gleaming, healthy hair coats and solid weight. Nodding in agreement, Jake stepped down and rubbed the back of his neck. "Know of anyone who could fill in as chute boss?"

"Lew."

"I don't think he'll work for me. He's had a rock in his boot over something since he showed up."

Bud snorted. "It isn't just you—he's charming as hell to everyone. But he does know rodeo and he's good with the livestock. He'll do."

"I'll talk to Kristen, and we'll get back to you. Speaking of charm, thanks for bringing Tucker along."

"Don't that kid ever talk?"

Jake scanned the area, finally locating Tucker up in the stands talking to a pretty young thing in a tube top and tight jeans. "I guess we aren't cute enough. Put him to work if you can. He'll be better off busy."

As he left the arena, Jake glanced at the back lot, where the teenagers were bathing horses for the Grand Entry. And toward the stands that would soon be filled with a crowd eager for a good show.

A sense of satisfaction flickered to life inside him for the first time since his injury. *This could be a decent career,* he realized, grinning to himself. *It's not a bad life, when everything goes right.*

The feeling lasted for exactly thirty seconds.

CHAPTER NINE

"WE'VE GOT A PROBLEM," Kristen muttered. Grabbing Jake's arm, she headed toward the back lot where they'd have more privacy.

At the tailgate of MRC's pickup, she glanced around and then took a deep breath. "Back in Mendota, the food theft could have been a prank—local teenagers causing trouble. Then there was the canceled radio interview, and Susie getting hurt. It's starting again. I've just had a phone call."

Jake hooked one boot on the truck bumper and an elbow over the tailgate. "The sheriff back in Mendota?"

"No. I'm sure he considered the case closed as soon as we pulled out of town. He didn't seem too concerned about the aspect of assault, or cruelty to an animal, even though Susie did get thrown in the process."

"Then what?"

"I've had two calls in twenty-four hours, canceling MRC rodeo dates for next year."

"Isn't that common—changing plans this far ahead?"

"These were rodeos MRC did last year. The arenas were both at county fairgrounds and had been reserved by those committees. There shouldn't be any reason to cancel.''

Jake tipped back his hat with a forefinger. ''Did they say why?''

''One guy hemmed and hawed, then said his committee decided they might not have a rodeo next year. I'll bet you five bucks that they do, with another company. The other guy said they'd decided MRC didn't 'instill confidence' anymore, with Roy and Guy gone.''

''You argued our case?''

From his wry grin, she could tell he figured she had probably fought tooth and nail to save the bookings.

She kicked a clump of dirt. ''There was never really any chance to change their minds. It was a done deal before they called—and neither one had signed a new contract yet, so they were home free.''

''Where were these rodeos?''

''Western Minnesota and northern Colorado.'' She paced a few steps away, then turned back to him. ''The thing is, they both made similar comments.''

''About what?''

''Apart from the change in MRC's management, they also knew about the troubles we had back in Mendota. And they *both* mentioned hearing that MRC's day money checks to the bull riders failed to clear last weekend.''

At that, Jake straightened. ''That's not true.''

''On the coattails of those other problems, it wouldn't be hard for an outsider to believe. I denied it, and offered to provide proof as soon as our canceled checks come back. But..." She hesitated, then plowed ahead. "I think they were both looking for an excuse to cancel, and they did."

He didn't look surprised, and she found herself thinking about his verbal agreement to buy MRC. The deal had hinged on her assistance through the season. Could he try to force a low price if the company took a downward slide before the deal was final? *Would he?* His word hadn't been much good ten years ago.

"You're thinking someone is behind this," he said quietly.

"Doesn't it seem strange?"

He didn't look impressed. "Cowboys leave one venue and by the next night they're two states away at the next one. Word travels fast. As for the bad checks, one angry cowboy, disqualified for one reason or another, could have started a rumor like that."

Over Jake's shoulder, Kristen saw Susie and some of the other teenagers heading toward the lunch wagon by the announcer's stand. As usual, the horses were wet and clean—the kids were wet and muddy from head to toe.

Kristen stepped closer and lowered her voice. "If there's one person responsible, I'm going to find out who—and you can bet I'm also going to find out why."

TOSSING HIS EMPTIED cup of beer to the ground, Tucker stared at the girl as she darted away to join a group of friends. *Score one for the champ.*

He hadn't even gotten to first base.

Slapping his hat against his thigh, he sagged

against the bleacher seat behind him and glared across
the rodeo grounds toward Jake, who was talking to
the hot chick he *claimed* was just a business partner.
As if Tucker was that stupid.

Over by the stock pens, Bud was talking to the vet.
The bullfighters had parked their trailer behind the
announcer's stand and were seated at a card table outside, where they were putting on makeup, looking
oddly mismatched in white T-shirts and colorful rodeo clown costumes from the waist down, with rain-
bow suspenders still drooping to the grass.

A steady stream of cowboys made their way over
to the announcer's stand, where Tina collected their
entry fees. Tucker had resolved to avoid *that* area—
if he got within twenty feet of Tina, she'd find something for him to do.

With a curse he stood, wobbling for just one dis-
orienting moment, then he started down the bleachers.
Being here as a—*spectator*—was so frustrating that
he almost wished he'd stayed at Guy's. But then Guy
would be trying to find things for him to do, too, and
Aunt Jennibelle would be hovering.

Six weeks. Six long weeks 'til his cast could come
off, if the bones healed well. Then longer until his
arm would be strong enough to ride. That day could
not come soon enough.

He wandered into the back lot, where cowboys
stood by the duffel bags and bronc saddles they'd
dropped on the ground, shooting the breeze as they
expertly adhesive-taped elbows, wrists and forearms
for support.

Nearly all wore loose jeans with just a knotted

string in place of a big trophy-buckled belt, choosing freedom of movement over style. The cast on his arm weighed heavier, as he watched the saddle bronc riders slip on the oversize, soft western boots that identified them as riders with common sense. A boot that slipped off easily was good insurance against getting hung up in a stirrup.

"Hey, Tuck, some girl's momma come after you?" Slim Hathaway, a young saddle bronc rider from Wyoming, grinned up him.

Slim had rosined the seat of his saddle and was now sitting on it with his long legs stretched forward on the ground, rocking back and forth to work the sticky substance into the leather.

"If that bull was some gal's momma, I'd hate to see what the gal looked like," Tucker shot back. He raised his casted arm as if to clunk Slim on the head. "You get a good draw tonight?"

"Nightdrifter. Good scoring horse—real consistent. I seen Denny Harmon try to ride her in Wichita. He went to the hospital on a backboard. Not," Slim added with a grin, "that I plan to do the same."

Tucker hunkered down next to him. "How's it going?"

Slim quit rocking in his saddle, reached for his duffel bag and pulled out a battered envelope. Withdrawing a trio of photographs, he cracked a wide smile that revealed missing front teeth. "My son."

Tucker dutifully admired the pictures of a roly-poly baby with even fewer teeth than Slim. "Good lookin' kid."

"I aim to be home to see him more, after this season. I figure I'll have a down payment on the place next to my folks by then.''

Tucker tried to visualize leaving the rodeo circuit for good, and couldn't imagine the boredom. ''You're quitting rodeo?''

''It's no life being on the road for months. Not with the baby, and with my wife trying to work two jobs.'' Slim took the photos back and slid them into a pocket of his duffel. ''We're gonna start raising beef.''

Tucker clapped him on the back with his good hand. ''Good luck tonight.''

He wandered through the growing crowd of cowboys, shooting the breeze with those he knew. Some of them were doing mental imaging of their next ride, going through the motions of a ride with a hand held high.

Just what Tucker himself would be doing right now if he hadn't got hung up in his bull rope and if that one bullfighter hadn't stood back and gawked while the other one tried to help.

Tucker's frustration welled up in his chest. *Damn.*

''Hey, kid!''

Bud. One more chore. Tucker kept weaving through the cowboys, heading in the other direction.

''*Tucker!*''

Tucker cringed. Bud had a good bellow on him, but his wife, Tina, had a voice like metal scraping across cement.

All heads turned toward her, then back to him. Some guys were chuckling, some appeared sympathetic, but all looked relieved that she hadn't been after *them.*

He was a *bull rider,* dammit—and he'd just been summoned like some snot-nosed school kid. Tucker halted, his anger surging.

"Hey kid, your mommy wants you!"

The taunt came from somewhere behind him.

Amid the laughter, Tucker blindly spun around. Focused for a bleary split second. Then hauled back and slammed a killer right cross into the astonished face of MRC's youngest bullfighter.

"PERSONALLY, I THINK you ought to leave him here." Kristen paced back and forth in front of the jail cell—one of just two at the sheriff's office.

The whole setup was like something out of Mayberry, Tucker thought, but the sheriff didn't look like an old-time TV star and he definitely wasn't happy.

Tucker sat on the metal bunk of his cell, glaring at the opposite wall.

"Well?" She glanced at her wristwatch, then stood still in front of the sheriff. "It's midnight, and I'd like to get this settled. Can we leave or not?"

"He broke a man's nose," the sheriff growled. "The other guy refused to press charges, but I oughta keep Tucker overnight just to teach him a lesson."

"I'm his brother, and he'll stay with me," Jake promised. "He won't get into any more trouble."

The sheriff shot a dark look toward Tucker's cell. "His blood alcohol was just over the legal limit, and I could also charge him with disturbing the peace."

"Aw, Sheriff, it was just a little misunderstanding among friends. Right, Tuck?"

Tucker closed his eyes as anger and humiliation welled up in his throat.

"*Come on,* Tucker." Jake moved up to the cell and braced each hand against a bar. "I'm leaving you here if you won't answer."

Tucker stubbornly turned his face toward the back wall. Nausea rolled through his gut from the beer…and from the strip-search he'd endured before being thrown in this hole.

Worst of all, he kept seeing the broadly painted happy-face of that bullfighter at the moment his fist connected.

Some kid up in the grandstand had started screaming—screaming that someone was killing a clown, for cripes' sake. Tucker had looked up into the stands in time to see the kid's dad punching a number into his cell phone. Five minutes later, a patrol car pulled in.

"Looks like a done deal to me, folks." The sheriff looked pointedly at the door. "He wants to sit here, and visiting hours are *over.*"

Kristen's lighter footsteps started for the door, but Jake's didn't follow.

"Look, I know you sorta needed to haul him in after that guy called 911, but we'll be leaving the state tomorrow night. In most small towns a little problem like this doesn't even go *this* far."

The sheriff glowered at Jake. "This is Pine Bend, and this is *my* territory."

"Please. I just can't leave him in here. He's my kid *brother.*"

After a long pause, the sheriff sighed. "I don't want to see him again, you hear? Any trouble, and the next time around he'll be standing in front of the judge—and I'll do my best to make sure he faces some serious fines.''

A wave of guilt and nausea and...sudden, overwhelming relief swept Tucker. Closing his eyes, he leaned his head against the cement wall and listened to the rustle of papers and hum of conversation out at the desk.

After what seemed like an eternity, footsteps moved back to the cell, and Tucker heard the sound of a key in the lock. He turned, knowing he probably looked like some sappy, stupid kid.

But Jake and Kristen weren't at the door. Just the sheriff. The man crossed the cell in two steps, grabbed Tucker's collar and slammed him up against the back wall.

Panic seized Tucker. *Defenseless as a baby rabbit,* an inner voice sneered at him. *He could knock your balls into next week and you couldn't do a damn thing.*

Taking a shaky breath, he resisted the impulse to fight back.

''You're learning, punk.'' The man's face was just inches from his own—eyes blazing, thin lips curled in a snarl. ''Now let's learn one more lesson. You're with that rodeo, and you're gonna be out at the rodeo grounds 'til Sunday. I don't want to see you in town. I don't want to find you drunk. And I sure as hell don't want to find that you're causing trouble.'' The man's meaty fist twisted Tucker's collar. ''Because if you do, you'll be right back in here with me, and next time you aren't going to like me near as much.''

Against the wall, with a viselike grip at his throat, Tucker could only gurgle a response. But the sheriff released him and stepped back.

"Good. Now you walk out of this jail and be careful, or there will be hell to pay. Got it?"

With a nod, Tucker sidestepped past him and headed straight for the door.

ANOTHER WILD SATURDAY NIGHT. And with Kristen and the crew still at the rodeo in Colorado, there wasn't a damn thing to look forward to. Roy poured himself two fingers of Scotch from the decanter on the sideboard, then headed for his leather recliner with both the bottle and the glass.

Moonlight filtered through the vertical blinds to paint bars of light across the bookshelves. The cluttered desk in the opposite corner. The open file drawers.

His office had once been as neat as an operating room—everything in its place, the bookkeeping posted in Ada's neat script. Now it looked like someone had pawed through everything in a hurry and left.

Somewhere in this mess were the feed bills he needed for taxes. The sales receipts for the last two loads of cattle he'd sold. Somewhere in here were registration papers on the gelding he'd sold today— *if* he could find the damn papers and a transfer form.

He tipped back the glass, thankful for the burn sliding down his throat, then poured another, impatient for the pleasant buzz to hit and the grim reality of his life to fade for just a while.

"Señor?" Maria rapped softly at the door and then

edged it open just enough to peer inside. "Your supper is still warm."

Roy took another deep swallow and waved her away, but she stayed there, her brow furrowed.

"You should eat something," she persisted, opening the door wider. "Come. You haven't had anything all day, and that is not good with your ulcer and—" Her hand fluttered toward the bottle he'd propped up against the chair. "The alcohol, no?"

Since dawn he and the boys had branded and vaccinated four-hundred-twenty calves, had loaded steers onto two semis, and had moved a herd of cows up into the northern meadow. A lot of work for a young man...exhausting work for an old one.

"Save it or pitch it," he muttered, leaning his head against the backrest of the chair.

He felt the warmth of the Scotch seeping through him, warming his bones. Another shot or two, and maybe he'd even get a good night's sleep...

A soft, warm hand stroked the side of his cheek. Drifting between wakefulness and sleep, he imagined it was Ada, her smile gently inviting, a sparkle in her eyes.

"*Señor*...please, don't do this every night. This isn't good for you."

Opening his eyes, he found lush breasts cradled within a soft curve of fabric just inches away. He forced his gaze upward to Maria's warm brown face. Even in the dim light of the single lamp burning over on his desk, he could see the concern in her expression.

"Please, let me take you up to bed."

Something stirred deep inside him. A memory of how good a woman felt when she was ready and eager. Would it be so wrong to find some small measure of comfort and satisfaction when there was so little of either to mark the days?

A flicker of heat pooled low, making him feel heavy and aroused for the first time in—was it months? Years? He could no longer remember, with the pleasant hum of good Scotch coursing through his veins and a lush woman just a heartbeat away.

Her eyes darkened, softened. "It's been a long day for you and for me. I hear the owl out in the old oak by the barn, and coyotes calling to the moon. Come with me...Roy. It's been so long for both of us. Too long, I think."

Sadness washed over her features, in memory of her late husband, no doubt. But still, she reached out and took Roy's hand.

He hesitated, then rose and looked down at her. "I'm an old man. Not young like your husband was."

"Sometimes it isn't the passion..." She looked up at him, her eyes glistening. "Sometimes the best gift is when you aren't lonely anymore."

An image of Ada filled his thoughts. Her gentle voice in the darkness as they lay side by side on their wedding night and dreamed of their future together. Her laughter as she swung a giggling toddler around and around.

It was over now. Some days, she barely knew him, and the emptiness in her eyes echoed the emptiness he felt in his chest when he thought of the years ahead. He was already sixty-eight years old. A lot of hard years, lean years, had bent his back and gnarled his joints into those of an older man. But inside beat the heart of a man who still needed more than an easy chair and a bottle of aged Scotch.

He focused on the woman in front of him and felt that heart kick into higher gear. "You understand that I'm not looking for a wife?"

"I know." Her eyes sparkled, and when she smiled her teeth shone white as ivory in the moonlight. "No more than I am looking for a husband."

His hand trembled at his side as he considered what he was about to do. But when he reached for hers, his grip was strong and firm. And together, they walked up the stairs.

The logic of want and need had seemed clear as a crisp Wyoming morning down in his office. Ada would never know. Her slowly progressing dementia would eventually leave her unable to walk, or talk, or even feed herself.

Day by day, he saw her slipping further into her own world—a world structured by mealtimes and medications, and the dutiful care Maria gave her. Already, she slept in a separate room because she tended to wander at night, and sometimes called out meaningless words in her sleep.

He told himself all these things as he led Maria up to his room. But at his bedroom door, the enormity of the moment weighed heavily on his soul. There had been women through the years, but they'd been in distant cities. Nowhere near his family.

To break this code in his own home seemed a far greater step.

"Maria..." Roy looked down at his hand on the doorknob for a moment, then fixed his gaze on the partly open door of the bedroom where Ada now slept alone.

Stepping around him, Maria covered his hand with her own and looked up at him with a sad smile. "You're a good man, Roy. If you do not want this, I understand. But perhaps...just to share the warmth of your bed would not be so wrong? Just once?"

If Eve had been half so tempting, it was no wonder that Adam followed her into sin. Roy locked the door behind them, then reached out and cupped Maria's face in his hand, traced her soft mouth with his thumb. She closed her eyes and leaned in to his touch, and he was lost.

"Come," he said softly, shutting away the warning bells in his head as he pulled open the door and led her inside. "Perhaps we both need this."

FOR THE FIRST TIME in months, he'd stayed in bed past the blush of dawn over the eastern hills. Roy pulled himself up to peer at the old Baby Ben clock ticking on the nightstand. Eight o'clock—how long had it been since he'd still been in the house past seven?

The nagging headache accelerated as he slid his feet over the side of the bed and dropped his head into his hands.

Full evidence of his indiscretion lay on the other side of the bed, sleeping.

He'd always told himself that what Ada didn't know couldn't hurt her. Yet now he had a woman in his bed—in his own home—while his trusting wife slept in a room down the hall. The thought sent the bitter taste of bile up his throat.

Rising gingerly to his feet, he slipped on his sheepswool slippers, then headed down the hallway to the bathroom.

Something's not right.

He stumbled to a halt at the bathroom door, then turned back to look down the hallway. Everything was just as it had been last night...except Ada's door was open.

She'd gone to the bathroom, maybe. Perhaps she was already sitting in her favorite chair in the living room, even though she hadn't attempted the stairs on her own in months. But if she'd gone that far on her own, she also might have come down the hall and heard...

Paralyzing guilt flooded through him.

Retracing his steps, he scanned Ada's room. Rapidly opened each of the bedroom doors. Ran downstairs to search every room. There was no sign of Ada.

And the front door was wide open.

CHAPTER TEN

"YOUR BROTHER is headed for big trouble." Kristen clenched her hands until her nails bit into her palms, trying to avoid saying too much.

"He hasn't had it easy." Jake picked up a box of files, brushed past her without so much as a smile and walked out of the announcer's booth. With the Sunday matinee performance over, they were packing up and heading back to Wyoming.

"But he's got to just deal with things and move on," Tina countered, closing down her laptop. "Haul a lot of past garbage around with you, and it just taints the rest of your life."

"It's also hard on the bullfighter population around here," Kristen muttered under her breath.

She looked over to the bottom row of the empty bleachers where Kenny sat hunched over, his head resting in his hands, a broad white bandage across his nose. Only by sheer luck had Tina been able to track down another bullfighter to cover the Sunday performance. The rules required two, and two were certainly needed for the safety of the contestants.

Jake came back in, limping more than he had a few days earlier. "Tucker's nearly twenty, and he's been on his own since high school. He doesn't think he has to answer to anyone.''

''But you're his brother.'' Kristen finished boxing up the printer and handed it to Jake. ''You're his best bet.''

''Not a good one. He barely talks to me, but you're sure welcome to try.'' He glanced around at the emptied office space. ''Are we set to go?''

Tina surveyed the area and nodded, her laptop cradled to her chest, then headed out the door. *Nobody* touched that laptop but her, and as much as she cursed when it locked up or lost data, she treated it like a treasured baby.

''Jake, Bud wants to talk to us before we leave. Want to head over to his truck?'' Kristen picked up her clipboard and checked off the last two things on her list, then started for the door.

She tapped the list with a finger as they walked across the rodeo grounds. ''Have you looked this over? It includes everything that has to be done before we pull out. Prize monies paid. Media releases. An equipment checklist—''

''I've seen it.''

''Good. I think you should start taking all of MRC's calls. You've been through two venues now—a total of six performances on this side of the rodeo business.''

''You can't quit.'' He didn't look down at her, but just kept walking.

All weekend Jake had been polite. Attentive to details. Distant, as if he'd never given that kiss another thought. Of course, with a man like Jake, there was always another town and another woman…so why would he?

Some things never change.

"I didn't say I was backing out on our deal," she retorted. "I'm saying that you're ready to take responsibility. The end of September will be here in no time—"

"Ten-and-a-half weeks."

"Uh…yes." *He was counting the days and weeks until she was gone?* "And the more you do now, the more ready you'll be."

"Fair enough."

Despite his damaged knee, he was walking faster than she could, so she hurried to catch up. "And you need to ask any questions you can think of."

"Okay."

"Well?"

He pulled to a halt so abruptly that she nearly ran into him. "Well, what?"

She blew her drooping bangs out of her eyes. "Is there anything you need to know?"

He leaned down until they were nose to nose. "I'd like to know how someone can respond with such emotion to a simple kiss—such heat—and then turn it off in the blink of an eye." Straightening, he started walking again. "Truthfully, it's sorta spooky."

"*Spooky!*" Her clipboard slid out of her grasp. Snatching it up, she started after him. "Because I'm not one of those easy chicks who surrender when you glance in their direction?"

He snorted. "You're hardly that."

They reached the lowboy trailer, where the crew

had just finished tying down the load of chutes and arena fence panels. Tucker slouched on the tailgate of a pickup parked on the other side of the trailer, his casted arm resting in his lap.

"Tighten that strap on the front end," Bud shouted. "Get it right or we're gonna be pickin' up this arena from here to the border."

"Personable guy," Jake said under his breath. "You two *are* related."

She looked up at him, ready to give a sharp retort, only to catch a twinkle in his eyes. "Well, at least Bud didn't spend an evening in jail."

"Score." Jake sighed heavily. "At this point, I'm wondering if I should have left him there."

They both glanced over at Tucker—who scowled in return—then looked back at each other.

"You did the right thing, and he's darn lucky to have you. I hate to admit it, but you're a good man, Landers."

He slid a sideways look in her direction, deepening the slash of dimple in his cheek. "And I'll save myself some grief by not taking that the wrong way." He lowered his voice so only she could hear. "You don't need to worry. I'm never going to touch you again, Kristen. I'm never going to move closer or take you into my arms. And I'm never going to kiss you until both of us are weak-kneed and on the verge of cardiac arrest."

She stared at him, speechless, because he'd just promised what she herself would have demanded if he'd made even one more move. Suddenly she realized it wasn't what she wanted, after all.

His eyes twinkled again. "Unless, of course, you ask."

Bud's voice boomed above the sound of the semi's motor. "Time to hit the road, boys." Four men headed for the pickup, while two climbed up into the semi tractor. "Hey, Lew!"

Halfway to the pickup, Lew turned back and sauntered up to Bud, his hat pulled low over his eyes and his mouth turned down in his trademark frown.

Bud clapped him on the back, then turned to Jake and Kristen. "Lew here agreed to work for us as chute boss."

Kristen stiffened. "We should have talked this over, Bud."

"Don't matter. We need him, and he's available." Bud spared a brief glance in her direction before turning his attention to Jake. The challenge in his eyes was unmistakable. "Got any problems with this?"

Jake met his gaze squarely, silently, for a good five seconds, as clear a macho stare-down as Kristen had seen in a good long while. "MRC is in transition right now," he said finally. "This will be a temporary position until we have all the other details worked out." He shifted his attention to Lew. "Does that work for you?"

"I guess I can stay a while." Lew spat on the ground.

"Bud is your boss, but I'll be his," Jake countered evenly. "Things will work out fine if we keep that straight."

Lew shrugged and headed for one of the MRC

pickups with the other guys. Bud headed for the cab of the semi.

In a few minutes, both vehicles were heading out of the fairgrounds in a cloud of dust, leaving only Jake, Tucker and Kristen, and the last MRC pickup truck parked a few yards away.

"That was cool." Tucker gave a derisive snort.

Kristen bristled. "Just who do—"

Jake held up a hand and gave her a warning glance. "I'm glad you thought so, Tucker," he said mildly, heading toward the pickup. "Bud overstepped his authority, but letting him save face in front of the boys was more important than making a point right now."

Raising both arms in exasperation, Tucker swore. "*Both* of those guys ran you over. Didn't you see that?"

Jake opened the driver's door of the truck, then turned back with a sad smile. "What would you have done—hauled off and knocked them senseless? Fired both on the spot? What would have been the best for MRC?"

"Lew hates your guts. And Bud—" Tucker broke off with a sound of disgust. "You don't even *defend* yourself. I've seen you walk away from one argument after another." He jerked open the back door of the truck and slumped in the back seat, then tugged the brim of his hat lower. "Some big shot *you* are."

Kristen glared first at him, then at Jake. "Aren't you going to say something?" she hissed. "If he was half that size, I'd want to give him a time-out in a corner until next Tuesday."

They were miles down the road before Jake finally

spoke. "It's family business—personal. But Tuck and I will discuss this later."

In the back seat, Tucker stirred, then stretched his legs sideways along the bench seat. "Yeah. I can see where you'd want to wait. I'm sure your *girlfriend* would be real impressed by our family."

Kristen took a deep breath and counted to ten. Slowly. "Your brother and I are *business* associates."

"Yeah, right. And we all know just how upright and moral Jake is." He snickered.

They were out in ranch country now. Mile upon mile of sparse grass and sagebrush, without a house, barn or cow in sight. Ahead there were low hills separated by deep ravines.

"I guess," Jake said on a long sigh, as he pulled the truck onto the shoulder near a ravine, "that 'later' just became *now*. Come along, Tuck—we're going to have that talk."

TUCKER'S HEART STILLED. Cold sweat trickled down his back faster than he could say "dammit," though he figured saying that aloud would be akin to waving a red flag in front of a bull.

Kristen turned around and gave him a sympathetic smile. "It'll be okay," she murmured. "He's a fair man."

If "fair" meant dealing out what someone deserved, then Tucker was in deep shit with no way out. They hadn't passed a town in fifty miles, and at the last one—Population 32—there hadn't even been a gas station.

All day, that incident yesterday had been eating at

him. The anger he'd felt at the taunting voice of some cowboy—*Hey, kid, your mommy wants you.*

The horror of seeing the blood on Kenny's face, contrasting so violently with his white clown makeup and that broadly painted smiling mouth.

The humiliation and fear he'd felt in the jail cell, when he'd been so totally powerless.

As a kid he'd wet himself sometimes when Dad came after him. Sometimes he had run off and thrown up behind the barn. For one dizzying moment yesterday, that sheriff had become his father, and that old, familiar nausea had started climbing up the back of his throat.

Jake opened the back door and waited. "You coming out?"

It was that or be dragged out by his ear and go face-first in the gravel—he'd had that experience often enough as a kid. Tucker climbed out and stood tall, his chin raised in defiance.

"C'mon, kid, if I didn't haul off and belt Lew, I sure as hell won't do it to you. We're just going to take a walk."

Jake lifted a hand as if to rest it on Tucker's shoulder, but Tucker jerked away. Jake sighed—again—and fell into step with him. "Let's go up onto that rise over there. Maybe we'll see some pronghorn."

At the top of the hill, they could see out over miles and miles of arid grassland that was already yellowed from a lack of rain. A handful of specks on the horizon might have been antelope.

Jake hooked his thumbs in his back pockets and stared out at the terrain for a long while before he finally spoke. "That first night—back at the Mendota rodeo—you were angry at me for leaving you behind with Dad. I've waited, figuring you'd tell me about it when the time was right. But maybe some things are just too hard to say."

A cold, hollow feeling filled Tucker's chest. He spun away and started down the hill. "I'm going back down to the truck. I don't have to listen to this."

Jake caught him by the arm in a grip that was at once gentle and unyielding. "*I'm* the one who's listening."

Not meeting his eyes, Tucker thought about the years and years when he'd wanted to run away but was too afraid. He'd tried to stay out of sight, but had always paid the price.

He'd idolized his rodeo champion big brother back then. Dreamed of the day he'd be old enough to escape home and become a star, just like Jake.

Of course, back then he'd thought he would be rich and famous the first time he plunked down his entry fee, not eking out each rodeo on dollars and dimes scraped together, living on cheap hot dogs and warm beer.

Jake swore under his breath. *"Tell me."*

Shaking his head, Tucker stared at his dusty boots, unable to find the words. After a lifetime of secrets kept from teachers and counselors and the ranchers next door, his tongue might as well have been made of lead. *I fell off my horse. One of the steers rammed into me.*

Minutes ticked by. They stood on the hill together,

staring at a landscape that faded away and left only an unspoken past between them.

"Did he drink?" Jake finally asked, never taking his gaze from the horizon.

Tucker shook his head.

"Did he...touch you?"

"Never," Tucker blurted out, feeling heat rise in his face. "God, no."

"But he was violent?"

Tucker kicked at the base of a wiry sagebrush, releasing its pungent scent into the air. "Yeah. He was...impossible to please. Ever." After the first words started coming, more and more followed, and suddenly he was telling about things he'd never even voiced to himself. "Nothing was ever done fast enough. Good enough. God help anyone who didn't do what he wanted, because he could haul you up against a wall and scream at you until your insides fried."

"Jeez, Tucker, I swear I didn't know."

"By the time I was nine, he had me ridin' green colts seven or eight hours a day. If I got bucked off, he made me get right back on. Didn't matter if I was bruised, cut or crying." Tucker gave a harsh laugh. "He said he was gonna make a man out of me."

"What about Mom?"

Tucker snorted. "He never hit her. Hell, I think she just wants to believe everything has always been okay. I used to have nightmares that he'd kill me someday. Sometimes I thought I'd be better off."

"Why didn't you tell me? I always came home at

Christmas. I could've found you a good place to stay.''

"I couldn't. Mom wouldn't go."

Jake stalked a few yards, then spun around and came back. "I never got along with him, either, but it wasn't that bad when I was still at home."

"You were gone before I even started grade school. He changed."

"Booze?"

"No. The ranch was on the verge of going under for a lot of years, and extra stress makes him crazy."

"And now?"

"I hear he got refinancing. Things are going better. I called Mom a while back when I knew he'd be outside.'' Tucker eyed the truck parked along the highway. "Think we oughta get going?"

"In a minute." Jake cleared his throat. "Hell, I'm not any good at this. Maybe you should be…uh, talking to someone."

"I don't need a shrink."

"Just talking to someone can help."

At the look of deep compassion and understanding in Jake's eyes, Tucker's own eyes burned. *Maybe now I have you.* He turned away, afraid Jake might see just how much that mattered.

"And fighting isn't the answer to anything, Tucker. It doesn't make a guy a bigger man just because he can deck someone. It makes him look like a jerk who can't deal with problems like an adult."

"You don't even stand up for yourself," Tucker shot back.

"Don't I? Look closer, Tuck. It's better to solve problems with words than with your fists."

"You wouldn't fight to stand up for yourself?"

"I would if I had to protect something—or someone—very important to me. If there was no other way."

Raising his chin, Tucker thought about the taunts back at the rodeo. That hulking bully of a sheriff who for one terrifying moment had become just like Tucker's father. "I'm not taking nothin' from *anyone*."

"Then think about this. Just how badly do you want to end up exactly like our old man?"

"JUST HOW FAR could a sixty-seven-year-old woman get on foot?" Roy slammed a fist against the steering wheel of his truck and scanned the hillside. "She doesn't even do the stairs alone anymore."

He'd discovered her missing this morning at eight o'clock, and now—six hours later—she was still nowhere to be found. All four hired hands, several neighbors and Doc Hollister had helped him comb the farm buildings twice. Now the rest of them had fanned out into the pastures surrounding the house.

Doc reached across the seat of the truck and rubbed Roy's shoulder. "She can't be far. We'll find her."

They both looked down the hill toward the farm pond—a half-acre of water created long ago by the damming of Little Sioux Creek—and then to the ranch buildings a quarter-mile beyond. Walking distance, even for someone who no longer walked very far.

"She used to take Kristen down there and put a life jacket on her." Closing his eyes against an unfamiliar burning sensation, Roy tipped his head back against the seat. "Made a big deal of dragging a picnic basket along and making it a party. 'Beach party,' she called it."

"We didn't find any footprints along the edge, Roy. I don't think she wandered into the water."

"What if she *wanted* to drown—stepped over the soft footing?"

"I haven't seen any signs of suicidal ideation. Not since—" Doc's voice halted abruptly. "Let's drive back up on the hill behind the house and then try the ravine one more time."

Roy shifted the truck into gear and headed across country, steering sharply to avoid the occasional boulder. They'd been down the ravine before, but they were running out of logical options, and the others were covering the surrounding area in an ever-widening circle.

Roy kept his eyes on the terrain, but Doc's words burned like toxin through his veins. "What were you going to say? When did Ada ever act that way? I never saw it."

Clearing his throat, Doc looked out the passenger window. "You'll have to ask her."

"A little late. Even if we find her, she doesn't have much to say anymore." The truck hit a bone-jarring hole. "Sorry."

Doc reached for his seat belt. "I don't often see dementia advance that fast. Such a wonderful woman, too. It has to be hard on all of you. She should have had many more years to enjoy having you off the road.''

They drove more slowly as they crested the hill past the house, looking for a glimpse of a pink robe, a lost slipper.

Nothing.

On the other side of the hill, they drove down toward the narrow creek bed that trailed between the hills and had created a deep ravine farther on. Roy parked the car, and they both started off on foot, calling Ada's name every few minutes.

After ten minutes of scrambling over rocks and brush, Roy sagged onto a boulder and braced his hands against his knees. "I need a rest," he wheezed, reaching for a pack of cigarettes in his front pocket. "Just a minute or two."

Doc watched him light up, a scowl on his face. "I thought you were quitting. After that last bout—"

"I need this," Roy snapped. He lit up, the routine somehow reassuring, and took a long draw. "And dammit, I think I have a right to know about my wife. You seem to think she was suicidal, but I just don't believe it."

"How often were you home during the past ten or twenty years—a few days here and there during the rodeo season? Longer during the winter?"

"I made a *living*. First as a competitor and later with the company."

Doc held up his hands. "I'm not saying you didn't have good reason. Just that Ada was here alone for a lot of years, raising Kristen on her own."

"She knew it would be like that. She understood."

"She might have known, but that doesn't make it any easier. The loneliness. Neighbors a dozen miles away. The endless wind that just blows and blows. Not everyone can handle this life."

"Without rodeo there were years we couldn't have kept ahold of this place."

"I'm not passing judgment. I'm just telling it like it was. Your wife was such a good woman, and I think she loved being with people."

And she'd been so beautiful, when she was younger. A familiar surge of jealousy burned in the pit of Roy's stomach. He'd been *glad* to know she was out here, away from the men who leered at her in town. "You sound like you know her pretty damn well."

"For cripes' sake, Roy. She was a good friend of my wife's. She was at our house a lot, and I was her doctor."

Roy fell silent, thinking of the times he'd caught her laughing with Guy, or smiling at some clerk in a store. As a young woman she'd been a lighthearted flirt who turned heads wherever she went.

"You think she was unfaithful to you?" Doc paced a few feet ahead and then turned back. "Since she can't speak for herself, I will. That woman *loved* you. I heard her talking to my wife over the years, and know she missed you every day that you were gone. There couldn't have been a sweeter, more gentle lady—and *never* was there even a hint of gossip about her in this town." Doc shook his head. "And believe me, in a town this size, everyone knows when someone sneezes."

Doc lowered himself to a boulder a few feet away. "I'll tell you something else, but only because I figure you're barking up the wrong tree. She grew depressed, over time. Especially after Kristen went off to college. I started her on antidepressants several years ago, though maybe you never knew. After she couldn't come into the clinic on her own, Maria started bringing her in for appointments, because you were always gone."

There were a lot of brown plastic prescription bottles in the cupboard above the kitchen sink, but all of them had incomprehensible generic names, and Roy had assumed they were all for her dementia and her heart. *When did I lose track of all of this?* "I…always thought she was stronger."

With a curse, Doc was on his feet and pacing. "Strength has nothing to do with it. She knew about you, Roy."

Oh, God.

"While you were out on the road, she was staying home year after year, faithful as a nun. But she *knew* about those women, Roy. One day years ago she broke down in my office, so I know. I hope—" Doc gave him a level look "—that you were having a good time, because *her* life was sheer hell after she found out."

CHAPTER ELEVEN

"THANKS FOR COMING with me," Kristen murmured to Jake, as they waited on a bench outside her mother's hospital room.

The weight of his arm around her shoulders felt warm and comforting, and after a few minutes she sighed and rested her head against him. They'd gotten into Bent Spur after ten last night, and had unpacked the truck. She hadn't noticed the blinking light on the answering machine until this morning—after Guy had come to tell her the news.

A nurse in a bright crayon-print smock stepped out of the room. "We've got her back in bed," she said, without looking up from the open chart in her hand. "The doc should be looking at those new X rays in just a few minutes, and then he'll come talk to you."

"Is she...does she seem okay? We were out of town and got here just after you took her down for X rays."

The nurse snapped the chart shut. "We hear some crackles in her lungs and she's running a low-grade fever, so that might be the start of a pneumonia. Poor thing, she could have tripped over all that brush and broken a hip. I wonder how long she was out there?"

"I haven't talked to my dad yet. The ward clerk said he went home to do chores."

"She gave everyone quite a scare, I'm sure. He and the doctor found her in some ravine not too far from the house. She's more oriented now that we have her hydrated, but her short-term memory is poor. Your father says that's her baseline."

Kristen nodded. "She's in her own world some of the time. Lethargic, and occasionally she says things that don't make sense—almost as if she's carrying on a conversation that happened long ago."

The nurse glanced up at the large wall clock over the nurses' station at the end of the hall. "Since she's awake now, I'll bring some things down from the kitchenette. Maybe she'll eat better with you here."

"She won't eat?"

"We admitted her after lunch, and brought her a late tray. She wouldn't eat a bite of lunch or supper. The second shift tried ice cream, pudding, toast—you name it. You'd think she would be starving by now."

Giving the nurse a smile of thanks, Kristen rose. "Come on in and meet my mom, Jake."

He shifted his weight and ran a fingertip around the brim of the hat in his lap. "I'll wait out here."

"Please?"

"Seems sort of personal, walking in at a time like this when I've never met her."

Kristen rolled her eyes. "She doesn't bite."

He stood and reluctantly followed Kristen into the room, hanging back a few paces with his hat in his hands.

She was thankful for his presence the moment she

saw her mother lying in the bed; even more thankful when he came up behind her and again put his arm around her shoulders as if he knew just how she felt.

Her mother lay like a wraith against the pillows, her face pale, the parchment skin drawn tight against the gaunt hollows of her elegant cheekbones and jaw. An IV bag hung above her bed. At the sound of their approach her eyes opened, and she made a move as if to sit forward, then fell back with a soft moan.

"Hi, Mom. I hear you're doing pretty well."

Ada looked up at her, slowly lifted a hand. Kristen took it gently, clasping it between both of her own. So cold—almost weightless, her mother's hand seemed to have no life at all.

"You had quite an adventure. I'm so sorry we weren't here earlier." Kristen looked up at Jake, emotion clogging her throat. "This is Jake Landers, Mom. He's buying MRC. Have you met?"

Ada nodded, but her expression remained blank.

Jake cleared his throat. "I haven't had the pleasure, Mrs. Davis."

The nurse bustled back into the room with a tray of toast, a cup of pudding, a carton of milk. "We don't have much up here and the kitchen is closed for the night, but we'd sure like to see her take an interest in eating again."

Kristen eyed the IV line snaking down from the stand and into Ada's gaunt forearm. "Is that giving her any nourishment?"

"Fluids, some calories. She came in pretty dehydrated—her electrolytes were way off." After checking the IV, the nurse headed for the door. "Hit the call button if you folks need anything."

Jake pulled a chair closer to the bed for Kristen, then took a chair in the corner of the room.

"Look what she brought you, Mom—nice hot, buttered toast. And you like chocolate pudding, don't you?"

Ada turned her face toward the wall. After five minutes of coaxing, Kristen sat back in her chair. "Maybe you're just too exhausted to eat. Could that be it?"

Silence.

Kristen rose and dropped a gentle kiss on Ada's cheek. "Maybe we should go home and let you rest. I'll be back in the morning, okay?"

When her mother didn't respond, Kristen tucked the blankets around her shoulders and then stood back to watch her, afraid that each breath might be her last.

Jake crossed the room and stood at the foot of the bed. "You sleep well," he said. "Tomorrow you'll feel a lot better."

Out at the nurses' station, Kristen leaned over the counter and waited until the nurse looked up from her charting. "How bad is she?"

The nurse looked up. "Doc Randal is down in the ER and hasn't seen the X rays yet, but he can give you a call if you two want to head home. You both look exhausted."

"If it's pneumonia?"

"He'll put her on antibiotics right away. We'd be catching it early, so she'll probably do fine."

"I couldn't get her to eat a bite, and she looks just awful."

The nurse closed the chart and folded her hands on the cover. "Your dad was here most of the day, and her caregiver was here for a while later this afternoon—Mary?"

"Maria. She's been our housekeeper for years."

"That's right. Don't worry. Ada has had good care and good support from her family. They were both here until shortly before you came."

"Should...I stay?" *Will she be all right? Is she going to die?*

The nurse gave her a sympathetic look. "I think you can go home. Your mom is tired from her ordeal and just needs her rest. I'll bet she looks a hundred-percent better in the morning."

"I don't know. Maybe I'll stay in the lounge tonight, just in case."

"You're welcome to stay. There's a couch in there, but it's vinyl and not very comfortable. Or I could have someone bring up a cot."

"That would be super." Kristen turned to Jake. "You go back. I'll be fine here."

"I can stay."

She knew he was even more tired than she was; she'd seen him favor his knee a little more with each passing hour. He needed a decent bed, not a cramped cot or uncomfortable couch. But his offer touched her heart.

"Thanks, but I think you should go back to Guy's. I'm expecting a number of phone calls tomorrow on some upcoming venues, and there are some advance publicity calls to make. The files are on the desk.''

He regarded her with troubled eyes. "Maybe you'd rather have someone here."

"If you're in the office, it will help a lot, really." She gave him a determined smile. "I'll call home if there are any changes."

She followed him to the ER entrance, watched him walk into the night toward the pickup. Turning back, she started for the elevators.

Before she reached for the button she heard the unmistakable sound of Jake's boots on the terrazzo floor.

"I forgot something," he said simply, laying a hand on her shoulder.

She turned and found herself enveloped in an embrace, crushed tightly to his chest. A janitor mopping the floor down the hall paused, looked up with interest. The admitting secretary at a nearby desk smiled.

He glanced up at them and then dropped a kiss on her mouth. "Good night, Kristen."

And then he was gone.

THE FOLLOWING WEEKS passed in a blur of promotion efforts and travel for MRC rodeos in the Midwest on the first and third weekends of June, followed by initial preparations for the annual Fourth of July venue near Bent Spur.

When they weren't traveling, Jake and Tucker stayed in the cabin at Guy's. Kristen stayed out at her family's ranch and drove back and forth each day to work with Jake on MRC business.

Just as well, Jake mused as he watched her pull up by the MRC office. Whenever they were together there seemed to be a spark between them at every accidental touch, their eyes met and time stood still. He found himself thinking about her when she wasn't there, watching for her to arrive every day.

Just three months more and she'd be gone—off to the new life in Dallas she had worked so hard for, and so justly deserved. No matter what undeniable chemistry lay between them, there was no place in her life for a crippled cowboy who'd just lost his rodeo career and was trying to start over at the age of thirty-four. He reminded himself of that fact every day.

"How's your mom?" he asked, sauntering over to her truck.

Shouldering a laptop computer bag, she pushed the door shut. "Fine."

"Is she more alert?"

Kristen smelled of something delicate, sweet. Wildflowers, maybe. He drew a little closer.

A shadow passed across her face. "The same…she doesn't say much, just sits. Doesn't want to get out of bed."

"Still the pneumonia?"

"She's still tired out, but frankly, I think she's really depressed." She started for the cabin housing MRC's business. "My dad disappears out the door by seven in the morning and doesn't appear until dusk. I swear he doesn't say more than three words a day to any of us. Maria is there, but for some reason

Mom won't talk to her. I'm gone all day. She won't really even talk to me when I'm there.''

Jake thought about the emotions that had been so rampant in his own childhood home—the anger and the arguments—and understood with sudden clarity that dysfunctional families came in many forms. Silence could be just as hard to bear.

''There were a couple of phone calls earlier,'' he said. ''A guy named Clint asking about the rodeo, and Tina wanting to make sure we'd arranged for the telephone lines out at the rodeo grounds.''

For the first time in several days, Kristen's smile was genuine. ''What exactly did he say?''

''Didn't make much sense. I got the feeling that he wanted to know something but didn't quite get around to it.''

She laughed. ''Stubborn fool. I could call and put him out of his misery, but maybe I should just let him suffer until the rodeo.''

''He's a friend of yours?'' Jake stared at her intently.

''An old friend,'' she said over her shoulder as she headed for the office.

He had no claim on her. Had no right to interfere in her life. But he suddenly found himself wishing that he'd told the guy to go straight to—

''He and Dixie were once quite an item. He's probably hoping that she'll photograph this rodeo.''

''Clint...*Williams?*''

''You remember him? It's been a long time. He left rodeo the season I barrel raced. Really nice guy.''

It had been ten years, but Jake remembered him,

all right. He'd been a darn good bronc rider, and Jake
had seen him at quite a few rodeos—until the man
suddenly dropped out of sight. Only a vow made to
Dixie had kept Jake from tracking him down later to
rearrange his face. "He lives around here?"

Kristen walked into the office and set the laptop
down on her desk. "Bought a ranch about twenty
miles from here after he quit rodeo. Raises cattle and
horses." She smiled wistfully. "I wonder if Dixie will
still show up for the rodeo."

Jake stared at her. "She's doing the photography?"

"Check the file. She signed up to do this rodeo,
and I invited her to stay with me, but last I heard she
was starting to get cold feet. She doesn't want to run
into Clint again."

The past ten years evaporated, and once again Jake
was looking down into Dixie's tear-stained face, making a promise that changed his life forever.

"Hey, is something wrong?"

Jake turned on his heel and walked back out into
the early morning sunshine, wishing he could forget.

DIXIE SHOWED UP at MRC's office early Friday afternoon, in her trademark yellow Ford pickup with Rodeos Inc., Rodeo & Equine Photography painted on
the sides.

Kristen took one look out the window and dashed
out to meet her. "You came, after all!"

"I figured it wasn't very professional to back out,"
Dixie admitted, giving Kristen a quick hug. "I'm a
big girl now. I don't need to avoid an entire Wyoming

county just to stay away from an old boyfriend. He's probably fat, bald and boring by now, anyway.''

Kristen bit back her first response. There wasn't a female heart west of the Mississippi that wouldn't skip a beat over that dark, brooding cowboy. If anything, Clint had grown more wickedly handsome over the years. ''You'll stay with us? Spend a few extra days?''

Dixie's smile faded. ''I wish, sugar. I need to be in Oklahoma on Tuesday for a shoot at a quarter horse farm, then back up to Laramie on Friday.'' She glanced around at the empty lot. ''Where is everyone?''

''They're all out at the fairgrounds, taking care of last-minute details. I sent Jake out there on his own. Figured this was a good time for him to solo, since we're on our home turf. I need to get out there in a few minutes, though.''

''How is he doing?''

''Health-wise? I can't believe how much better he is. He barely limps unless he's tired. I don't think the doctors ever expected him to do so well. Want a cup of coffee?''

She led the way into the office and gestured toward a love seat near the window. Then she poured two cups, handed Dixie one and settled into an easy chair in the corner.

Dixie took a sip and cradled the cup in her hands. ''Does he like this business?''

''There have been times, I think, when he misses competition terribly—he gets this sad, far-off look, like he wants nothing more than to ride again.'' Kristen smiled a little. "On the other hand, he's a natural at promotion and public relations. He can charm just about anyone, and really gets the job done."

"And you. Are you completely charmed yet?" Dixie flashed a smile. "Or are you still planning on going back down to Dallas?"

"This whole situation hasn't been easy. There's this…force that's still there, after ten years. I just keep reminding myself of how he stood me up—the ultimate betrayal—with another woman on the day we were to get married. And that pretty much takes cares of my libido. I may not be very perceptive, but at least I learn from my mistakes."

Dixie took a long swallow of her coffee, then set her cup down and glanced at her watch. "And I learned from mine. Looks like it's time to head out to the rodeo and set up. Are you ready?"

"I think so." Kristen gathered up a sheet of sponsorship scripts to be read during the performance and glanced around the office for anything else that needed to be taken along.

"There's just one thing…" Dixie worried at her lower lip with her teeth. "I know you've kept tabs on Clint over the years because of me. If he turns up at any of the performances, I don't want you trying to get us together, okay? I came here to do my job and to see you, and that's it."

"No problem. If I see him headed your way, I'll have one of the pickup men run him over. Would that be okay?"

"No blood, no major wounds." Dixie's laughter was brittle.

"Fair enough. I'm sure Rowdy and Tom can handle that just fine. Though in all fairness, I have to tell you—Clint definitely didn't change for the worse over the past few years."

At the door, Dixie hesitated with her hand on the knob, then gave her outfit a rueful look. From her skintight red slacks to her crimson-and-gold satin blouse, she was vintage Dixie—all sass and brass. "Funny thing is, people probably think I'm caught up on appearances, but this is all just sort of my trademark, so people remember me and can spot me easily at rodeos. But I wouldn't much care if Clint had put on fifty pounds and lost his hair."

"Then why won't you at least try to see him?"

"Years ago I lost something that would have meant a lot to him, and now—" Dixie's breath caught, and she bowed her head. "I'm waiting to hear on a repeat biopsy that I had this week. There's a chance that I might not be much of a bargain for anyone wanting a long-term relationship."

Kristen heart clenched. "Oh, no, surely that can't be true."

"That's why I hesitated to come here, knowing Clint might show up. We were as different as sunlight and shadow, but he's always held a big corner of my heart." She laughed softly, rested her forehead against the edge of the open door. "I guess maybe I've grown up enough now to know that we both could have made compromises and worked things out. Stubborn pride is cold comfort, now that it might be too late. Ironic, isn't it? Even if he was still interested, I'd probably just have to turn him down."

CHAPTER TWELVE

ROY STARED OUT the kitchen window, watching Maria carry a basin of food scraps out to the barn cats. They came running, as always, tails raised straight as flagpoles, at least a dozen in colors he'd never bothered to remember, nameless—if they'd come along after Ada began to fail.

She'd loved her cats, and they'd often come to sit in her lap when she drifted back and forth on the porch swing on summer evenings just like this one.

They're like my grandchildren, she'd tease Kristen, *until you give me some that live close by.*

Maybe by now, if he hadn't meddled, there *would* be grandchildren running through this old house. Only one person knew what Roy had done. Lord help him if the truth were ever told.

As he'd expected, Maria lingered at the fence, talking to one of the younger hands. Roy turned from the window, took a deep breath and headed for the living room where Ada would be sitting as she always did.

She was more alert now. At the hospital her medications had been adjusted, and though she'd relapsed some since then, she still seemed brighter, more aware, though she rarely spoke to either Maria or him. During the seven weeks since she'd been discharged, he'd intended so many times to sit down and talk to her, but had always found a thousand excuses to stay away from the house. From her.

From the truth.

But night and day, Doc Hollister's words circled in Roy's chest like a hungry coyote, chewing away at the edges of his heart, leaving him to bleed a little at a time.

He'd been so blind.

He found her in her favorite chair by the window. At his approach, she looked up from the seed catalog in her lap, searching his face as if she were reading there all of the lies and half truths he'd given her over the years. As if she were seeing through to his very soul.

Then her eyes turned soft and expectant, and her mouth curved into a faint smile.

The years fell away, and he saw her in this room as a young woman. With a baby in her lap and a soft smile on her face.

Oh, God, how he'd betrayed them.

He pulled a chair up next to hers and found he couldn't speak through the tightness in his throat. She set aside the catalog and laid a hand on top of his, like a silent benediction.

"Ada, why did you stay with me all these years?" he finally managed to say.

Her eyes filled with understanding as she shook her head slowly, and he waited for her to say she'd had nowhere else to go, that she'd been trapped by circumstance in a life that had gone terribly wrong. That her life had been wasted.

She gave him a sad smile. "Because I loved you."

He closed his eyes, Hollister's words tearing at his heart.

"But all those years, when I was gone...?"

A silence lengthened, marked by the ticking of the old mantel clock, and when he looked at her again he saw her eyes were glistening with unshed tears.

And he knew, with absolute certainty, that she'd known about the women he'd had through the years, in towns he couldn't even remember anymore.

"Why do you ask me now?" she whispered.

Because he'd come so close to losing her when she'd disappeared from the house. Because the uncertainty of life had never been more clear.

He looked down at their hands, gnarled and deeply veined with age. "I never realized how much you've meant to me over the years. I had a gift and threw it away, and there's no way I can go back and make it right."

A tear sparkled, then spilled down her cheek.

The words came hard. He could have delivered a breech calf or fought a blizzard to save livestock, or dug a mile of fence posts by hand—any of those would have been easier than coming up with what he had to say.

"I'm sorry, Ada. I love you."

Her hand tightened on his. "I know."

BENT SPUR'S BIGGEST social event of the year was traditionally the annual Fourth of July rodeo. This year promised to be the biggest and best yet. Though the Friday night performance didn't start until eight, by six-thirty the parking lots were filling up fast, and the food stands and beer tent were doing land-office business.

Dixie lurked nervously at the door of the announcer's stand, eyeing the early arrivals.

"I think we could save you some time by just calling him on the loudspeaker," Kristen said dryly, looking up from her notebook.

Tina peered around the cowboy waiting to pay his entry fees. "Call who?"

"I'm, uh...I need to deliver prints to someone from a rodeo last weekend," Dixie mumbled.

"I can check the day sheets to see if he's coming here," Tina offered. "What's his name?"

"Uh...Slim."

"Slim who? There must be three or four that I see regularly on these lists."

Kristen choked back a laugh. "Don't worry about it. I think Dix sees him out in the parking area."

Dixie gave Kristen a grateful look and escaped out into the gathering crowd behind the chutes. With the lineup of cowboys crowding into that small space, plus Tina and Kristen, she hardly wanted to announce that she was watching for the arrival of a man who'd spurned her once before and would likely do so again.

She wanted to see him just one more time. Talk to him. And find out if she'd dreamed up all that magic from long ago.

"Hey, Dix—gonna make me real pretty tonight?" Fred Gallagher, one of the up-and-coming bull riders, winked at her as she passed. "I could use some good publicity shots."

"Only if you ride better than my grandma this time," she shot back. "Remember to stay *on* the bull until the buzzer sounds."

Some of the cowboys laughed. Some were already so focused on their upcoming rides that they didn't even notice the banter swirling around them.

Dixie nodded at Tucker, who raised his hand in salute and smiled back at her. He was shooting the breeze with some of his friends, and seemed a lot less tense than he had at the last rodeo. Happier, too, since his cast had come off last week.

There were a lot of cowboys here, but not the one she had come so far to see.

He's not coming, after all, a mocking voice whispered inside her head. *Did you think he still cared? Should he care, after what you did?*

Susie rode past on her palomino mare and grinned down at Dixie. "Can you catch my hippodrome ride this time? I'd love a picture for my mom. We'll be starting in a few minutes."

"I'll be there."

"Thanks." She continued past, then twisted in her saddle and rested one hand on her horse's rump. "There's some guy looking for you. He seems familiar, but I can't remember his name."

Dixie's heart took an extra beat. "Tall guy, dark hair?"

Susie grinned and swiveled back to face forward, just as someone touched Dixie's shoulder.

Without turning around, without hearing a word, she *knew*. Awareness shimmered through her, a soul-deep feeling that made her blood race and her insides quiver. "Clint," she said softly. "It's been a long, long time."

He moved forward, and her gaze traveled helplessly up, past his lean hips and that broad, hard chest, to the enigmatic gaze she remembered so well. Kristen hadn't lied. He was all that he'd been before, only more so. The years had added muscle mass to his body and fascinating little lines to his dark, cleanly sculpted features. He had definitely improved with age.

He looked down at her with a haunting blend of warmth and sadness in his eyes, and she knew he was thinking about the past. Maybe he was regretting the wasted years between them.

"It's good to see you," he said, his voice raw. "I suppose you won't be here long…"

She took his hand, feeling a surge of warmth at the contact with his warm, callused flesh, and led him to a far corner behind the chutes, where they talked of the past and their lives since then. The old magic was there just as strong, and she knew he sensed it, too.

You have to tell him, an inner voice whispered. *He deserves to know.*

Taking a deep breath, she gathered her courage. Too many people knew, and if they saw the two of them together, someone else might say something to him. *Better from you than someone else.* "Clint…"

From the arena came the sound of the announcer's voice, welcoming the crowd. The soaring notes of "The Star Spangled Banner" rose into the evening air.

He touched her cheek. "Can I see you after the rodeo?"

"I'd love that." She looked up at him, feeling complete—as if a part of her had been missing all these years and was finally back in place. *He's got to understand.* "But right now I've got to get out there."

A palomino horse approached at an extended trot through the shadows. Susie looked down at Dixie with a pout marring her pretty features. "You were going to take pictures of my ride, but you *missed* it."

"I'm sorry, honey. I promise I'll get you the next time, and I'll do it for free. Okay?"

With a last, regretful smile at Clint, Dixie headed for the bright lights of the arena. And prayed as she never had before.

JAKE GRINNED at the senior citizens running the food stand, and then stood on the side to watch.

Two of them had spent forty years running a local restaurant, one still ran the weekly bingo parlor for the local Catholic church, and the rest had been local businessmen. They worked together with astonishing speed and efficiency, all the while bantering with the crowd lined up outside and cajoling customers into larger purchases.

They'd volunteered to run the food stand to raise money toward remodeling the town's senior citizens' center. At the rate they were going, they'd have enough money to build an extra wing.

Satisfied, Jake headed to the other end of the arena to check in at the announcer's stand. So far, he'd talked to two newspaper reporters, introduced a few of the local sponsors to some of the rodeo stars, settled a dispute at the beer tent, and helped one panicked mom find her runaway four-year-old.

Out in the arena, tonight's specialty performer—a top-notch rope act out of California—took his bow, and the crowd erupted into applause.

Tina finished recording a stack of entry checks. "How's it going?"

He rapped his knuckles on the wood frame of the building. "So far, so good. Great crowd. No fights out behind the beer tent."

"Yet." She placed the checks in the cash box at her feet and turned the key.

"Need anything?"

"If you could stay here for just a minute, I'd like to take a two-minute break—unless the line is too long." She rose and peered out the door toward the line of portable facilities behind the grandstand. "Looks good. Be back in a second."

Jake waved her off and leaned against the wall. Through the big open window, which was only two feet away from the fence, he had a full view of the arena.

The ring men were rolling out the barrels now, toeing around in the dirt for the deeply buried stakes marking the precise location for each barrel. Before the rodeo began, the judge and Bud had been out there with a tape measure for a good fifteen minutes.

Stan, at the microphone in the booth above Tina's office, began his spiel—delivered in his trademark booming, melodramatic voice—about the daring young ladies who would soon be racing out into the arena at breakneck speed in pursuit of the top money in the barrels event.

The crowd roared as the first horse and rider flew into the arena and started the cloverleaf pattern around the barrels. A collective gasp rose when the horse skidded around the first one. Followed by a groan as the rider's stirrup caught the second barrel, sending it into a tipsy wobble. By the time the girl rounded the last barrel and started her run for home, the second barrel had steadied, and everyone was cheering.

Stan's voiced blared through the loudspeakers. "And that was a great 14.66 seconds, folks. Great job, Melissa! Next up, we have Katie Stover, on Sonny!"

"I'm back," Tina called out. "Anyone stop in?"

"Nope." Jake straightened. "Have you seen Kristen?"

"Over along the arena fence—other side, close to where Dixie is—last I saw." Tina shook her head. "I don't know what's going on, but Dixie missed shooting the Grand Entry and didn't get out there until half the bareback event riders were through."

That was strange. As a rodeo photographer, Dixie received the right to take pictures, but her money came only from the prints she sold. The time and expense of getting to each venue dictated the need to be taking good action shots at every opportunity, and she'd always been one of the more aggressive rodeo photographers around.

"I'll wander over there and see if everything's okay."

"Wait..."

He turned back and waited.

"I…" She bit her lower lip. "I guess I should tell you that Bud isn't in the best mood tonight. He's been riled about something and…sometimes by the end of the night…well…"

Jake understood. He'd seen Bud at the end of a rodeo in that frame of mind. Bud didn't drink during the rodeo, but afterward he sometimes hit the bottle hard and got meaner as the night went on.

"I'll keep an eye on him. Thanks."

On the way, Jake stopped in at the VIP seating area—box seats close to the chutes, where most of the rough-stock action was centered. "Howdy, folks. Having a good time?"

The local car dealer and his family, a group from the Chamber of Commerce, and the owner of a local bank were here tonight. One of the kids, a boy of maybe nine or ten, gave Jake a thumbs-up. "This is so cool!"

"If there are any cowboys you'd like to meet afterward, I'll try to arrange it for you. I'll stop back after the bull riding. Some of these boys head down the road right after the events are over, but we might be able to catch a few."

"Thanks, son." The banker gave him a wink and lifted a cup of cola in salute. "It's been great. Hey Marge—" He turned toward his plump wife. "This here is Jake Landers. Remember reading about him? He was the World—"

Knowing he was in for a long conversation, Jake sighed, and hitched one hip against the edge of the fence surrounding three sides of the VIP section.

Without good support from sponsors, staging a rodeo was a huge financial risk, and keeping them happy and well-recognized was a key to having them agree the next time around.

Jake had started to enjoy this business much more than he'd ever expected to. The challenges were different from those he'd faced riding bulls, but there was as strong a sense of satisfaction when everything went well.

Public relations, however, took considerable time.

KRISTEN WATCHED the last bull burst out of the chutes. The rider, a kid from somewhere in Oklahoma, made it to seven seconds before being airmailed into the dirt.

As usual, Hoot was right there—in good position, turning back the bulls when they first came out of the chutes, distracting them after they ditched the riders. Kenny was there, too, not hanging back as much as he had at first. Kristen smiled, recalling some of the routines the two had been working on.

During breaks in the rodeo action, Kenny had taken to nimbly leaping up on the arena fence and briefly joining the crowd, as if quaking in his boots at the sight of Hoot's trick mule. They'd even developed a routine involving an explosion of gunpowder hidden in Kenny's loose clown pants—resulting in a cloud of smoke and noise that echoed through the rodeo grounds.

As bullfighters, their main mission was to keep the cowboys safe, but they were crowd pleasers, as well. Hoot had been right to encourage Kenny's dreams.

Jake appeared at her elbow. "It was a good night."

"Sure was. The dirt was just right, and the stock bucked really well. No injuries. No disasters. Tomorrow night should go just as well, if the weather holds."

"Any word?"

"The Weather Channel says we have a good chance for thunderstorms tomorrow morning and afternoon. I'll keep my fingers crossed. We've got rain insurance, but I'd rather have a good rodeo."

Jake grinned and motioned toward the gate of the arena, where Tucker was joking with Kenny. "I guess ol' Tuck must be growing up just a tad. He must have finally apologized."

"Kenny must have accepted," Kristen said dryly. "Or Tucker would be wearing a bandage across *his* nose."

"And he'd deserve it." Jake watched his brother disappear into the crowd, his expression pensive. "He has a lot to learn. How is Dixie? I was headed over to see her and got waylaid by the businessmen of Bent Spur."

She chuckled. "I'll bet. You're lucky they let you go."

"About Dixie..."

Kristen gave him a curious look. "I saw her during the intermission. She says she's gotten some really great shots tonight, and should have a good collection of proofs to show tomorrow. Some of them might even be good enough for a portfolio she's working on. Why?"

"Tina said she started late tonight."

"Yes, well…she ran into an old friend."

"Clint."

"Good guess." The look of concern in his eyes surprised her, made her wonder about the history he and Dixie might have shared. The little shaft of jealousy that shot through her was unworthy of her, she knew. All of them had their own lives, now. She had no right to question what Jake or Dixie might have done over the years.

"What happened?" he asked.

That surprised her even more. Cowboys rarely talked about feelings, relationships. For most of them, it was as if the entire emotional realm were a foreign language. "You'd have to ask Dixie," she said tactfully.

"He shot her down?" There was an edge to Jake's voice now. A glitter of anger in his eyes that suggested a deep concern for Dixie that, oddly enough, involved another guy.

Mystified, she hedged a little, unwilling to betray a confidence. "I…don't know. She was busy in the arena all night, and I haven't seen him in a while."

Jake swore under his breath. "Excuse me," he muttered. "I need to find her."

Watching him go, she wondered if he'd ever felt as strongly about his own behavior on the day she'd waited in her wedding dress, while he was in another state, perhaps with another woman.

Probably not.

They'd both been young and impulsive, caught up in a whirlwind affair of just three short months. He'd handled it badly.

But ten years later he'd become a strong, caring man—one who shouldered responsibilities and watched out for those he loved. He'd make someone a wonderful husband, now, she thought wistfully.

And if she hadn't grown so much wiser over the years, she might almost wish she was that someone.

BETWEEN SHOTS of bronc riders, calf ropers and steer wrestlers, Dixie had some time to think. By the time the bull riders were done, she knew her options—and wasn't happy with any of them.

Enjoy a few more hours with Clint after far too many years apart, and then drop a few hints. Tell him and be done with it. Or not tell him at all.

Her jittering stomach and shaking hands tele-graphed the only decision she could make. If she didn't tell him the truth soon, she was going to fall apart.

An hour after the rodeo ended, they slid into a booth at The Lone Steer. And again, the old magic was there—in that twinkle in his eyes, his subtle sense of humor, in the way his bone-deep integrity seemed to touch everything he said.

When the conversation faltered, he regarded her with troubled eyes. "I suppose you want to get going. You've had a long day."

Startled, she looked up from the patterns she'd been tracing in the condensation on her glass of iced tea. What he must have interpreted as boredom was a major case of nerves. Closing her eyes briefly, she willed him to understand and forgive. Why had she waited so long?

"There's something I never told you—There wasn't a chance, when you left for Wyoming so abruptly after we broke up. I didn't know where you were. No one seemed to know either…"

He stared across the table at her, his bottle of beer suspended halfway to the table.

"I—I didn't know, when we broke up. But…a few weeks later I found out I was pregnant."

His eyes widened, then narrowed and grew cold.

"I…I was so scared—young—I didn't know where to go or what to do. I didn't know where you where, just that you didn't want me anymore…"

Her voice trailed off into an endless gulf of silence between them, marked only by the rapid beating of her heart.

"You had an abortion." His voice was like shards of ice. "Why are you telling me now? So I can tell you it was *okay?*"

She stared back at him, absorbing the chill in his voice, and knew that he'd never really understood her. "That's what you think?"

"I've thought about you all these years. Regretted that I didn't try harder to work things out." He swore softly. "You could have tried harder to find me, when you found you were pregnant. I would have taken him in a split second. And I would have loved him every day of his life."

"Or her," she whispered sadly.

"Nothing has ever meant more to me than family. It's what I've wanted—wished for—for years, but no woman ever quite measured up after my knowing you. But you didn't even give that child a chance."

He gave a short laugh. "I guess I set those standards way too high."

Her old grief gave way to anger. "Then you're more arrogant than any cowboy I've ever met. There can be reasons—compelling reasons—that a pregnancy must end. But I don't think you even care to know."

His expression etched in granite, he stood up, pulled his wallet out of a back pocket of his jeans and dropped a ten on the table for the bill. "I've got to go. I need to get back to check on a couple of sick calves."

"I understand. Completely."

Not meeting her eyes, he turned away and headed for the front door.

And she knew she'd never see him again.

TINA'S PREDICTION about Bud's temper came true.

He leaned against the chutes as the stock trucks pulled out and lifted his bottle in salute. "Well, boys, another rodeo, another party. Who wants to join me down at The Lone Steer?"

Shaking his head, Hoot turned to leave, but most of the other crew nodded in assent and headed out toward the parking lot.

Jake sauntered over to the announcer's stand and propped an elbow on the open windowsill. "You need a ride home, Tina?"

"Thanks. The kids already went home with my truck, so I could use a lift."

Now that the crowds and cowboys were gone, Bud's sarcasm carried through the silence. "We can all drink to the success of MRC—and just hope it survives another season. If not, we'll all be back to riding fence and herdin' cows.''

Lew's voice was already slurred. ''I sure as hell hope not.''

''Is Bud going to be okay?'' Jake frowned.

''I could go along with him and try to baby-sit, but that never helps, anyway.'' Tina shrugged as she packed up to leave. ''He just gets a little meaner as the night wears on. Can you help me move my files? I don't like to leave anything important overnight, even though this place is locked.''

Jake walked in and lifted the box of files. ''Anything else?''

''Just the cash box.'' She shouldered the strap of her laptop case and bent to retrieve the box under the desk—

She froze. Then she dropped to her knees and searched wildly under the desk, her face white. ''Oh, my God,'' she whispered as she stood up. ''It's *gone*. The money is gone!''

CHAPTER THIRTEEN

"THE DOOR was always open, of course. Anyone could walk in here, but the office was never unattended. I only left once, and Jake stayed while I was gone." Her face pale, Tina looked from Bud to Jake, and then to Kristen. "It had to be someone we all knew, someone who could walk in and shoot the breeze, then sneak out at the right moment."

Bud scowled at Jake. "It could be someone we know damn well."

"And why would he do that?" Kristen snapped, one hand on her hip. "Wouldn't that be a bit odd, stealing from the company he's buying?"

Jerking his chin up, he sent her a look of pure contempt. "Why not? The final papers aren't signed. If MRC was in trouble, he could threaten to back out and try to drive the price down."

Kristen felt a sliver of guilt pierce her. Not so long ago, she'd had a similar thought, but now she knew Jake too well to believe it. "You're a fool, Bud."

Bud took a step forward, his face a dark red. Even as kids, she and Bud had never gotten along, but the glint in his eye spoke of feelings that went well beyond mere dislike. "I suppose you think that sleeping with—"

"What?" Anger burned inside her at the implication.

Bud glared at Kristen. Lew, Hoot and the others gathered around.

"Arguing isn't getting us anywhere," Jake said mildly, as he moved between them. "Tina wrote out day money checks right after the bull riding, and then most of those boys probably just cashed those same checks right away."

Tina nodded. "I write them checks to keep the bookkeeping straight, but then I'm sure glad to cash those checks if the cowboys prefer currency. A lot of the boys pay their entry fees in cash, and it makes me real nervous having much cash in the box during a two- or three-day rodeo."

Jake eyed her thoughtfully. "So the remaining money was still here after the bull riders were paid out."

"Does this mean we don't get paid on Sunday?" Kenny lifted off his hat and ran a hand through his tousled hair.

"'Course not, you fool." Hoot gave him a good-natured punch on the arm. "The secretary doesn't handle your pay. Bud or MRC writes those checks."

"Did anyone see anything suspicious?" Kristen asked. "Anyone in a hurry—anyone who shouldn't have been hanging around this area?"

"I seen that brother of Jake's up here a while back," Lew sneered. "He's probably a little low on cash."

Tucker broke free of the crowd and went toe-to-toe

with Lew, his one good fist clenched. "I never stole nothing from anybody."

Jake stepped forward and pulled him back. "Easy. We're just asking here. Who else?"

The cowboys looked at one another. Shrugged.

"Wasn't really looking this way," one mumbled.

"We was out loading up the stock."

"I was following some gal out the gate, but her boyfriend turned up and I skedaddled back here," one drawled.

A ripple of strained laughter spread through the group.

"Both Bud and Lew were up here, too," Kristen said quietly, her gaze on Bud's face. "But that doesn't mean they're guilty—"

Flashing lights sent ribbons of crimson across the darkened arena as a patrol car pulled up at the gate.

"Stick around for a while, everyone," Jake said. "I called the sheriff, and I'm sure he'll have some questions. The more answers, the better."

Lew snorted. "And how the hell is he gonna figure it out? The cash box is gone, along with the fingerprints. You can just kiss that money goodbye."

"How much do you figure, Tina?" Kristen asked.

For all of her sharp wit and tough shell, Tina appeared ready to burst into tears. "I can figure it all out to the penny once I go through the books. Of course, the extra prize money put up by MRC is in the bank, not here. Maybe…several thousand. But the food stand group had just brought up their cash box for safekeeping, too."

She sniffled, her eyes wide, wary, and riveted on

Bud's face. "And earlier, I took off my wedding rings. They felt loose today, and I was afraid they might slip off. I put them in with the money."

"There's no insurance to cover the stolen money, and the rodeo secretary is responsible for every last penny that disappeared," Bud growled. "If I find out who did it, there'll be hell to pay."

AT MIDNIGHT, Jake leaned back in the desk chair back at MRC's office and gave Kristen a weary smile. "Heck of a day."

Lifting her cup of decaf in salute, she toed off her boots and sighed. "And to think it was all going so well."

"I'm sorry about what Bud said to you."

"About sleeping with future management to get ahead?" Kristen gave an impatient wave of her hand. "Bud is a complete jerk. Give him a few beers and he's ten times worse. I swear, I don't know why Tina has stayed with him all these years."

"I figured he knew about…Dallas."

"He knows I'm heading south this fall. Once he starts drinking, he loses his common sense. What are you going to do about him next year when you own the bucking stock?"

Jake propped both boots on the desktop. "It sure won't be a one-man job. Guess I'll need to see how he likes working for me."

"In all fairness, you do get a package deal with Bud. He's good with the stock. Tina is one of the best rodeo secretaries around. And their girls do a great job with the Grand Entry and helping everywhere else.''

Kristen glanced out the darkened window toward Guy's house. Dixie's yellow pickup was parked under a security light at the edge of the yard, its interior camper lights off. ''Dixie must have turned in already. I know she left the grounds right after the bulls last night, so she could run her proofs at a one-hour photo place down in Fairfield. Did you track her down tonight? You sure seemed worried.''

Jake shook his head, gave her wry smile. ''Things got a little busy there at the end.''

''Did you two…ever date?''

His mouth quirked up at one corner. ''She's like a little sister to me after all these years. Rodeo gets to be like a big family when you travel a lot.''

Though it didn't really matter at all, Kristen felt the anxious little flutter in her stomach settle down. *I'm leaving in a few months, anyway, for the life I really want. Why should I care? Jake and Dixie are two people I like. Maybe they'd be happy together.*

A surprising sense of loss overwhelmed her as she contemplated his lean, chiseled features, knowing that she and Jake would soon go their separate ways.

But then Dixie's words about biopsies and worries and uncertain futures came back to her for the hundredth time that night, sending that same agitated butterfly into action against Kristen's ribs. ''Dixie… might need a good friend, in a lot of ways. Not just over Clint.''

He stilled.

''Just talk to her sometime.'' Too close to betraying

a confidence, Kristen launched into a recounting of the night's highlights.

"It's late," Jake said quietly, when she paused for a breath.

Startled, she glanced at her watch. "Oh, you're right. I'd better hit the road."

"Don't."

Her heart skipped a beat. "I, uh—"

"Why not just stay here? You used to, until I showed up. Tuck and I are still down at the other cabin."

She felt her cheeks warm. Of course, he hadn't meant anything more. How could he? With Guy and Jennibelle up at the house, and Dixie and Tucker and all the hands likely to awaken at the crack of dawn...

Flustered, she stood. "It isn't that far to the ranch."

"Fifteen miles, well after midnight on a Friday night."

A night when a lot of the cowhands from neighboring ranches headed for town in their dusty pickups to shoot pool, drink and flirt with the female population of Bent Spur...and drink some more. "I'll be fine."

The old desk chair creaked as he slid his long legs off the desktop and rose. And an old, all-too-familiar sensation shimmered through her as he approached.

"Stay."

"No, I..." *If I stay, I'll lie awake in this cabin and remember, and wonder. And wish.*

He trailed his hand against the side of her face, then let it rest on her shoulder. "You're safer here."

Safer? For a man so large, corded with muscle and

sinew, with work-roughened hands, he had the tender touch of someone who could gentle a colt or soothe a child or…awaken the emotions of a woman who'd denied those feelings for far too long.

There was nothing safe about the way he made her feel.

He smiled as he stepped around her and crossed the room to flip on the light in the back bedroom. ''Jennibelle told me that she keeps linens in the closet for unexpected guests. There's clean towels in the bathroom.''

It was crazy to drive all the way home, when she'd have to turn around in the morning and come right back. ''Thanks.''

Her mind sped through dozens of memories, all the reasons why she would never trust herself or Jake for any long-term commitment. The reasons were all still there. But when he headed for the front door of the cabin, then spun back and crushed her against his chest, not one of those reasons mattered.

His hard, mobile mouth was on hers, his hands strong and sure, drawing her hips against his own, then tangling in her hair. Awareness and need and a kaleidoscope of emotions filled her.

Even as she laid a restraining hand against his broad chest, she knew with blinding clarity why her brief marriage to Steve had failed. Why none of her other relationships had lasted. She'd only been fooling herself.

No matter what he'd done on the cold November day ten years ago, on the day they should have been married, no one had ever come close to making her feel the way Jake Landers did.

And no one ever would.

"IT IS LATE," Maria said softly. "You've worked so hard these past days. I could...make you a late supper?"

She hovered at the kitchen door with a wounded look in her eyes, reminding Roy he'd made a terrible mistake—one of a long list of mistakes in his life that could not be undone.

"No," he said gruffly, not meeting her eyes. "I'm going up to bed." *To Ada's bed, where I should have been all these years.*

There had been no miracle cure—there would be none for Ada's slowly progressing dementia—but during the past week she'd regained some of her sparkle. Because Ada would no longer speak to Maria, Roy had taken over her medications and much of her care. The time together had brought back a comforting feeling of togetherness for them both.

And at night, when they wrapped their arms around each other and drifted off to sleep, the feeling of peace and contentment made his heart ache for all the time he'd thrown away.

"I thought...I hoped maybe..."

Maria wanted more—a relationship, a future—but he couldn't give it. He stopped at the living room door and took a deep breath, frustrated because the right words skittered just out of reach, like some damn fool flock of chickens.

"I can't, " he finally said in frustration, looking over his shoulder at her. "Ada is my wife."

"But maybe—"

"No." He gentled his voice, wanting her to understand. "How many years have you been here— thirty?"

Her faint smile told of unspeakable sadness. "I was a new bride of sixteen when I first came here, and my husband, he was not yet your foreman. But I have been your housekeeper for fifteen years, now."

"You're a beautiful woman, Maria. Beyond this ranch there's so much more…"

"You are firing me?" Her voice rose with anger and alarm. "Letting me go?"

God help him, he was making a mess of this, too. "No. You're like family." He suppressed a wince. "You can stay forever. But…you shouldn't feel *obligated* to us. If you ever decide to try something different, my wife and I will find a way to get along."

Maria whirled away in a flash of crimson skirts and disappeared down the short hall to her room, a flurry of rapid and incomprehensible Spanish following in her wake.

Roy rubbed his neck and sighed, then headed for the darkened living room. He sat in the recliner in front of the television, reached for the remote, then set it back down.

He'd never meant to hurt Maria, and God knows, he'd never meant to hurt Ada. He only hoped somehow he could set things right. Set *everything* right. His thoughts turned to his daughter. He'd figured things would work out when Guy first brought

up the idea of Jake buying MRC. Jake would arrive,
Kristen would take off for Dallas. Roy never expected
Jake to insist that Kristen help him get started, much
less that she'd end up traveling to the rodeos with
him.

From that first trip, to the Mendota rodeo, Roy had
felt a growing prickle of fear that she might make the
same mistake twice. Leaning back, he closed his eyes
and swore softly under his breath.

Yesterday morning, Jake and Kristen had come out
to the ranch. He'd caught Jake watching Kristen with
that soft kind of look that boded no good. And Roy
had seen her eyeing Jake in the same way.

Telling her would forever destroy Roy's relationship with his daughter, but it was time Kristen found
out the truth about Jake Landers.

TWO WEEKS after the Bent Spur rodeo, Jake looked
out over the Bear Creek, Colorado, arena from his
vantage point in the VIP section of the bleachers. *Another weekend, another rodeo,* he thought with satisfaction. The parking lot was nearly full already, the
weather perfect.

He caught sight of Tina on her way to the secretary's office. "Hey, Tina," he called out. "Have you
seen Kris?"

Tina slowed her pace. "I think she just ran into
Dixie. I saw her near that yellow camper truck, anyway." She jerked a chin toward the entrants' gate
beyond the chutes. "Over there."

Jake turned back to the local businessmen already
seated. "During the intermission I'll come get you,"

he reassured them. "You'll go out into the arena and be recognized for your support of this rodeo. Has everything been okay so far?"

Six gray heads nodded, and their wives all beamed up at him. "We've got a great lineup of contestants tonight. We'll be ready to roll in just a few minutes."

He winked at the women, and then set off in search of Kristen.

The previous weeks had passed in a blur. When he wasn't dealing on a new venue for the coming year, he was working on countless arrangements and promotion efforts for a different one—and most of this went on while he and Kristen were working on a rodeo in progress.

This side of the rodeo business was worlds away from settling onto the back of a ton of muscle and attitude in a chute, but he'd found a different kind of satisfaction with MRC. A feeling of accomplishment at developing a good promotional campaign. The feeling of victory when all the pieces finally came together, and a committee signed on the dotted line.

Scanning the parking lot and rodeo grounds for Dixie's truck, he admitted to himself that the feeling of satisfaction had definitely *not* followed through on a more personal level.

A flash of bright yellow caught his eye—the camper truck, parked in the shade. Dixie and Kristen were leaning against the hood, deep in conversation.

He passed the cowboys unpacking gear, starting their arm wraps, but barely noticed their banter.

"Hi, stranger!" Dixie smiled at him as she shouldered the wide black strap of her Nikon. "Perfect evening for a rodeo, don't you think?"

He touched the brim of his hat in greeting, his attention riveted on Kristen. "We need to talk. Do you have a minute?"

Kristen gave Dixie a mystified palms-up gesture as she turned to follow him past the truck, past the livestock semi, to a knoll at the back of the parking area.

"What's up?" She glanced around. "Afraid of spies?"

"This is hardly a secret."

"What, then?" Her eyes widened. "Not another theft!"

"No."

As usual on these hot summer days, she'd caught her heavy blond hair into a high ponytail and settled an MRC Rodeos cap on her head. In the shade of its bill, her gray eyes reflected worry. "Bud isn't drinking, is he? Already?"

Bud had been hitting the bottle more with each passing week, and had been fined by the Association at the Twin Pines rodeo last weekend. The more he drank, the more vocal he became against Kristen's role in MRC.

"I'm not sure Bud will have much time with the company once I take over," Jake said, reaching out to tuck a stray strand of hair behind Kristen's ear. "But that's not why we're out here."

She looked up at him as if transfixed by that simple gesture. "Then why?"

"At Guy's, or at your dad's ranch, we're surrounded by people. Traveling, we have Tucker with us and maybe a couple others. And during the ro-deo—'' he looked back at the crowds filling the stands, the cowboys milling around behind the chutes ''—there are people everywhere.''

Her eyes twinkled. ''And that's a problem be-cause…''

''I want you, Kristen. I have wanted you since— hell, probably since the day I was born. I just didn't know it then.''

He leaned over and brushed a kiss against her mouth. And then another. ''Maybe we met too young to make this work. Maybe things would have been a lot different if—'' He lifted her cap, caught the fluffy tie thing holding her ponytail, and slid it down until her hair cascaded free and wild down her back. ''If we hadn't been so impatient.''

''I remember. In just months we were talking about marriage.'' Her dark eyelashes fluttered shut as she leaned into his kiss.

''I've never wanted anyone as much as I want you.'' He nuzzled the soft curve of her ear, trailed kisses down the slender column of her throat, reveling in the vibration of her moan beneath his mouth.

She framed his face with her hands and brought him back up for a kiss that grew deeper, hotter, until he was trembling. ''I guess we still have that fire,'' she whispered against his mouth.

''It's been hell, being with you and not being close.'' He pulled back a little and cupped the back of her head to cradle her against his chest, letting her feel the crazed pounding of his heart. ''There's a clock over the announcer's stand, and I want you to

watch that clock tonight. With each passing minute,
I want you to think about what it could be like tonight, after these people are all gone. Right here—
under these trees, under the stars.''

''Here? Outside?''

''But you have to *tell* me that you want this. It's
up to you.''

''But—''

''Bud has a guy who stays overnight with the stock,
but he'll stay up by the holding pens. He sure isn't
going to patrol this field, as well. Most everyone will
be at the rodeo dance.''

She frowned as if deep in thought. ''Hard decision.
Go to the dance, or meet you. I don't know…''

''Think about what you'd like me to do, how you'd
like to be touched. Held.'' His gaze slipped briefly to
her parted lips, then back up to meet her eyes, and
he winked. ''Whatever.''

She rose on tiptoes to kiss his mouth, trailing her
fingertips down his chest and across his championship
belt buckle with deliberate care. ''I'm looking forward to *whatever* a whole lot.''

It dawned on him that he'd wasted too many years
being proud and stubborn and thinking he knew what
was best.

Instead of listening to his heart.

CHAPTER FOURTEEN

DIXIE CROUCHED LOW, her back to the Bear Creek arena fence. As soon as the cowboy tipped his hat, the action would burst out of chute 4 not thirty feet away.

With the night sky as a backdrop, the red chutes, the bright green Skoal banners and the pale cream of Cropduster's hide would all be beautiful, and the talented cowboy who'd drawn him this time might just stay on long enough for a great shot.

She adjusted her 80-200 zoom lens. Held her breath. Adrenaline raced through her veins. Friday night had been a little hazy, but tonight was crystal clear. *This will be the night.*

The bullfighters were in position, ready for action. The cowboy's head nodded once. The gate flew open.

Cropduster blew out like an atom bomb, then corkscrewed his massive body and turned back toward the chutes with a sharp spin to the left.

Click...click...click... Dixie grinned as the film sped through her camera. *Perfect!* She crouched lower for a better angle as the bull exploded skyward, then slammed back and shook the earth. *Keep with him— keep with him—*

Through the lens she saw the cowboy's upper body

tip into his riding hand. Another second or two and he'd be airborne, she knew. Her peripheral vision picked up Kenny and Hoot moving in.

It happened too fast to catch, though later the film would reveal every key second. The rider, his face twisted in a grimace of fear and pain as he ejected like a fighter pilot from the top of the bull. His hand, caught in the rope on the other side of the bull's back....

Hoot moving in quick, slipping, being hooked high into the air. And Kenny, moving in with a practiced ease he hadn't shown until this night.

The action dropped to slow motion. Kenny struggled to release the bull rope. The bull bucked, dragging him along. Finally, the rope fell away.

The cowboy staggered, then launched himself up onto the arena fence as if the hounds of hell were nipping at his heels.

The crowd came to its feet and roared, as Kenny danced with the bull, luring it deftly away from Hoot, who lay motionless in the dirt. With a last defiant shake of his horns, Cropduster trotted toward the gate.

Dixie sank back against the fence, her heart still beating in her throat, as the doc and EMTs rushed into the arena. Hoot had always maintained that Kenny had the talent and courage of a bullfighter, and he'd been right.

"Thank God," she whispered, when Hoot gingerly sat up.

Listening to the applause and cheers of the audience, she cradled her camera and rose to her feet—

"Dixie?"

A hand dropped onto her shoulder, and she spun away, startled. "I didn't hear you, darn it—" Her breath caught. *"Clint?"*

"I was just in the area and…" His eyes somber, he hooked a boot heel on the bottom rail and leaned forward to rest his arms on a higher one. "Thought maybe I'd stop in."

Confusion and shock swept through her. *"Stop in? We're a good eight hours from Bent Spur!"* The distant sound of the announcer's voice barely registered. "Are you here for the weekend? Just today?"

He dropped his gaze to his boots. When he looked up, she saw an expression of determination in his eyes that hadn't been there before. "You're working, but I'll be back."

"But it's almost over. Just one more bull rider."

"I'll be around."

"Wait—"

"Save me a dance." Summoning the same, lazy grin that had stolen her heart so many years ago, he touched the brim of his hat and disappeared into the darkness.

She looked back toward the arena, just as chute 2 opened on Sierra, an average bull, not a consistent performer. Twice she'd seen him just run down the arena instead of turning back by the chutes and bucking so a cowboy could score higher.

The rider looked fifteen and green, though he had to be eighteen to enter. There was just enough time to click off two shots with him aboard. Then one of him in midair.

The moment he landed, Dixie stowed her equip-

ment and scrambled to the top of the fence behind
her.

The back lot was dark, save for the security lights.
Clint was back there, maybe talking to old friends.
Maybe she wouldn't wait 'til the dance to look him
up.

BUT SHE DIDN'T FIND HIM until the dance even though
she'd walked through the back lot looking for him
until most of the cowboys were gone.

Stepping out of the American Legion hall, away
from the pounding rhythm of a local rock band, the
clink of beer bottles, the smoky haze, she saw him
leaning against a lamppost with his hat tipped low
over his forehead and one boot propped back on the
post.

He lifted his chin, and a quiet smile lit his face.
"Dixie."

"It—it's good to see you again. Enjoy the rodeo?"

"Didn't see much of it."

"You just happened to be in the area, huh?" she
teased, crossing the sidewalk.

Dropping his gaze, he stood there, clearly still as
uncomfortable with small talk as most of the cowboys
she knew. He tipped his head toward the Ford four-
wheel-drive truck parked across the street. "Want to
go for a drive?"

"Sure." The truck was a good ten years old and
the upholstery was a little threadbare, but he'd taken
it through a car wash, and the interior was spotless.
The effort he'd made was not lost on her.

In the wink of an eye they were beyond the city

limits of Bear Creek and heading into wide-open rangeland. In the daylight, the Rockies were a narrow band of jagged blue teeth on the horizon, but now the darkness blended sky and land into a endless sea of black, marked only by the wash of stars overhead.

Close scents of sagebrush and damp dust and the more distant scent of cattle blew in through the open windows. Comfortable, familiar scents of ranching. When he reached forward and turned on the radio, soft strains of Faith Hill's "Breathless" surrounded them.

She studied the strong planes and angles of his face, carved deeper by the passing years and shadowed by the dim glow of the dashboard lights. For years she'd thought she would never see him again and had made herself believe that it was for the best. She'd lied to herself.

He'd said they needed to talk, but he sure didn't seem to be in any rush.

"Why did you come to Bear Creek?" she finally asked, curling one leg beneath her and draping an arm over the back of the seat.

Another mile passed before he answered. "I had to."

"Why?"

He sighed heavily. "You."

"And I can see that your enthusiasm is *boundless,*" she retorted dryly.

His hand flexed on the steering wheel. "I made a mistake a long time ago, and it's time to set it right."

"Really?"

"All I ever wanted was ranching and a family. The

family more than anything else.'' He gave a short
laugh. "I got the ranch and the mortgage, anyway."

"And what did you think I wanted?" she asked
quietly.

The glance he gave her arrowed straight to her soul.
"You sure as hell didn't belong on some struggling
ranch, where the bills come and the profit doesn't,
and where the closest neighbor is ten miles away."

"You didn't think I'd want to help? Work beside
you?"

"I figured you'd come to hate that life. And...I
knew I couldn't handle it when you walked away."

"So you did, instead." Dixie closed her eyes
briefly against the painful memories. If she'd tried
harder, if they'd compromised somehow, maybe they
could have been together. Maybe even had a family
by now.

His voice went raw and low. "I swear I never
knew...I didn't know that you were..."

"Pregnant?"

"I would have come back. Married you. Given you
money to help out. Anything."

After all these years, she didn't think she had any
tears left, but now she felt them burning beneath her
eyelids. "Is this what this visit is all about? Your guilt
because you think I went out and decided to abort
your baby?"

"No. Yes. I...I left you in trouble, and that wasn't
right. I should have been there. Helped you."

That hurt. "You really do see me as some shallow,
irresponsible twit. Pull over."

He gave her a startled look, but kept driving—

slower, as if searching for a quick place to turn around.

"Pull over. Now."

His jaw clenched. "I'm not leaving you on some deserted highway in the middle of the night."

"And I have no intention of letting you do that. *Pull over.*"

He drove slower yet, until the headlights picked out a narrow gravel road intersecting the highway, where he pulled well off the road. "It's time to get back to Bear Creek. It's late. You're upset."

She unbuckled her seat belt. When he shifted to face her, she moved across the bench seat and grabbed at his shoulders to get his complete attention. "I didn't know I was pregnant until you were gone. But I *loved* you then, and I loved that baby from the first moment I knew I was pregnant."

"Then why—"

"You assumed wrong. I had emergency surgery for an ectopic pregnancy, not an abortion. I was young and scared and broke, and I couldn't go back home." She released his shoulders and retreated to the opposite corner of the cab, trying to hold back her tears. Even after all these years, she mourned for the baby, remembering each anniversary of her due date…and each anniversary of her loss.

"Dixie—"

"I didn't have insurance and I waited way too long. A friend made me go to the hospital. It all came to over ten grand, but he helped me out and would never let me pay a penny back."

Clint blanched. He reached up and took her hands in his. "Oh, God. I'm sorry."

"I just wanted you to know the truth...before anyone else told you." She swallowed with difficulty, not wanting to tell the rest. "The doctors said I might never be able to have a child again, because of the scarring."

Leaning his head against the headrest, he closed his eyes, his fists clenched on his thighs. "You shouldn't have been alone."

"There's something else. Seeing you like this brings back a lot of old feelings, but it can't happen."

He drew in a sharp breath. "You have someone else."

"No." The question nearly made her smile. *There's never been anyone else but you.*

"Then maybe things can work out."

She bit her lip. "I'm not a very good bet for the long haul," she said, striving for a lightness she didn't feel. "I've had some...abnormal tests. Nothing conclusive yet, but I have to go back to the University Hospital again."

A silence lengthened between them, dark and frightening and filled with the unknown.

"That's it?"

"Isn't that enough?"

"Come here." He reached for her, pulled her to him with one arm and lifted her chin with his other hand. That soft smile was back, lighting his face with hope. "Honey, I lost you twice because I was bullheaded—ten years ago, and again back in Bent Spur.

You think I would walk away again? We'll go through this together.''

"I'm not much of a bargain."

"Nothing in life is guaranteed."

"But a family…"

"What matters to me is you." He dropped a gentle kiss on her forehead, her nose, and then settled his mouth over hers.

After a while, he pulled back. "I'm sorry about what I said back in Bent Spur. I should have known you wouldn't…" He gave her that boyish smile, then wrapped his arms around her and held her close. "All that ever mattered was you. It just took me a long time to figure it out."

BEAR CREEK'S local pizza joint doubled as a bar, and was still packed at midnight with a large crowd from the rodeo plus a Saturday-night herd of local cowboys. Kristen waited until Tucker left the table and headed for the men's room, then leaned forward. "I called Roy and Guy tonight."

"Why?" Jake cocked an eyebrow, his gaze steady.

"I was careful not to say much. They don't need to be worrying. But I keep thinking that there's some connection, some piece of the puzzle that we're missing. None of MRC's problems have been isolated incidents. I'm sure of it. Tomorrow I'm faxing Guy some names to see if he remembers anything that could give us a clue."

He nodded. "I've been checking around. Quite a few cowboys have been at every MRC rodeo where there's been an incident. A couple of them had disqualifications in their events back in Mendota.''

"Any of them wearing new boots this weekend?" she retorted.

"Nope. And I hung around Tina this afternoon while she was taking entry money. At least two of them seemed strapped for cash."

"Could be just an act."

He shook his head. "I don't think so. I've been down that road myself. If either of them could act that well, they could head for Hollywood."

"Those cowboys are still a possibility, though."

"True. Along with some of the regular crew...plus Bud, and Lew and Vance."

"But Vance was fired before the money disappeared."

"He could have slipped back. Who knows? If Tina was distracted, contestants might have seen him around but not realized he'd been fired and not given him a second thought."

"True." Kristen took a sip of her cola and lowered her voice. "Bud's a jerk, but why would he steal from his own wife?"

"They had to cover the loss. But if he had the money anyway, it wouldn't be a hardship—and he would have managed to drive another chink into MRC. In case you didn't notice, he isn't very happy about you running the show this season."

"'Isn't very happy' is putting it mildly. But what's the point? I'm only around a few more months and then you'll take over. It isn't like he's in line to inherit the job."

"Lifelong jealousy?" Jake took a swallow of his Coors and set it aside. "Competition?"

"Maybe. What about Lew? No one seems to know much about him."

"Bud says he was an old rodeo buddy from way back. Does some headin' and heelin' at the rodeos down in Texas, but mostly does ranch work. Nothing much on him in the statistics, so he hasn't done real well in the past few years."

"Luckily for him he knows cattle. He sure isn't one for conversation. I can't get a word out of him."

A scuffle escalated over by the jukebox. Jake and Kristen met each other's eyes, then rose as one to look over the crowded room.

Through the smoky haze she could see Tucker standing with his fists cocked and chin raised belligerently. The cowboy he was facing down—a guy she'd never seen before—looked like a steer wrestler, a good four inches taller and fifty pounds heavier, and too drunk to have any common sense.

"Heaven help him, he's going to die this time," she said under her breath as she started across the room.

"Wait." Jake grabbed at her arm. "I'll get him."

He edged past her and eased between the tightly spaced tables and chairs through the center of the room; she followed in his wake. Some of the cowboys glanced at Jake, then looked at the situation at the jukebox and moved out of the way. A few others called out some encouragement.

A woman in a skintight halter top and dangly

beaded earrings headed for the phone—which meant the local sheriff could be here any minute.

Jake moved to Tucker's side. "We've got to leave," he said quietly.

Tucker's glare slid briefly from the other cowboy to Jake, then back again. "I don't need your help."

"I know you don't. I'm just saying that we are leaving *now,* and we're your only ride back to the motel."

"I'm not going."

"Who's this, your keeper?" The burly cowboy threw back his head and laughed. "Lucky he showed up."

Tucker took another step forward. Jake grasped his arm with a viselike grip. "No, Tuck." He gave the other guy an apologetic look. "There was probably a good reason to argue, here, but he can't afford any more fights this year."

"What, you don't want your little friend gettin' hurt?"

Jake lowered his voice. "I don't want *anyone* getting hurt. Especially me."

The cowboy looked around the room for support. No one met his gaze. His fists lowered a few inches.

"Maybe we should take this outside," he sneered. "Just you and me."

Jake gave an apologetic shrug. "I don't think so."

At the periphery of her vision, Kristen saw Hoot stand up a few tables away. And Kenny. Then a couple of cowboys from Bent Spur who were competing this weekend. Across the room some others rose, though she couldn't see who they were.

"None of us wants any trouble," Jake said quietly, jerking his chin toward all the rodeo cowboys now on their feet. He held the other man's gaze, his silent warning clear.

The man's fists lowered to his sides. "Guess it helps to have a lot of buddies, don't it."

Tucker stepped forward, a muscle jerking in his jaw. "I don't need—"

"Tucker!" Jake's quiet command was pure steel.

The front door of the building opened, sending a patrol car's rays of eerie crimson light sweeping through the smoky room and highlighting the bulky frame of an officer. His partner stood farther back.

"Time to go," she said, giving Tucker a nudge. "*Now.*"

The noise of conversation and clinking glasses hushed.

"Any problems here, folks?"

The rodeo cowboys all sat down and casually resumed their conversations as if nothing had happened. Tucker's shoulders slumped. The cowboy Tucker had confronted muttered something under his breath and turned back to the jukebox.

"Just a little friendly conversation," Jake said mildly. "But we're leaving now, if you'd like our table."

He started for the door with Tucker behind him. Kristen followed.

The deputy eyed Jake and Tucker with suspicion as they passed, then touched the bill of his cap as Kristen approached. "A woman called from here, ma'am. Said there was trouble. Was that you?"

"Gosh, no. I didn't see anything at all. Seems like a nice place." She smiled at him, then winked as she sidestepped past him. "I recommend the pepperoni with extra cheese."

Outside, she breathed a deep sigh of relief and climbed into the MRC pickup parked a few spaces down. Tucker climbed in after her and slammed the door.

"Well," she said brightly. "Good place for supper, don't you think?"

Muttering something incomprehensible, Tucker slouched in the corner of the cab. Jake threw the truck in reverse and backed out slowly, his eyes on the rearview mirror, then headed toward the highway, his jaw set and eyes narrowed.

"Just say it," Tucker said flatly, after several minutes of silence.

Jake drove another mile before replying. "How long has your cast been off?"

"What, you want me to hit the road? If that's what you—"

"No. Just tell me how long it's been."

"Maybe a month."

"What do you want out of life?"

Kristen felt him rebelliously jerk a shoulder. "I've been working my arm. It's getting stronger. I can join my traveling buddies in another week or two."

"What happens if you end up in a brawl and break it again? Or end up with jail time?"

Tucker didn't answer, just slouched a little deeper. Flicking a glance at Kristen, Jake seemed to choose his next words carefully, and she knew he was trying to avoid revealing too much about their family.

"We learn from example. But we've got choices. We can choose which ones we follow. Be smart, Tucker."

"So I should just stand there and let any stupid jerk walk all over me?" Tucker swore under his breath. "You don't get it."

"I just hope you get it before you do something that can't be undone."

A few blocks later, Jake slowed and pulled into the motel, where he and Tucker shared a room at the far end. Kristen had one near the office. He snagged a room key from the dashboard and tossed it to Tucker. "You go on in. Kristen and I have some things to discuss."

Tucker caught the key in midair as he stepped out of the truck. "I'll bet."

"We'll be at the truck stop down the road if you get lonely," Jake said mildly. "But I do have an extra key, so don't wait up."

He watched until Tucker disappeared into the room. "Now I know how parents must feel when their kids finally go to sleep," he said wryly, turning to face her.

"Total relief."

"So tell me, Kris…" His eyes were dark, expectant, filled with wicked sensual promise and a spark of unexpected humor. "Now that we've got some privacy. Is there anything you'd like to do?"

CHAPTER FIFTEEN

OH, YES. Kristen looked up at him, her thigh still pressed against his, feeling the heat of him through the layers of their denim jeans, and wondered if he'd thought about this moment as much as she had over the past few hours. Months. Years.

"I guess," she said carefully, "it might not hurt to check things out at the rodeo grounds. You mentioned, um…stars overhead, and…"

Curving an arm around her shoulders, he drew her closer. His blue eyes darkened with desire. A corner of his mouth tipped upward, deepening the slash of one dimple, as he lifted her chin with a forefinger. "I've thought about this for a long, long time. Are you sure?"

As sure as her next breath, as sure as the steady beating of her heart.

Twisting within his embrace, held back by the steering wheel of the truck, she slid her arms around his shoulders and kissed him. Knowing that everything in her heart was in her eyes—the want and need and…love that had started so long ago and had never really diminished despite the years.

Had there ever been a day when she hadn't wondered about what he was doing? Where he was? If they would ever meet again?

He pulled back a little, his hands trembling against her back. ''Krissie.'' His voice was low and raw, as if it hurt to speak.

Shifting, he tried to move closer, but his elbow connected with the steering wheel. A wry smile lit his eyes. ''Trucks were never meant for much of this. Though I remember...''

''Montana?''

She eased back and smiled, remembering the wild passion they'd felt for each other that summer, when there'd never been enough time, enough places to go. When they'd been so crazy for each other that some days they hadn't even seen sunshine.

They'd made love twice in the cab of her pickup.

Nostalgia gave way to wistfulness, as she realized that nothing could ever equal the eager anticipation of being young and in love for the first time. How could reality ever compete with memories made all the more incredible by the passing years?

When she and Jake made love again, it would probably be...disappointing.

''You suddenly look sad,'' he said gently, releasing her from his embrace. He laid his arm across the back of the seat. ''You don't have to say yes.''

She was half afraid to tarnish her memories with reality and disappointment, but the concern in his eyes proved more compelling than sheer masculine desire. This was *Jake*.

Her gaze drifted downward, across his lean, tanned face, to his sensually cut mouth and the strong jaw now shadowed well past five o'clock like that of some dark and dangerous gunslinger on the silver screen. And she knew without any doubt that the greatest danger was to her heart.

"I was just...remembering." Reaching back, she fished in her pocket and withdrew her motel room key. "There's the rodeo grounds, or my room," she whispered, dangling it in the air.

"So what is it—sheets, or the stars?"

She laughed, suddenly feeling nearly giddy with anticipation. "Tough decision."

He followed her into the room. Watched silently as she locked and chained the door.

Even if the room had been pitch dark, she would have known exactly where he stood, who he was. She felt his presence in the tingling of her skin and the awareness that shimmered through her like cool spring rain. His subtle woodsy aftershave. The soft sound of his breathing.

"These rooms aren't the greatest," she said as she switched on a lamp.

Two double beds with a table and lamp between, a mirror-topped dresser and a single straight-backed chair filled the available floor space. A framed Charles Russell print on the wall, an old-fashioned phone. "The phone doesn't work consistently and this room doesn't even have a television," she added apologetically. "I'm sorry—"

"We don't need either one."

He stood behind her, scooped up her hair and draped it over her shoulder, then slid his large, callused hands slowly, ever so slowly down her arms.

Capturing her wrists, he reached around and locked their hands together over her hips, drew her back against his chest until she could feel him against her, from head to foot, enveloping her with his size and strength.

Her nervousness faded as his warm breath tickled the stray wisps of hair at her nape, sending shivers down her spine. Tipping her head to the side, she gave him access to the tender flesh of her neck and moaned aloud when he kissed her there, then trailed a series of kisses down the length of her neck.

In the mirror she watched as his hands moved higher, to her waist. But her eyes drifted shut as he nibbled at her ear and started whispering all the things that he planned to do to her, for her, on that bed.

And the floor.

And in the shower beyond.

Erotic images flooded her, sending heat spiraling through her belly, curling her toes. Frustrated, she twisted in his arms to face him.

"Not fair," she said, lowering her voice to a seductive whisper. She curved a hand behind his head and drew him down to her level, until their mouths met.

Each tried to get closer, deeper, with hands searching and bodies arching, until they finally broke apart stunned. Breathless. And stared at each other in shock and wonder.

"I remembered," she finally managed, "that we had something so far beyond anything else I'd ever experienced. But I thought, well..."

"That it was just a memory."

"And I was even a little afraid—"

"Of being disappointed?"

Laughter bubbled inside her as she looked help-lessly up at him, her heart still racing, her pulse still leaping in her wrists. "You, too?"

He cupped her head with one large hand and drew her against his chest, where she felt the heavy pound-ing of his heart. "I guess we didn't need to worry," he said dryly. "Five minutes, and I'm already on the verge of a heart attack."

She ducked her head, suddenly feeling unaccount-ably shy, wishing she had packed filmy negligees in-stead of serviceable cotton, wondering at the beautiful women a man like Jake would have been with over the years.

"What's this? You suddenly look ready to run." He smiled down at her, then tipped his head toward the bathroom door. "You think about tonight while I take a shower. If you want me to leave when I come out, just say the word. Deal? No hard feelings."

She nodded, not looking up, as memories of soap-suds and laughter and slippery, searching hands and mouths came back to her. When she raised her gaze to meet his, she knew he was remembering, too.

"Maybe," he said thoughtfully, his hand poised at the first button of his shirt, "we should consider this together." He unfastened one button, then lowered his hand to the next. "What do you think?"

The next button opened beneath his fingers, and then the next, until his shirt hung open and she could see the soft black shadow of hair on his chest.

"I think you're right." She pried off one boot and

kicked it toward the door. Then the other. "Collaborating on this decision-making process could only be of benefit. And—" she reached for his silver belt buckle "—mutual aid might help speed up the process."

"Honey, this is definitely not a timed event."

She grinned up at him, suddenly feeling as though she were eighteen again and at the absolute top of the world. Exhilarated. Excited. And head over heels in love.

They left the lights off in the bathroom, so just dim illumination came from the lamp in the other room. The cramped confines of the shower, the slippery little sliver of soap, the steam, the rising desire and the laughter—all brought back a thousand memories.

The added years brought a depth to their emotions that hadn't been there before, because neither had realized just how precious their gift was…and how rare.

Hours later, as they finally lay entwined together, spent and satisfied, Kristen snuggled closer and laid her hand across his broad chest. So warm and strong… He'd fulfilled every fantasy she'd ever had, and even a few she hadn't.

As the first pale flush of dawn broke the horizon, she blinked back the sting of her tears as she mourned the loss of the years they'd been apart.

And tried to ignore the tiny, unwelcome voice echoing in her heart. *Can you really trust him, when he left you once before?*

A SHRILL SOUND split the air. Danced savagely on his pounding brain. Fighting back a wave of nausea,

Tucker grabbed for the extra pillow on his bed and smashed it over his head to block out the sound, but it kept coming, and coming....

Bleary-eyed, he finally raised his head and peered at the bedside clock. *Who the hell would call at seven on a Sunday?*

It took another few ear-splitting rings for him to realize that Jake's bed was untouched, and that he was alone in the room. *We're going to talk,* he'd said.

Yeah, right.

The noise and the pounding in Tucker's head and the scenes from last night jangled together in his skull as he reached for the phone, more in self-defense than out of any desire to talk to anyone, any time, ever again.

After two false tries, he knocked the entire thing to the floor. Hanging partway out of bed, he retrieved the receiver by its cord, as if reeling in a dead fish.

The process escalated the pounding in his head to roughly the sound and force of a speeding train. *"What!"*

A vaguely familiar male voice chuckled. "Is this Jake?"

"No."

"Tucker, then. Kristen called me, and I need to talk to her, but the phone in her room isn't working. When you see her, tell her—"

The voice faded, as nausea started working up Tucker's dry throat and his head filled with an ever-greater jungle beat. A vague sense of embarrassment and anger over last night's events roiled together, mowing down whatever sense and tact Tucker possessed.

Dragging himself to the side of the bed, he eyed the distance to the bathroom and hoped he could make it in time. "Jake isn't here—he spent the night with Kristen. Who's this?"

But there was no time for replies.

Dropping the phone, Tucker stumbled away from the bed and headed for the bathroom, regretting the margaritas and beer he'd had the night before. The Singapore Slings he'd shared with some cute barrel-racer babe from Denver.

Long afterward, he lay gingerly back on the bed and tried to remember if he'd just dreamed it, or if there'd really been a phone call...and who it could have been.

What the hell. If it was important, the person would call again.

THE SUNDAY MATINEE performance of the Bear Creek rodeo brought out even greater crowds than that of the night before. The bright blue sky with a scattering of white puffball clouds provided a stunning backdrop for the colorful flags and promotional banners, the bright western shirts of the contestants, and the sparkly ruby outfits worn by the girls during the Grand Entry hippodrome ride.

As the crowd rose to sing the national anthem, Kristen scanned the back lot of the rodeo until she found Jake. He stood tall and tanned, his hat in his hand and his black, wavy hair gleaming in the sunshine.

He'd come so far. The limp was almost imperceptible, except at the end of a long day, and he seemed to be in much less pain. Not that he would have told her otherwise.

And he'd thrown himself into his new career. He definitely had the communication skills and personality to succeed as a producer.

The thought made her smile slip. Last night had been incredible, but neither one of them had mentioned the future.

He'd been footloose forever, chasing trophy buckles and championships, with little responsibility beyond the next rodeo. A new career didn't mean he was ready to take on any lifetime commitments.

And she still had her condo and job opportunity waiting in Dallas. By the first of October she'd finally be pursuing her own dreams. Security. Advancement. A bright future. That was still what she wanted, right?

As the last notes of the national anthem faded away, she started toward Jake to discuss the sponsor introductions during the intermission. Tina's wildly waving hand caught her attention, instead.

"Me?" She pointed at herself, and Tina nodded vigorously.

The Bear Creek rodeo grounds had been built solely for horse shows and rodeos, and boasted excellent facilities. The secretary's office filled half of a long building that housed an elaborate food stand on the other end and *real* rest rooms—with running water—in the center section.

As soon as Kristen stepped into the office, Tina held out a phone. "It's for you. Guy."

"Hi, honey," Guy greeted her. "I got the fax you sent after we talked last."

She crouched low against the wall and cupped a hand around the receiver at her ear, raising her voice to be heard over the announcer's enthusiastic introduction of the first bareback contestant. "What do you think?"

"You're *sure* those incidents are connected in some way?"

"Call it intuition, but yes…I do think so."

He paused, and she knew he was again looking down the list of names she'd sent him. "None of these old boys are church choir prospects. But I can't see any of them setting out to destroy MRC's credibility."

"Not even Bud?"

"He still have the sale stuck in his craw?"

"I don't think he likes me any better than he did when we were kids."

Guy chuckled. "I heard your dad tell a few tales. I surely wish I could have seen you back then, going at a boy twice your size, like some pigtailed avenging angel."

"Bud deserved it."

"I bet he did, honey. But now he's got a business reputation to keep up. A mortgage to pay for, and a family. From what I've seen, his wife keeps him in line."

Kristen glanced over at Tina, who was now at the door with her hands braced on her hips, lecturing one of her teenage daughters. "She tries."

Guy went down Kristen's list of suspects, expressing doubt over each one. "These boys would have more sense than that. Heck, how would they win if MRC went under? They'd be risking arrest over something that couldn't benefit them either way."

"That's why this is baffling. Jake is buying the company, and everyone seems to like him really well. There's just no profit to be made by causing trouble."

"A couple of names aren't familiar, though. This Randy, out of Oklahoma…Walter…Lew—this one is an employee, now?"

"Bud's idea. Not mine."

"When did he come aboard?"

"Back in Pine Bend, but he had some other commitment before he could start. He wasn't at the Bent Spur rodeo. Too bad—you could have met him while we were in town."

"Did you fax this list to your dad, too? He might remember something I don't."

"His fax machine bit the dust and he hasn't replaced it. I'll talk to him when we get back."

Guy fell silent, and Kristen held her breath, hoping.

"There's maybe one real hostile guy I can think of through all the years Roy and I rodeoed together and the time we were runnin' MRC. Not from around this part of the country, though. California, maybe. And his name sure wasn't on your list."

"What was it?"

"Ron…Rich…Ray…" Another long silence. "It was Sonny Ray."

"His last name was Ray?"

Guy thought hard. "Nope. Williston, maybe. Masterson…Galveston… It's been a long time. Probably dead by now, ornery cuss that he was. I'll give your dad a call and see if he remembers.''

After discussing MRC business for a few minutes, she wished Guy well and hung up, then stepped outside.

Jake was still over by the chutes, watching the men move livestock into position at the far end of the arena for the steer wrestling. As if sensing her presence, he turned a little and his eyes surveyed the area.

When he saw her heading toward him, he grinned and held her gaze, his eyes intense with desire and a depth of emotion so powerful that her stride faltered.

At that moment, all her doubts were swept away.

THE MATINEE went off without a hitch. The stock bucked well. The overflow crowd proved wildly enthusiastic. No one got hurt—Security hadn't had to tactfully escort a single drunk out the gate.

Kristen threaded her arm through Jake's as the first bull rider hovered over his bull, crossed himself in silent prayer, and then eased into position. Out in the arena, Hoot and Kenny were ready for action.

''Wishing that was you up in the chute?'' she murmured.

She felt a sigh go through him.

''Always.''

She playfully bumped against him. ''You're doing so well—not even limping by the end of the day anymore. That's got to be a relief.''

''But not satisfaction. Not like I'll have when I get back out there again. It's…a rush. An adrenaline high.''

The cowboy in the chute nodded once.

The gate swung wide.

The bull—Hit Man—erupted into the arena, an impossible mass of muscle suddenly airborne, then twisting and plunging to the earth, only to take off again, corkscrewing his immense body with the agility of a hula dancer.

The cowboy lost his rhythm on the second jump—showed daylight on the third, and was in the dirt and running for cover a second later. He'd already scrambled up the fence when the eight-second buzzer sounded.

The bull circled, feigned a charge toward Hoot. Kenny darted in, rolling his red, white and blue-striped barrel, clowning for the crowd with broad gestures to convey terror.

The bull did charge then, but Kenny jumped nimbly aside, and the bull hooked only the barrel, tossing it high. The crowd roared, and Kenny swept a deep bow.

"He's come a long way," Jake said.

Kristen nodded. "He's done well for his first year. You're lucky to have both of them working with MRC. They're decent guys, good bullfighters and they also please the crowds."

The next three bulls dumped each of their riders in less than three seconds, followed by two riders who made it to the buzzer with respectable scores, and one who was disqualified for touching the bull with his free hand.

The announcer's voice boomed through the loudspeakers. "Okay, folks, last one up is Slim Hathaway. Slim comes to us from—"

Kristen tuned out the announcer's voice and held her breath. Slim had drawn Hit and Run, a tough bull known for trying to hook anything on two legs. A good draw for scoring high. A bad draw if a cowboy was looking forward to a long and healthy future.

Slim nodded. The judge at the chute released the latch and the gate swung wide open.

The bull took a powerhouse leap, then went into his trademark hard spin to the right. Dropped his front end. Shifted lightning-fast into a left spin.

Slim landed flat in the dirt a good ten feet away.

The instinctive reaction for a bull rider, hurt or not, was to hit the ground running and head for safety. Sometimes they staggered and dropped to all fours, too dazed or concussed to find the arena fence.

For a cowboy to land like Slim—without any defensive effort to break his fall—and not move, was bad. Really, really bad.

Slim raised his head and chest a few inches. Then dropped face-first in the dirt in an awkward tangle of arms and legs, limp as spaghetti.

A cry of dismay rose from the crowd, followed by silence. Kenny moved in front of Slim, and Hoot darted out to distract the bull.

To watch a good bullfighter work a bad bull was to watch a dance of death—one skilled but defenseless partner in face paint, one angry partner armed with two-foot horns and the agility of a ballet dancer.

Kenny dodged within a few feet of the bull's horns, taunting him, drawing him away. The bull lowered his head and shook it. Pawed great clods of dirt high into the air. Then charged. Again Kenny nimbly leapt to one side.

Skidding to an abrupt halt, the bull took one look at the open gate and—even though he'd been through this routine a dozen times before—spun away instead of heading out of the arena.

Cowboys standing along the fence reached in unison for a high rail and scrambled up beyond the reach of the horns.

The bull shook his head, pivoted. Charged the fence at the far end of the chutes and slammed his head against the bars. The crowd in the bleachers gasped. A woman grabbed her kids and screamed.

The bullfighters and pickup men moved in closer, the pickup men slapping their bat-wing chaps and shouting, sidestepping their horses to create a greater visual barrier.

Hit and Run barreled between them and raced down the arena fence a dozen yards, then stopped, angrily twisted his horns into a fence panel and jerked his head upward.

The panel—pinned securely to the ones at either side and always, *always* wired together for added safety—lifted away.

It teetered, still suspended on the bull's horn. The bull bellowed and tossed his head again, jerking the panel completely free. One end swung wildly into an older man sitting in the front row.

Suddenly Jake reached up, and with one swift motion launched himself over the fence and ran toward the bull.

The crowd screamed. People rushed backward, up higher into the stands. Pushed and shoved down the narrow walkway between the arena fence and the first row of seating.

Bellowing, the panicked bull tossed his massive head and neck. Fought to free himself from the predatory object now caught on his horn.

Kristen stared in horror as the pickup men galloped forward, circled to the other side of the bull. Cowboys rushed down the arena, Hoot and Kenny in the lead. Bud, too burly for speed, came after the rest, shouting a litany of curses.

Jake grabbed at the fence panel. Hoot arrived a split second later, caught the other end.

"Now!" Jake shouted. "Lift it!"

But just then the bull leapt into the air, breaking free of them both. Bellowing, he slammed into the ground. The section of fencing fell away.

Twisting his massive head and neck, he cut back to the left in a blur of motion. Rammed his horn at Jake's chest. Half the shirt tore away, as Jake stumbled backward. Before he could dodge, the bull was right back with another hook at Jake's thigh.

Kristen cried out, unable to look away, the fury of the bull and the movement of the bullfighters unfolding in sickening slow motion, as Jake scrambled to his feet and darted to the left.

Enraged, Hit and Run feinted a charge toward Hoot, then Kenny. Yelling, the pickup men danced their horses closer and closer—until the bull finally halted. Blew loudly. And then broke into a disjointed lope toward the open gate by the chutes.

The buzz of terror in the crowd faded at the sight of the ambulance crew working over Slim.

Stunned into silence, they sat back in their seats and watched the doctor as he rushed in. The crowd of EMTs and cowboys. The backboard and cervical collar being retrieved from the ambulance—surely signs of hope.

With her heart jammed in her throat, Kristen watched Jake dust himself off and then hunker down with Hoot and Bud to examine the damaged fence. *"Thank you,"* she whispered, glancing heavenward. *This could have ended so differently.*

Her gaze flew back toward Slim. Renewed fear sent tears spilling down her cheeks. *Please don't cover him up. Please let him be okay.*

After what seemed like an eternity, the crew lifted the gurney into the ambulance. The doors shut. The ambulance slowly turned around and headed out the back gate.

The cowboys on horses waiting outside the arena parted to let the ambulance through, all eyes on its progress, most of them holding their hats in their hands.

The vehicle pulled out onto the highway, not going nearly fast enough. *Sirens. Turn on your sirens!* Kristen pleaded silently.

But no frantic wail filled the air.

When Jake appeared at her side and slipped an arm around her shoulder, Kristen turned in to his chest and tried hard not to cry.

CHAPTER SIXTEEN

"I CAN'T STOP THINKING about Slim's family," Kristen said, pacing the floor of MRC's office. "And someone in the crowd could have been badly hurt when that bull hooked the fence last night." She shuddered, remembering. "*You* could have been killed out there!"

"All I lost was a good shirt," he said wryly.

Folding her arms across her chest, she frowned. "And I nearly had a heart attack when that happened. I can't believe you aren't limping—or worse."

"Guess I was lucky."

They'd arrived back at the ranch at three o'clock this morning, exhausted and saddened. Conversation on the trip home had been solemn, cursory at best. Too tired for a drive back to her parents' ranch, she'd stayed in the small bedroom in the MRC cabin.

"Last night sure as hell wasn't an accident," Jake mused. "I've helped put up the arena, and the boys always reinforce each panel's connection to the next one with a triple wrap of heavy wire. It takes a wire cutter and muscle power to take that arena apart."

"Bud says he has the crew check the arena every day, yet almost a third of that wiring close to the chutes was removed before yesterday's performance.'' She sighed, and cocked a hip on the edge of the desk. ''Several bulls in the lineup are known for hooking at the fence when they get riled. Someone was *hoping* this would happen.''

''Unless Bud...''

They looked at each other, sharing a moment of doubt.

''If someone has been hoping a bull would hook the fence at other venues, as well—''

''—then the crew should have been noticing missing wires when they took down the arena.'' Kristen frowned. ''You've helped them tear it down. Ever see anything unusual?''

''Bud's crew takes off all the wiring before we start loading, so all we do is unpin each section.'' Jake ran a hand through his hair. ''We can hardly ask him.''

''The next rodeo, then. You can ask the guys, be offhand so they don't get suspicious. And we'll both keep an eye out for anything unusual.'' She slid off the desk and went to stare out the picture window across the room, her thumbs hooked on the back pockets of her jeans. ''Sure wish we could've gotten fingerprints from that panel. It might have helped.''

''Yeah—to identify the few hundred spectators who walked along that fence all weekend.''

She fell silent for a few minutes. ''Come look outside.''

Tucker sat on the top step of the porch in front of Jake's cabin, his head in his hands. He'd been sitting out there for the better part of an hour.

''I've got to go talk to him,'' Jake said.

''He's taking Slim's death hard. These young guys

think they are invincible until something like this happens.''

''I always traveled alone—or with buddies who talked even less than me. Since Tucker showed up, I seem to be turning into his counselor at every turn.'' He tried for a smile and knew he hadn't come close. Kristen laid a comforting hand on his arm. ''I'm not good at this—I don't have a clue what to say.''

''Just getting him to talk will help.''

''I can't make things better for him.''

''Having a big brother to look up to—''

Jake snorted. ''Last I heard, he thought I was spineless for not decking someone.''

''He's *lucky* to have you as a mentor.'' She glanced at her watch. ''I've got to call a guy about the rodeo dates for next June. Come back after you talk to him, okay?''

She settled down at the desk, suddenly all business, and briskly flipped through the contents of a file in front of her, then reached for the phone.

Halfway to the door, Jake turned back. He moved up behind her and rested his hands on her shoulders.

Startled, she looked up at him, her eyes wide.

''I get the feeling that you're sorry about what happened between us,'' he said softly.

''No—of course not.''

He lowered his mouth to hers and gave her a swift kiss, then met her eye-to-eye. ''Good. Because I'm not sorry at all.''

There had to be a hundred ways to say this right, but he couldn't think of a single one. Slim's death had reminded him of just how fragile—how *tempo-rary*—life could be.

"I just want you to know that…you mean a lot to me."

A delicate pink flush rose in her cheeks as she twined her arms around his neck and drew him back for a longer, far more intimate kiss.

At the squeal of hinges and scrape of the front door against the cabin flooring, they both looked up. Straight into the furious eyes of Roy Davis.

"Dad!" Kristen abruptly released Jake, the pink in her cheeks deepening to dark rose. "I didn't expect you here."

"Guess not." He scowled at Jake, then jerked his chin toward the door. "I need to talk to my daughter. Alone."

JAKE HEADED across the yard toward his cabin, knowing only too well what Roy was saying to his daughter.

When the MRC opportunity came up, Jake had known he would have to face the past. Heaven knew, Kristen had a right to be angry, but he'd figured they could work together for a few months as part of a business deal, plain and simple.

Which showed just how obtuse he was. At the end of September, she'd be leaving for Dallas and taking his heart right along with her. And there wasn't a damn thing he could do about it.

Years ago, a promise to an old friend had cost Jake his future with the woman he loved, and that promise still stood. But a man was no better than his word.

Sitting on the top step of the cabin porch, head bowed, arms braced on his thighs, hands clasped, Tucker didn't look up when Jake settled down on the step next to him.

"Guy says he could use some help moving cattle this afternoon. I figured you and I could both use a change of scenery," Jake said.

"I suppose."

Jake took off his hat, ran a hand through his hair and put his hat back on. Hooked one booted foot over the opposite thigh. Studied the clouds building along the horizon. Dark clouds promising rain.

"I knew Slim," Tucker muttered.

"Friend?"

"Sorta."

"Real hard, seeing someone die." Jake leaned back on his elbow. "Especially someone young, healthy. One of us."

Tucker kept staring at his hands. "He had a baby boy. He was so proud of that kid—showed me pictures. I keep thinking about how proud he was."

Jake thought back over the guys he'd known who hadn't walked out of the arena. Young lives cut short at twenty, twenty-two. "Everyone knows the risks. Figures it just happens to someone else."

"But it don't." Tucker held out the arm he'd broken during his ride in Mendota. He'd been lifting weights to bring it back into shape, and had claimed it was better than ever.

Jake had his doubts.

"This arm was nothing. But look at you—your career ended after a wreck. And Slim…" Tucker swallowed, looked away. "I keep wondering if I'm gonna see him out there in the dirt, when I get on my next bull. If the fear…"

"Any bull rider with a lick of sense feels fear. It isn't a matter of *if* you'll get hurt, it's *when.* You just get tough and keep going until you're too old or too broke to fix."

"This was gonna be Slim's last season. He thought he'd have enough for a down payment on a place near his folks. He was just so darn proud of that boy… Makes a guy wonder about the price he paid."

"I know." Jake hesitated, then added, "Maybe you'll want to stay at Guy's a while longer and sort things out before you join your buddies."

"What else would I do—go back to Dad's ranch?" He gave a bitter laugh.

"Heck, you're not even twenty. Go to college. Trade school. Head for Sheridan and find a job. Check into the Air Force." Jake stood up and stretched. "Work for Guy. Or I could sure use good help with MRC. You could work with me."

"There's nothin' I love more than rodeo. My friends are there—it's like *family.* And that rush, when you make it to the buzzer on a tough bull…"

"I know."

"I'm gonna make the finals someday. I'm not a quitter."

Jake gave him a wry smile. "Then I guess you've just made your decision. Come on, let's go catch some horses out of the pasture for this afternoon."

They started off for the barn together, side by side. After a few moments, Jake slung his arm around

Tucker's shoulder and gave him a awkward brotherly hug. "Someday, when you're old and feeble and finally decide the bulls can buck without you, promise you'll come back and look me up. There will always be a place for you in MRC if you want it. Deal?"

Tucker looked him square in the eye. "Deal."

KRISTEN TURNED AWAY from the window after Jake reached his cabin. "Did you hear about the performance last night?" she asked, turning to face Roy.

Roy blinked and took a deep breath. Maybe discussing business first would give him a chance to cool down. He needed to be calm...and tactful. "Trouble?" he asked.

She told him about Slim's death and the sabotaged arena fence, then handed him an updated list of dates and locations of problems that had occurred for the company. "What do you think?"

He looked at her blankly, then forced himself to concentrate. "I've been thinking since Guy called. You never know what could be in someone's mind— an old argument, someone angry over suspension or disqualification. Could be a hundred different cowboys over the years. But to do all of this? Heck, I just don't know."

"Guy mentioned someone named Sonny. Masterston? Williston?"

"I didn't even remember his first name until Guy mentioned it."

"What happened?"

"Guy and I were at a night rodeo in Oklahoma. We found a contestant down in the holding pens with the stock. The Association rules are pretty darn clear on that score. He had no good reason to be in there. They didn't find any evidence of drugs or weapons on him, but the judge disqualified him from the entire rodeo. I heard later that he'd been suspended for a while, too. Lost his standings toward making the circuit finals.''

Kristen sighed. ''That doesn't seem like enough motivation to take revenge on your company years later.''

''Nope, it sure don't.''

''How's Mom doing?''

Roy looked away. ''Good.'' He cleared his throat. ''Better. Since, ah…her medicine's been adjusted.''

Pulling up a chair next to the desk, she smiled at him. ''Since being in the hospital? Or did the doc start her on something else?''

''Maria left last Monday.''

''*Maria left?*'' Kristen sat forward. ''She's been at the ranch forever. Why did she leave?''

He shrugged and avoided her eyes as he gave the same excuse he'd given everyone else at the ranch and in town. ''Said she wanted to go back to Mexico and live with her sister. Told me to tell you good-bye.''

The truth was that she'd wailed and clung to him, wanting far more than he could give, insisting that Ada could be moved to a nursing home.

Since then, he'd cursed himself for being ten times a fool for ever getting involved with Maria.

''I'm going to miss her so much! And what about Mom? Who's taking care of her?''

"I'm helping her more, and now we have an old friend of hers from town—the preacher's widow. She's giving us a trial run to see if things will work out."

"Gladys *Dillon?*" Kristen reached for a can of cola on the desk. A mischievous twinkle lit her eyes. "She'll make everyone stay in line. She taught Confirmation and even kept the rowdy boys under control. They called her The Marshall behind her back." She paused, considering. "But what does this have to do with Mom's medicine?"

"I reckon Maria didn't understand the directions very well." *Or maybe intended to keep Ada snowed and docile.*

"But didn't you notice—needing refills more often?"

Roy felt a flush creep past his collar. "The ones for anxiety or sleep are given 'as needed,' but Maria must have been giving them every day. Gladys figured it out, looking back at refill dates." *And gave me hell, too, for not being more careful.*

"This is wonderful! Mom's really doing better? Wanting to go to town? Is she talking more"

"Yeah, but the dementia is still there," Roy warned. "Don't expect miracles."

Kristen shot to her feet. "I think I'll head out to the ranch earlier."

"Wait—" Roy realized he hadn't had a chance to say what he'd come to say. Now was the time.

He'd had a decent rodeo career for almost twenty years, faced a lot of rough bulls and tough steers. He'd been a damn good contractor for over twenty.

But he'd also made a few mistakes along the way, and every one of them was coming back to roost in the space of a single summer. Life just wasn't fair.

Kristen was waiting.

"I saw you and Jake. When I came in."

A rosy blush sped up her cheeks. "Yes, well..."

"Did you forget what he did when you were eighteen?"

"No, but I—"

"A man like that ain't worth your time."

"I'm twenty-eight, Dad. I can decide for myself." Her eyes flashed with anger. "If you think he's so bad, why did you trust him in the MRC sale?"

Roy had resolved to be calm. Now, in the space of a few heartbeats he lost that control. His anger came rushing back like a stampeding herd.

"*No!* Guy set it up. Jake is *his* nephew, not mine. When Jake insisted on your help, I figured you'd just be at this desk, helping with the paperwork for a while." Roy snorted. "I never thought you'd end up traveling with him."

"Where is this all coming from?" she cried. "You were sure nice to him when we came out to the ranch last time."

"That's before I walked in to find him pawing you," Roy growled.

"Pawing me!"

"I heard you're even *sleeping* with him, dammit!"

"*What?*"

"I called the motel in Bear Creek one morning and found that you sure as hell weren't alone."

Kristen's face turned white. "I don't have to listen to this." She stalked to the door and flung it open.

"Wait." Roy felt his heart twist, knowing that his next words would end whatever chance he might have of getting close to his daughter. "You need to know the truth about Jake Landers. And...about me."

She paused, leaned her forehead against the edge of the door.

"You thought you were in love, but you were only eighteen—practically a baby. He was *six years older*...no steady income...just another bull rider whose only goal in life was a damn gold buckle." Roy sucked in a deep breath. "He had only as much money as his last ride. What would you have done—lived out of the back of a pickup for ten years? How could I let that happen? You've always shown so much promise, Krissie."

She slowly turned, her face still white, her voice cold as a Montana blizzard. *"What did you do?"*

He talked faster, hoping she would see the truth, wanting her to understand. "You've got your whole life in front of you—a career in Dallas, a nice place to live—you can meet the *right* kind of men. Jake Landers is no more than a stray dog."

"What did you do?"

She was shaking now, and Roy wished he could pull her into his lap as he had when she was a little girl with bruises and scrapes. "I waited with you at that church. But I knew he wouldn't be there."

Her face paled. "Why?"

"You thought he would stand by you forever, in sickness and in health? I knew what he was after—

some starry-eyed young gal with money, someone with a big ranch to fall back on after he couldn't chase the rodeo circuit anymore.''

"Jake? You're crazy!''

"I offered him ten grand to walk out of your life.'' Roy met her eyes. "I did it to protect you—to be sure he wanted you. He took that money without a second thought.''

JAKE AND TUCKER GOT BACK at six o'clock that evening, dismounted and ground-tied their horses in front of the barn. A few hours of trailing cattle up into the hills had given Jake a lot of time to think, but he still wasn't prepared for the sight of Kristen standing on the front steps of the MRC office, her arms folded across her chest. Even from a distance he could see she was furious.

Tucker glanced in her direction, then cocked an eyebrow at Jake as he uncinched his saddle. "Doesn't look like she's very happy.''

"No.''

"Need some advice about women?''

Startled, Jake looked over the back of his gelding and caught a twinkle in Tucker's eyes. "No, but I think I'm gonna get it.''

Tucker deftly unsaddled his horse, then came around the back of Jake's horse with his saddle and saddle blanket propped against his hip. "Listen.''

"Listen?"

"Yep. They all love to talk.'' Tucker disappeared into the barn, then came out empty-handed. "If you listen a lot and say 'uh-huh' now and then, they'll think you're *great* company.''

Jake smiled back at him. Tucker was finally losing some of that chip he'd been carrying around. He and Jake had talked about the past, about their dad, about Tucker's future. They'd become almost…friends.

But Tucker's advice would be of no help with Kristen. Not after Roy had talked to her. Jake had known this time would come. Now he needed to know if she'd be able to forgive him.

It wouldn't take long to find out, he realized, as he saw her heading in his direction. ''Uh, Tucker? Jennibelle must have dinner on the table. Would you tell her that I'll be a little late?''

Tucker glanced at Kristen, then gave Jake a knowing smile. ''Okay. Just remember—*listen.*''

Touching the brim of his hat at her approach, Tucker led his horse to the corral and turned him loose, then headed for the house.

''Kristen.'' Jake lifted the saddle from the gelding's back and carried it in to the tack room. She waited outside, her face pale and arms once again folded defensively across her chest.

''Do you know why my dad wanted to talk to me?'' Her voice was brittle as ice. ''Do you have any idea?''

Picking up the gelding's reins, he shrugged. ''I can guess.''

''Tell me why you didn't show up at our wedding.''

There were more reasons than even her father knew, reasons Jake couldn't talk about. So he gave her the most basic truth of all—the one that had convinced him years ago and was true even now.

"You deserve so much more."

"Well, you apparently got plenty," she snapped.

He flinched but plowed on, anyway. "You were bright, heading off to college and a great future. You were only eighteen. You deserved everything that's good in your life. I didn't have more than a beat-up truck and a bull rope to my name back then. What kind of life could I offer?"

"Noble to the last, Landers. Yet you never bothered to explain, or to contact me later. And you gladly took a lot of money as reward for never seeing me again."

"Even before that, I knew it would be wrong to get married," he hedged.

She'd looked up at him with those shining eyes, eager to set a date, and he'd been overwhelmed. Flattered. Swept along on a tide of his own youthful passion and her excitement. If anything, she had been more in love with the *concept* of love than anything else. But he doubted she wanted to hear that now.

"So I was worth, say, what a decent cutting horse would bring at auction—" Her voice broke, her eyes filled with pain. "Did you dicker? Decide what the market would bear for a Roy Davis daughter? Only, you were wanting to get rid of one, not buy—and that makes it all the more humiliating."

"I'm sorry."

She lifted her chin. "I've called Dallas. I can start my new job on September fifteenth, so I'm leaving MRC two weeks earlier than originally agreed. I assume you won't object. I'd leave immediately, but unlike you, I keep my word." She turned toward her pickup. "You have to keep your bargain with Roy and Guy regarding MRC, though. Deal?"

"Deal."

Jake watched her stalk away, her long blond hair swinging against her back, and wished there was a way to set things right. But a vow made couldn't be broken, and he couldn't hurt someone else even to save his own heart.

CHAPTER SEVENTEEN

THE LAST TWO WEEKS of July passed with hundred-degree days, but subzero temperatures between Jake and Kristen.

On the last weekend of the month, Kristen stayed behind when the crew left for a rodeo in Coulter, Colorado. By Thursday she'd completed a detailed five-year plan for the company. By Friday morning she'd dealt with all the current invoices, cleaned out the files and alphabetized the books on the shelves. If not for the steady phone calls regarding promotion and public relations projects for the remaining rodeos of the year, she would have been pacing the floor.

When Guy showed up at the office door on Friday afternoon with two cups of coffee and a smile, she felt pathetically grateful for company.

"Bored?" he said mildly, looking around the office. "Unless you're planning on doing surgery in here, I think you've probably got it just about as clean as it ever needs to be."

"I've got six weeks left, and when my last day comes I'll be out of here faster than Cropduster leaves a chute." Settling back into the chair at her desk, she gave him an apologetic smile. "Not that I haven't enjoyed seeing you and Jennibelle more often."

He took a sip of coffee. "That eager," he marveled, shaking his head slowly. "I would've thought that maybe you had a little more spunk than that."

"Spunk!"

He shrugged. "Not my business. Speaking of business, how's the schedule for next year?"

"Not bad." She leaned down and blindly groped beneath her desk, then withdrew a rolled, two-by-three-foot, one-year calendar. "I need to get this up on the wall."

Standing, she unfurled it and held it for him to read. "We've got seventy percent of this year's rodeos rescheduled, and have picked up a few new ones. Several cancellations, but not bad."

Guy studied the dates, then lounged back in his chair, holding his cup in both hands. "Looks good. You and Jake are a good team."

"He'll do fine on his own," she said breezily, rolling the calendar back into a cylinder and sliding a rubber band over it. She tossed it onto the desk. "Probably better."

Guy snorted. "Have you heard from Tucker?"

"It's just been a week since he left, and he's already called twice. He's still sure his arm will hold out and that next year's All-Around buckle is within his grasp. Youthful optimism is wonderful, isn't it," she said wistfully, gazing out the window. "When you first start out, you think even the moon is within your reach."

"Sometimes a guy can get carried away," Guy agreed. "Big plans, all the excitement... Then he starts to see reality creeping in and can be over-whelmed.''

Kristen glanced back at Guy. ''I don't suppose we're still talking about Tucker.''

''I just hate to see something good lost. You might want to look a little closer at what happened between Jake and your dad. Sometimes there's more than one side to a coin.''

''There's *always* more than one side to a coin,'' she sputtered, trying not to laugh.

''You see?'' Guy gave her a triumphant smile. ''Now you just need to figure it out.''

''I do love you and Jennibelle.'' She leaned down to give him a quick hug. ''You two were always like an aunt and uncle when I was growing up. I even used to wish that you were my dad, sometimes.''

Holding his cup off to one side, he gave her a one-armed hug in return. But by the time she crossed the room and sat back down on the edge of the desk, his eyes were filled with concern. ''You know your dad means well.''

''We could talk about the weather, instead,'' she countered. ''Think it'll rain tonight?''

Guy doggedly continued. ''He's a good man. A hardworking man who's made mistakes. Some,'' he added with a sigh, ''bigger than others.''

''I know about his affairs.''

''Your dad didn't...just sleep around. There were several...special friends, and—''

''*Special friends?*'' Kristen shot back. ''He broke his vows to my mother, left her home alone with me. I'll bet he never once cared about how she felt.''

"I'm not saying that he wasn't wrong."

Kristen snorted. "Between him and Jake, I guess my views about male fidelity are at the low end of the barometer."

"Are you sure that Jake was unfaithful? Did you ever have proof?"

"I heard."

"Was that enough—to have heard?"

"He didn't show up at the church when we did. I heard later that he was with another woman. Now I learn that my loving father gave him a lot of money not to show up." Kristen gave a short laugh. "That's probably enough to convict him right there."

"Still…sometimes there's more to things," Guy mused. He glanced at his watch, then rose abruptly to his feet. "Just thought I'd stop and sit a spell, while Jennibelle was getting ready for town." He reached out and rested a hand on Kristen's shoulder. "You'll do what's right, honey."

"I already have," she whispered, as he walked out the door.

Her new job was secure, the old friend subleasing her condo would be out by September fifteenth. In six weeks, she'd be well on her way to a new life. The only thing that could make her happier would be to leave for Dallas right now.

SHE'D STAYED HOME during the Coulter rodeo, but two weeks later when the first rodeo in August rolled around, she was the first one packed and was in the truck with the motor running before anyone else was ready.

This time they were leaving a day later—on the Wednesday—because the Granite Creek Chamber of Commerce had done most of the advance work on its own.

"A little eager, are we?" Jake murmured as he climbed in.

"I'll go crazy if I stay here another day," she admitted. "Bring on the bright lights and excitement!"

She'd maintained a tough, professional attitude for the past few weeks, teaching Jake basic accounting, pertinent business principles gleaned from six years of college, and all she knew about the running of a rodeo company. He'd absorbed the information with sharp perception and endless curiosity, and many of their intense discussions had lasted well past midnight.

It was just too hard to stay completely aloof with someone who possessed such a burning desire to learn, someone who could debate intelligently for hours without ever becoming defensive or angry. And so they'd slipped back into an awkward friendship.

But there was never any flicker of warmth in his eyes these days, and Kristen carefully continued to maintain her distance. That was exactly how it should be, now and forevermore. So why did she feel such a hollow place in her heart?

As soon as Hoot and Kenny climbed into the back seat of the truck, she floored the accelerator. "How far is this, again?"

"A little over two hours," Kenny piped up from the back seat. "Just like the last time you asked."

"Thank you," she said dryly, flicking a look at him in the rearview mirror.

"Glad to be of service." He winked at her. "We're all gonna miss you at the rodeos. Me and Hoot took a vote and decided that you have to stay on. Jake may know how to run the company, but he ain't near as pretty."

Kenny's words played through her mind during the first two days of preparation for the rodeo. Just an advance case of nostalgia, she told herself firmly as she surveyed the grounds on Friday evening. In a little under two months, Roy and Guy's business would change hands, and the only rodeos she'd see would be the ones where she got in line to pay for a ticket, like everyone else.

But tonight was going to be perfect.

A balmy August breeze fluttered the promotional banners and flags lining the arena. The rich scent of frying chicken filled the air.

Cowboys resplendent in bright shirts strewn with logo patches prowled the area. Some lined up to pay their entry fees. Others were pulling safety vests and adhesive tape out of their duffel bags. Several stood with a boot heel hooked on an arena fence rail, shooting the breeze with their slim-hipped, long-legged buddies.

Kristen felt a smile of satisfaction come clear from her soul as she breathed in the sights and sounds and anticipation in the air.

"Good to see you Kris," called out one of the guys hunkered down by his duffel. "Missed you at the Coulter rodeo."

A few of the cowboys looked up at her with shy grins, several more said hello.

"Hey, Kristen!"

Tucker sauntered up, his post-adolescent bravado back in place, but with a warm look in his eyes. *He's going to be quite a heartbreaker when he's a little more grown-up,* she realized. "Are you entered in the bull riding?"

"Nah." He gave her a sheepish smile and held up his left arm. A heavy bandage looped across his palm and ended at his elbow. "Guess I tried to start back a little too soon."

"That's got to be a disappointment."

He shrugged. "Uncle Guy went on the Internet and looked into some community colleges, got me some information about financial aid. Jake went to college, so I figure maybe I should, too." He gave her a rueful smile. "Rodeo isn't proving to be a very steady income."

"Not when you're so breakable!" A cowboy jostled Tucker playfully as he passed.

"I've gotta keep myself in one piece for all those college gals I'm gonna meet," Tucker shot back.

A month ago, he might have tried to deck the guy. *Progress,* Kristen thought.

Sunlight reflecting off a glittering gold lamé blouse caught her eye, and she looked up.

Dixie, laden with photography equipment, flashed a smile at her as she crossed the arena. "I've got to get set up here—we'll talk later!"

Rodeo. Action. Excitement. A host of old friends. Feeling as though she'd come home, Kristen gave a last glance at the familiar faces and activity behind the chutes, then looked down at her clipboard and got to work.

And hoped that nothing at all would go wrong tonight.

"WELL," DIXIE SAID as she eyed with unabashed delight the crispy fried chicken heaped on the paper plate in front of her. "Things are going *real* well in my life. How about yours?"

After clicking a few photos of the specialty act in the center of the arena, she'd joined Kristen during the intermission, swearing that she could never pass up the chicken at Granite Creek. They'd found an empty picnic table down by the parking area and—ignoring the swarm of kids playing tag and screaming bloody murder just a few yards away—settled in for a quick visit.

Kristen looked at Dixie's plate and smothered a laugh. "First, I've got to ask how come you can eat all that and stay as tiny as you are. And next, I want to hear about Clint."

"Honey, I'm packed so solid that one of those bulls couldn't knock me over." She blew a cloud of platinum bangs out of her eyes. "As for Clint, I guess I've already died and gone to heaven." She lifted her left hand to display a diamond ring. "That man is more stubborn than I am."

"Oh, Dix—that's wonderful news!" Kristen leaned over to give her friend a huge hug, barely missing the plates of food between them.

Dixie grinned from ear to ear. "He wants to stay

on the ranch, but I'll still cover the rodeos I want to.
And I should have time to work on my photo-essay.
Even better—my tests are looking pretty good.''

''That's incredible! You must be so relieved!''

''Yeah. It was pretty scary.'' Dixie shuddered.
''After an abnormal Pap and a biopsy that didn't look
good, I was really worried. I still have to go back in
six months, but my doctors say they aren't expecting
any problems.'' Her eyes lit up. ''Now I get to hear
about *you*.''

The announcer's voice echoed through the grounds,
warning of the next event.

''Oops, gotta go!'' Dixie scooped up her plate.
''Just tell me quick—you two back together where
you belong? When's the wedding?''

Kristen gathered her own plate and pitched it in a
nearby trash can, the food untouched. ''There isn't
going to be one. Believe me, it's for the best.'' *Funny,
how the feeling in her heart never matched those
words.*

''What?'' Dixie grabbed Kristen's arm. ''What on
earth happened?''

''You've heard the phrase 'the price of true love'?
Well, I found out how much I was sold out for, and
I guess it wasn't nearly enough.''

''Huh?''

''My dad paid him ten-thousand dollars to embar-
rass me at my own wedding. I stood there waiting for
a guy who valued the money more than me.''

Dixie's face paled. ''But didn't Jake give you an
explanation? Surely—''

''Nope. Just some line about how 'I deserved so

much more' than him. But it's clear enough—his so-called love was bought off pretty easily.''

Dixie gave Kristen a quick hug. "I'm so sorry. But don't write him off so quickly. We need to talk after the rodeo, okay?''

And in a flash, she was gone.

THE LATE EVENING LIGHT was perfect. Just a few really good shots of steer roping and the saddle broncs, and she'd have enough to stay off the road for a while, work on her photo-essay book.

But none of that mattered right now.

She stopped at her truck and stowed her photo equipment inside, then headed for the secretary's booth. Tina looked up as Dixie entered the small building.

"I need to find Jake.''

"Hi, Dix. He was in here a while ago. He might be up with the VIPs...or over by the chutes.''

Dixie stepped outside and shielded her eyes against the bright halogen lights overhead. Kristen was talking to a reporter by the back gate, so Dixie circled wide to avoid her and moved faster through the crowd.

He wasn't by the VIP section...nor at the chutes... She glanced across the arena and spied him with the judges, checking the setup of the barrels for the barrel racers who were up next.

The moment he stepped out of the arena, she grabbed his elbow. "Come with me.''

He looked down at her, clearly startled, but didn't

argue. At soon as they were well beyond the chutes, she stopped.

"What's up, Dixie?"

She frowned. "Jake, I owe you my life. I would've died if you hadn't taken me to the hospital." She took a deep breath. "You've got to tell me where you got the money to pay those bills."

His jaw tensed. "No."

"Jake!"

"That was our deal, remember? No questions."

She hit her forehead with her open palm. "It's *okay*. I...I was afraid back then. Afraid Clint would hear about it all and that he would never forgive me. I was scared and sick and embarrassed. But we don't need secrets anymore. Tell me."

Jake looked down at her with a crooked smile. "No."

She tossed her hands up in exasperation. "Twelve-thousand dollars didn't just come out of *nowhere*. It was Roy Davis's money, wasn't it. Ten grand, at least."

"Dammit, Dixie, it's not important anymore."

"It's true. The timing is right. He gave you that money to stay away from his daughter, and then you..." She froze. "Oh, my God, Jake. You walked out on her because of me? Because I needed the money?"

An unspeakable sadness filled his eyes. "It's more complicated than that."

Her chest tightened. "I know you wouldn't have taken that money for yourself."

He shrugged away the truth as if it didn't matter.

But Dixie knew what accepting the money and letting Roy Davis think he was lower than dirt must have done to Jake's pride.

"Kris and I thought being in love was all that mattered," Jake murmured, his eyes fixed on something in the distance. "But then I stopped and looked— really looked—at what I had to offer her. *Nothing*. Not a home, not a future, not even a decent income. I'd already decided that I couldn't go through with it."

"You told her?"

Jake rubbed the back of his neck as if to ease tension there. "I planned to. But then you got sick, and Roy came barreling down to Colorado to shove his money in my face..." He hooked his hands in his back pockets and stared up at the stars. Swallowed hard. "Roy's deal was that I could never tell Kris about the money, couldn't talk to her for at least a year—preferably ever. He had papers drawn up and everything."

"A contract?"

"Eighteen-percent interest and repayment in twelve months if I failed to cooperate." He sighed. "I don't suppose it would've held up in a court of law, but you needed help, and I knew walking away from her was the right thing to do."

"But my medical bills were over twelve-thousand!"

He grinned. "I got lucky on a bounty bull at the next rodeo. At the time, I was so depressed I was hoping he'd send me to kingdom come. Instead, I won a six-thousand-dollar bonus."

"You were my hero, you know. The brother I never had." Dixie gave him a hug. "So now you can just go talk to Kris, and explain!"

"Explain what? I didn't show up. Her dad has already told her about the money. What can I say that will change anything?"

"Just what you told me!"

"Right. I was so concerned about her welfare that I went ahead and took the bribe from her father."

"You have to tell her the truth," Dixie pleaded. "Otherwise, she'll go on thinking exactly what her father has all these years. That you would be low enough to take money to hurt her."

"The irony," he said softly, "is that it's still better to leave it buried. Why make things harder? She has her MBA and a bright future, and has made it clear from the start that she wants to move on. She belongs in Dallas, I don't. If she stays in Bent Spur because of some misguided emotional tie, how long will it be before she's restless? Resenting the fact that she never got away?"

"You can't know that."

He reached out to lay a hand on Dixie's arm. "I helped you once, now you need to help me. Promise me that you'll stay out of this."

She stared up at him—six feet of resolute male without a clue—and hoped her answering smile was enough. *Sorry, cowboy, but that's one promise I just can't make.*

KRISTEN PACED the rodeo grounds, feeling an odd sense of...urgency. Mid-August in Wyoming could be as hot as anywhere else in the West, but usually the humidity was much lower and by evening the temperatures dropped to a comfortable level.

Tonight the air felt close. Charged. As if an electrical storm were brewing in the dark sky overhead. But there were no clouds. When she moved away from the bright lights, she could look up and see the stars.

However, even the livestock seemed edgy tonight. The bulls usually stood dozing, or idly watched the passersby through the fence. Tonight they were milling around, and one of them bellowed for the second time.

The broncs were nervous, too. With a pecking order long-established and close quarters in the holding pens, they usually stood in relative peace, each with a rear hoof idly cocked and head lowered.

One squealed, kicked, and the others scattered in a rush like birds taking flight, stirring up dust. Another one whinnied, and the whole herd milled about, anxious, as if they sensed an impending storm.

The barrel race was over, the arena cleared of barrels, and the first bull rider's name and stats came over the loudspeakers. A crowd of cowboys stood slant-hipped along the inside of the fence.

The pens behind the chutes were dark.

Feeling an inexplicable sense of unease, Kristen crossed the back lot and looked around for any of the crew. A sliver of white flashed in the darkness.

She walked faster. ''Bud?''

But Bud would be up in the chutes, watching the

positioning of the bulls, overseeing the handling of his stock.

The horses startled at her approach and shied back. In the next pen, she could pick out Cropduster's light coat—a ghostly silver in the dim light—as he jostled his way to reach the feeder along one side of the pen. The rest followed him anticipating their meal. Except that Bud never fed them until after the rodeo.

A shadowy figure moved away from the feeder.

"Hey, what are you doing back here?" she called out.

With the loud music and the announcer's patter coming through the loudspeakers lining the length of the arena, she could barely hear her own voice.

The figure—a man dressed in black—froze. Muttered a curse.

Trapped by the configuration of holding pens on three sides, he started up over the fence behind him. Inside, Tornado Alley—still penned alone, still hostile as ever—rushed forward and slammed into the fence.

Cursing, the man dropped back to the ground.

The bulls in the other pen lined up at the feeder and lowered their heads, starting to eat. The man gave them a quick glance, and she suddenly knew exactly what he'd been doing.

Alone. In the dark.

"Oh, my God," she cried. "Bud! Jake!"

Thundering applause for the first bull rider shook the bleachers. She rushed toward the feeders, tried to scare the bulls away.

Rough hands hauled her back—one tightening on her arm, one clamped over her mouth.

"Little girls really shouldn't be back here," he growled in her ear. "It's a good place to get hurt."

She tried to twist free. But the hand across her mouth and nose hauled her backward until her head was pinned against the intruder's chest. She fought against his grasp. Fought for air.

With a raw curse, he pivoted. Slammed her against the metal bars of the fence. Her head snapped back, hit a bar with a force that sent her reeling, dizzy, to the ground.

He hauled her to her feet, one forearm across her throat. "You make one sound—*one sound*—and you ain't gonna see tomorrow."

Clawing at his arm, she tried to kick back at him, fighting the nausea and darkness and pain throbbing in her head. Her knees buckled.

His grasp loosened, and she slid lower as her entire weight fell into his arm. Grabbing her opposite fist, she rammed her elbow full force into his crotch.

Caught unaware, he groaned and doubled over. She spun away—then kicked with every ounce of strength she possessed, and landed another direct blow with the toe of her boot in the same vulnerable part of his anatomy.

With a guttural cry he dropped to his knees.

Someone else moved up behind her. A scream rose in Kristen's throat. But the person gently moved her aside and then reached for her attacker's collar. Hauled him to his feet with one hand.

And delivered a powerhouse blow to the man's jaw.

The guy crumpled to the ground without a whimper.

Stunned, she sagged against the fence and looked up into Jake's enraged face. *Jake,* who'd once sworn that he would never lay a hand on another man.

At his side she saw Tucker, who was staring at his brother as if an alien had landed.

"I guess this is what you meant about being willing to fight for what matters," Tucker whispered, almost too softly to be heard.

Jake ignored him. "Did he hurt you, Kris?" Jake asked hoarsely. "Are you okay?"

She shook her head, trying to clear away her muzzy thoughts. "The...bulls. He gave something to the bulls."

Jake spun and charged toward the fence, shouting and waving his hat into the startled faces of the bulls lined up along the feeder.

The animals scrambled backward, their eyes rimmed white with fear at this strange apparition. All but Cropduster, who loved just about anyone who wasn't on his back. He took another mouthful of feed and watched Jake with mild interest.

Over the loudspeaker came the last bull rider's score, a hearty farewell to the crowd and a burst of music.

Several cowboys materialized out of the darkness. Then others, all glancing first at Kristen and then glaring at Jake with narrowed eyes.

"Keep the bulls back," Kristen shouted. "We've got them away from the feed. I think it's been poisoned. Maybe the horses, too. Someone find the vet."

Her attacker groaned and curled into a defensive ball on the ground, his face still hidden in the shadows.

While the other cowboys rapidly moved the bulls into another pen, Jake turned back to Kristen, cupped a hand under her chin. "Are you okay? *Really?* If he hurt you…"

Wrapping his arms around her, he held her close to his chest. Her head throbbed. Her throat hurt. But she'd never felt more secure.

"Thank you," she whispered.

He tucked her head beneath his chin and held her even closer. "I don't know what I'd do if anything ever happened to you."

The man on the ground stirred again. They both looked down at him, then back into each other's eyes.

"I think we're going to find out who's been causing our problems," she said.

Jake leaned over and grabbed the man's collar, then hauled him to his feet.

CHAPTER EIGHTEEN

BUD APPEARED, followed by Hoot, Kenny, Dixie and most of the crew. "What the hell is goin' on here?"

Jake gave Bud a measured glance, then turned his attention back to Lew, standing a few yards away, slumped over, his hands braced on his thighs. His face was gray and sheened with perspiration as he looked up, his eyes darting over the assembled crowd as if he were seeking an escape route.

Bud moved closer, scowled at Jake, then peered at Lew. "And what the hell have you done to Lew?"

"You might ask Lew what he just tried to do to the bucking stock," Kristen snapped. "Check out what's in that feed."

Kristen's suspicions about Bud had vanished. He always treated the bulls and broncs better than his own family, and would *never* cause those animals harm.

"Hey, look here," Hoot called out. He stepped into a pool of light beneath a security light and held out an empty gallon jug. "The label says it's antifreeze."

With a roar, Bud lurched toward Lew, but Jake held him back.

"Lew isn't going anywhere," Jake said quietly. "Kenny, I want you to find the vet covering tonight's rodeo. Hoot, tell Tina to call the sheriff. The law will take care of this.''

"Not nearly well enough." Bud jerked his arm away and stood ready, breathing hard, his fists clenched at his side.

Kenny reappeared with the vet a few minutes later.

Frowning, the vet took the empty gallon jug from Hoot and inspected the pink residue on the rim, then ran a forefinger inside the opening and rubbed the slippery substance between his fingers. "Damn. I was hoping maybe something else was in this jug, but it's definitely antifreeze. Did the animals ingest much of it?"

"It's dark back here, but I saw Lew moving along the entire length of the feeder," Kristen said. "I don't think most of them got much, though. Except maybe Cropduster. He ate more grain, but it's hard to say how much."

Tucker walked over to the feeder and returned with a handful of corn. "Seems pretty dry, where he was standing.''

The vet frowned. "Ethylene glycol is serious stuff. It shuts down the kidneys pretty fast. There's a medication that came out a year or so ago that we can try, and we can run a lot of IV fluids to flush out his kidneys." He looked from Kristen to Bud, then back again. "No guarantees, though. It's your call—but if he was mine, I'd get him to the clinic right away.''

"Do it." Kristen and Bud spoke in unison.

They looked at each other, startled. And then she offered him a smile. "Thanks.''

"Hell, he's worth twenty-thousand." But the look

in Bud's eyes told her that he would have made the same decision no matter what Duster was worth.

"What are you going to do about him—?" Bud demanded, jerking a thumb toward Lew.

"Tina says the sheriff will be here in ten minutes," Hoot called out as he made his way back through the growing crowd.

Kristen's anger grew as she studied Lew's hunched figure, and recalled all the problems MRC had endured during the past few months. "Why would you do this? The fence panel wiring, Susie's horse—you did all of that, too, didn't you!"

He lifted his gaze, and for one brief moment she saw the hatred burning in his eyes. Then he looked back at the ground.

"Why?" she insisted. She could hear her voice rising, knew she was losing control.

A large, warm hand curved over her shoulder. Jake had moved next to her, but even that didn't temper her anger. "All of these animals could have suffered horrible deaths. People—*children*—could have been killed if that bull at Bear Creek had escaped into the crowd. Why would you want that to happen?"

When Lew was finally handcuffed and in the back seat of the sheriff's patrol car, she stepped close to the door and tried one more time. "Just tell me why."

She barely caught his raspy whisper above the noise around them.

"Your daddy ruined my life." The cold, hateful look in his eyes sent a chill down her back. "So I've done my best to return the favor."

AT THE END of the Sunday performance, Kristen lingered in the secretary's office and waited until Tina finished writing out prize money checks.

"We should have known," Kristen said dully. "Lew had a chip on his shoulder from the start. Roy and Guy were trying to think of the guy who might have held a grudge over the years, but they were thinking it was Masterston or Galveston, not Lewiston. Lew must have put his full, correct name on the W-2 income tax forms he filled out when he was hired."

"Bud never gave it a second thought—a lot of these guys go by nicknames." Tina stood up and stretched. "I checked with the Association. Years ago, Guy and Roy were competing at a rodeo and caught Lewiston in with the bucking stock so they reported him.

"Was he trying to tamper with the animals?"

"No one proved anything, though there was some strong suspicion. He had an empty syringe in his pocket but *claimed* he'd used it on his own horse. Said his horse wouldn't load and trailer without a little Ace to calm her down."

"Everyone knows the Association rules—no competitors are ever allowed in the holding pens."

"True. He was disqualified from the rodeo and lost his chance at a hefty purse. That was the one year he was high in the standings for the circuit championships. Missed out on the circuit finals by just a hair."

"He did it to himself."

"And the following year he didn't compete well at all." Tina shook her head. "A couple of the older team ropers said he never did make a comeback with the rough stock, and didn't do well in the timed events, either.''

"So he blames Guy and Roy for missing his one chance at fame and glory.''

"Yeah, and he'd been letting it fester for years. Some of the guys said he drifts around as a cowhand. They think he's gotten sort of off balance.''

"Could be." Tina looked up from her laptop. "But still capable of trouble. Bud thinks maybe Lew paid Vance to start causing us problems—and when Vance wasn't aggressive enough, Lew stepped in. Taking Vance's job gave him an ideal set-up.''

A shiver slithered down Kristen's back. "At least they're both gone. Have you heard any more?''

"Jake and Bud both went into town to talk with the sheriff, so I guess he's grilled Lew pretty hard. Lew has confessed to the theft of the rodeo money, and to hurting Susie's horse at the Mendota rodeo. Jake said something about him canceling a rodeo interview, and interfering with next year's schedule, too.''

"Did he say anything about the food theft at our first rodeo?''

"Jake called Mendota, but the sheriff out there has nailed some local teenagers on that one. I believe the boys will be sending MRC money to pay for what they took.''

"I wonder what they did with forty pounds of hot dogs." Kristen managed a smile. "They must have all had a good case of indigestion.''

Tina rolled her eyes. "Apparently they had a beer party out at a quarry."

"Make that major indigestion." Kristen hesitated. "By the way, Jake and I had a talk last night. He's letting me out of our deal. When we get back to Bent Spur, I'll be packing and heading down to Dallas."

Tina's mouth fell open. *"What?"*

"I told him he could call me if he had questions. And both Guy and my dad are around, too. Heck, Jake is doing fine, anyway. He's taken over most of the work, and I'm just helping. He'll do fine."

"Now that's just about the dumbest thing I've heard all year." Dixie walked into the room and gave Kristen a look of complete amazement. "I'd like to know if there could be two more misguided, stubborn people on the planet."

"Jeez, Dixie, thanks for your support."

"Support? You need *counseling.*" Rolling her eyes, she grabbed Kristen's arm. "Come with me."

"I know you mean well, but—"

"March! We're gonna talk up in my office." Dixie raised a brow. "If you don't come with me, I'll go use the microphone up in the announcer's booth and let everyone hear me."

From the militant look on Dixie's face, Kristen believed her. She followed Dixie from the room, the sound of Tina's snickers fading behind them.

When they reached the top row of the empty bleachers, Dixie settled primly on the seat, the effect muted by her skintight gold lamé blouse and jeans.

"You say you want to move to Dallas and have that career. Fine. But people can commute these days, work things out. If you truly loved him, you'd find a way.''

''That's a little hard to imagine. Remember, I grew up with a dad who traveled with the rodeo circuit...and had tawdry affairs. Even Jake did. The...the weekend of our wedding he was with some other woman.''

''Was he?''

''He's never denied it. I'd rather live alone than have a life like that.''

''But he never told you what happened?''

''Believe me, those are details I'd rather not know. I loved him so much...and now, after being with him this summer, a lot of those feeling are back. It already hurts to leave.''

''Go talk to him. Tell him how you feel.''

''Actually, I feel pretty upbeat about going back to Dallas.''

Dixie rolled her eyes. ''But will you be truly happy there? Will you have absolutely no regrets, never wish you could have the one man who made you happy?''

''Would that be the one who got *paid* to skip out on his wedding?''

''You were just kids, immature... Not ready for commitment at any rate. But now...''

Kristen smiled and hoped it looked real. ''I know. I understand. But it was for the best back then, and really, it's for the best right now.''

She started to rise.

Dixie caught her arm and pulled her back down. ''I was so stupid. Stupid and stubborn and afraid—

but I'll never admit it to anyone else on the planet except you and Clint.'' She gave a self-deprecating laugh. ''Because of that I wasted *years* when I should have been with the only man I ever loved. I almost lost him forever.''

''I'm happy you two are back together, truly. But the circumstances are different.''

''Are they? Look at Jake. Really look at him. He's the most honorable guy I know. Ask yourself about the circumstances back in Las Vegas.''

It had to be the late-afternoon sun, because there seemed to be a sheen of tears in Dixie's eyes.

''Did you ever wonder *why* he would take money from your dad?'' Dixie continued. ''Jake would do anything to help someone else, but did you ever see him accept so much as a *favor?* Even a cup of coffee? Hand one to him and he accepts with thanks. Offer to get him one, and he politely declines.''

That was Jake. Kristen closed her eyes, remembering his efforts to reach out to Tucker; the quiet, sad smile he'd worn when he thought she wasn't looking.

''He kept a promise to me for ten long years,'' Dixie continued. ''A secret that hurt his pride and took from him something that he loved very much. That kind of man is worth your heart.''

''What—''

A tear skidded down Dixie's cheek. ''He says I have to stay out of this. He made me promise, because he thinks it's for the best. How can I break a promise to the man who saved my life?''

''Who *what?*''

Dixie took a deep breath and stared down at her

fists. "I...got pregnant ten years ago. I didn't find out until after Clint had left for Wyoming, and when I got really sick, I had no one to turn to. Jake gave up everything that mattered to him, just to help me—a friend. Now, you think real hard about that, and then you go talk to him. If you walk away from that man, you'll be making the biggest mistake of your life."

KRISTEN FOUND HIM behind Tina's pickup, loading boxes of office supplies. The livestock semis and crew pickups were pulling out onto the highway. Across the arena, workers were clearing the food stand and picking up trash under the bleachers.

He looked up and smiled as he hefted a box into the back seat, but his smile didn't reach his eyes. "Eventful weekend."

She nodded, not knowing quite where to begin. "The vet says Cropduster is looking good so far. They've had him on IVs since last night, and that new medication. Bud will send a truck back to get him in a few days."

"That's good." Jake hooked a heel on the running board of the truck and leaned against the door frame, his thumbs jammed in his front pockets.

"The numbers on this rodeo look good."

"Great."

"I guess I'll be leaving for Dallas after we get back to Guy's place."

He tipped his head in acknowledgment, but it took a long time for him to answer. "Probably for the best."

Moving closer, she rested a hand against the hard

wall of his chest and looked up into his eyes. "Is that what you want?"

He didn't move, but she felt his breath falter. Saw his eyes darken before he closed them and turned his head away.

"I've made a lot of mistakes in my life," she said softly. "I've been thinking about how to do better in the future. For starters, I need to be honest with myself. Whatever I've tried to tell myself over the years, I've loved you, Jake. I always will."

She rose on tiptoes and captured his face in her hands, then kissed his mouth with all the love and hunger she'd held inside for too long.

She stepped back and searched his face, but he only turned away, his jaw set.

She gave him a bittersweet smile that didn't begin to convey the pain in her heart. "I should have come back after you, Jake. We could have figured this out long ago, but I let stubborn pride keep me from making my life complete. Someday, maybe you'll realize you're doing the same thing."

"I GUESS I'M PACKED," she said sadly, casting an eye around her old bedroom at the Davis Ranch. She'd cleared out her things at the MRC office, and had to get some boxes of winter clothing she'd stored. "I'll go say goodbye to Mom, and then I'd better get started."

Roy stood in the doorway of her room. Looking away, he cleared his throat. "I—I'm sorry, Kris."

"I'll be back at Christmas," she said brightly, taping the last box shut. "I'll call, and I'll write."

"I was wrong."

She froze.

The pain and awkwardness in her father's voice told her just how hard it was for him to go on. "I—I only wanted the best. You were so young—just a baby—all caught up in the fun of being out on the circuit. And then he came along…"

Kristen looked up and saw the tears in her dad's eyes.

"You were too young to be running off. I *was sure* he was just looking for a meal ticket. But now—" He paused. "I've seen how you two look at each other. All these years I thought I'd figured him right because he took that money and ran." He bowed his head. "Dixie told me what he did for her. And because I wrote up that damn contract, I maybe stole a lot of years from you both."

"He and I just weren't meant to be." Kristen smiled at Roy in what she hoped was a reassuring way. "It's over with, now."

"No, it isn't."

Jake.

He sauntered down the hall like a gunslinger, his stride long and steady and hell-bent for trouble. Roy stepped aside, and Jake stopped in front of Kristen, his eyes burning into hers.

"We've come so close, yet we always mess up," he growled. "We've wasted an awful lot of years. So this time—" he nodded toward the hall behind him "—I've brought witnesses so we get it right."

Kristen peered around him. Her mouth fell open. Her mother was coming slowly toward them, hanging on to Dixie's arm. Behind them, Tucker was grinning like a kid at Christmas.

"Kristen, we should have been together since we first met." He gathered her into his arms, hauling her so close that she could feel his heart beating in time to her own. "All summer I've been thinking that I had to ride one more bull to the eight-second buzzer. I was convinced I needed that to be happy. Now I realize I was wrong. All I need is you. Nothing else matters."

His dark lashes drifting shut, he lowered his mouth to hers. Sensations shot through her, of love and heat and longing so intense that she felt tears slipping down her cheeks.

When he drew back, his own eyes were shimmering. "I love you, Kristen Davis. Whether you want to stay here in Wyoming or start your career in Dallas, we are going to work this out. Because darlin', I'm not going to live another day without you."

She looked up into his eyes, cradled his beloved face in her hands, and knew that this moment was her truest taste of heaven on earth.

Then she pulled him down into a kiss that swept them both into a life that would never again be the same.

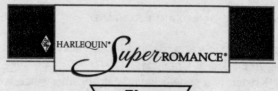

Silhouette
bestselling authors

KASEY
MICHAELS

RUTH
LANGAN

CAROLYN
ZANE

*welcome you to a world
of family, privilege and power
with three brand-new love
stories about America's
most beloved dynasty,
the Coltons*

*Brides
of
Privilege*

Available May 2001

Silhouette®
Where love comes alive™

Visit Silhouette at www.eHarlequin.com
PSCOLT

Harlequin truly does
make any time special. . . .
This year we are celebrating
weddings in style!

To help us celebrate, we want you to tell us how wearing the
Harlequin wedding gown will make your wedding day special. As
the grand prize, Harlequin will offer one lucky bride the chance to
"Walk Down the Aisle" in the Harlequin wedding gown!

There's more...

For her honeymoon, she and her groom will spend five nights at the
Hyatt Regency Maui. As part of this five-night honeymoon at the
hotel renowned for its romantic attractions, the couple will enjoy a candlelit
dinner for two in Swan Court, a sunset sail on the hotel's catamaran, and
duet spa treatments.

Maui • Molokai • Lanai

To enter, please write, in, 250 words or less, how wearing the Harlequin
wedding gown will make your wedding day special. The entry will be
judged based on its emotionally compelling nature, its originality and
creativity, and its sincerity. This contest is open to Canadian and U.S.
residents only and to those who are 18 years of age and older. There is no
purchase necessary to enter. Void where prohibited. See further contest
rules attached. Please send your entry to:

Walk Down the Aisle Contest

In Canada	In U.S.A.
P.O. Box 637	P.O. Box 9076
Fort Erie, Ontario	3010 Walden Ave.
L2A 5X3	Buffalo, NY 14269-9076

You can also enter by visiting www.eHarlequin.com
Win the Harlequin wedding gown and the vacation of a lifetime!
The deadline for entries is October 1, 2001.

Makes any time special ®

PHWDACONT1

1. To enter, follow directions published in the offer to which you are responding. Contest begins April 2, 2001, and ends on October 1, 2001. Method of entry may vary. Mailed entries must be postmarked by October 1, 2001, and received by October 8, 2001.

2. Contest entry may be, at times, presented via the Internet, but will be restricted solely to residents of certain geographic areas that are disclosed on the Web site. To enter via the Internet, if permissible, access the Harlequin Web site (www.eHarlequin.com) and follow the directions displayed online. Online entries must be received by 11:59 p.m. E.S.T. on October 1, 2001.

   In lieu of submitting an entry online, enter by mail by hand-printing (or typing) on an 8½" x 11" plain piece of paper, your name, address (including zip code), Contest number/name and in 250 words or fewer, why winning a Harlequin wedding dress would make your wedding day special. Mail via first-class mail to: Harlequin Walk Down the Aisle Contest 1197, (in the U.S. P.O. Box 9076, 3010 Walden Avenue, Buffalo, NY 14269-9076, (in Canada) P.O. Box 637, Fort Erie, Ontario L2A 5X3, Canada.

   Limit one entry per person, household address and e-mail address. Online and/or mailed entries received from persons residing in geographic areas in which Internet entry is not permissible will be disqualified.

3. Contests will be judged by a panel of members of the Harlequin editorial, marketing and public relations staff based on the following criteria:

   • Originality and Creativity—50%
   • Emotionally Compelling—25%
   • Sincerity—25%

   In the event of a tie, duplicate prizes will be awarded. Decisions of the judges are final.

4. All entries become the property of Torstar Corp. and will not be returned. No responsibility is assumed for lost, late, illegible, incomplete, inaccurate, nondelivered or misdirected mail or misdirected e-mail, for technical, hardware or software failures of any kind, lost or unavailable network connections, or failed, incomplete, garbled or delayed computer transmission or any human error which may occur in the receipt or processing of the entries in this Contest.

5. Contest open only to residents of the U.S. (except Puerto Rico) and Canada, who are 18 years of age or older, and is void wherever prohibited by law; all applicable laws and regulations apply. Any litigation within the Province of Quebec respecting the conduct or organization of a publicity contest may be submitted to the Régie des alcools, des courses et des jeux for a ruling. Any litigation respecting the awarding of a prize may be submitted to the Régie des alcools, des courses et des jeux only for the purpose of helping the parties reach a settlement. Employees and immediate family members of Torstar Corp. and D. L. Blair, Inc., their affiliates, subsidiaries and all other agencies, entities and persons connected with the use, marketing or conduct of this Contest are not eligible to enter. Taxes on prizes are the sole responsibility of winners. Acceptance of any prize offered constitutes permission to use winner's name, photograph or other likeness for the purposes of advertising, trade and promotion on behalf of Torstar Corp., its affiliates and subsidiaries without further compensation to the winner, unless prohibited by law.

6. Winners will be determined no later than November 15, 2001, and will be notified by mail. Winners will be required to sign and return an Affidavit of Eligibility form within 15 days after winner notification. Noncompliance within that time period may result in disqualification and an alternative winner may be selected. Winners of trip must execute a Release of Liability prior to ticketing and must possess required travel documents (e.g. passport, photo ID) where applicable. Trip must be completed by November 2002. No substitution of prize permitted by winner. Torstar Corp. and D. L. Blair, Inc., their parents, affiliates, and subsidiaries are not responsible for errors in printing or electronic presentation of Contest, entries and/or game pieces. In the event of printing or other errors which may result in unintended prize values or duplication of prizes, all affected game pieces or entries shall be null and void. If for any reason the Internet portion of the Contest is not capable of running as planned, including infection by computer virus, bugs, tampering, unauthorized intervention, fraud, technical failures, or any other causes beyond the control of Torstar Corp. which corrupt or affect the administration, secrecy, fairness, integrity or proper conduct of the Contest, Torstar Corp. reserves the right, at its sole discretion, to disqualify any individual who tampers with the entry process and to cancel, terminate, modify or suspend the Contest or the Internet portion thereof. In the event of a dispute regarding an online entry, the entry will be deemed submitted by the authorized holder of the e-mail account submitted at the time of entry. Authorized account holder is defined as the natural person who is assigned to an e-mail address by an Internet access provider, online service provider or other organization that is responsible for arranging e-mail address for the domain associated with the submitted e-mail address. **Purchase or acceptance of a product offer does not improve your chances of winning.**

7. Prizes: (1) Grand Prize—A Harlequin wedding dress (approximate retail value: $3,500) and a 5-night/6-day honeymoon trip to Maui, HI, including round-trip air transportation provided by Maui Visitors Bureau from Los Angeles International Airport (winner is responsible for transportation to and from Los Angeles International Airport) and a Harlequin Romance Package, including hotel accomodations (double occupancy) at the Hyatt Regency Maui Resort and Spa, dinner for (2) two at Swan Court, a sunset sail on Kiele V and a spa treatment for the winner (approximate retail value: $4,000); (5) Five runner-up prizes of a $1000 gift certificate to selected retail outlets to be determined by Sponsor (retail value $1000 ea.). Prizes consist of only those items listed as part of the prize. Limit one prize per winner. All prizes are valued in U.S. currency.

8. For a list of winners (available after December 17, 2001) send a self-addressed, stamped envelope to: Harlequin Walk Down the Aisle Contest 1197 Winners, P.O. Box 4200 Blair, NE 68009-4200 or you may access the www.eHarlequin.com Web site through January 15, 2002.

Contest sponsored by Torstar Corp., P.O. Box 9042, Buffalo, NY 14269-9042, U.S.A.